257

Acknowledgements

My thanks to my editor Marion Donaldson for her help and
forbearance

CHAPTER 1

Katy Molloy stared at her reflection in the mirror, idly twisting a tube of Tangee Gay Red lipstick round and round in her hand. Was she mad, or what? Why had she let her mam and Margaret Kelly coax her into going to the dance at the Cashmore Hotel? It was only six months since her elder brother's death in November of last year and the anger she'd felt then at the senselessness of it was still hot in her, for Vincey had been a vibrant joy of a man – her best and closest friend. When he had received his call-up papers in 1943 to fight in the war, she had been devastated.

Two years later, when he returned unscathed, Katy had made her way to her secret 'Wishing Tree', the big oak tree in the far field, and climbed up to perch on her favourite branch, to thank God for his safe return. She was so happy that life was back to normal and they were a whole family once more. True, Vincey didn't smile as much or tease her as often as he used to do, and there were times when he disappeared for hours, in one of his strange moods, but she had accepted the change in him.

The blinding headaches had started a year after Vincey's demob, accompanied by bouts of sickness. Katy quickly realised that her mother was very worried and was trying to hide it, and when Vincey was rushed to the Mater Hospital in Belfast after collapsing she knew that it was serious; within hours he was dead. The doctor told them he'd had a subarachnoid haemorrhage, and when they looked puzzled he gently explained in simple terms that it was a brain haemorrhage. In any case, what did a name matter? Vincey was dead. What made it worse was knowing that he had come through the war without a scratch, only to die of a bloody brain haemorrhage.

1

Katy threw the lipstick onto the dressing table with force then started guiltily as her mam called out: 'Katy! Margaret is here.'

She hastily dabbed some powder on her nose and made her way downstairs, acutely aware that she owed it to her parents to make an effort. She stood by the kitchen door for a moment and peeked in. Her old school friend Margaret, who was now in her first year at Queens University, was standing by the huge scrubbed table, her hands cuddling a cup of buttermilk. She was a tall, willowy girl with jet black hair and those blue Irish eyes that were different to any others on God's earth. Katy's mother, her face eased of sorrow for a moment, was listening to something Margaret was saying and nodding her head in agreement. They are talking about me, Katy thought as she walked in.

'You look great!' Margaret cried. She put the cup down and steered Katy to the door, throwing Annie a wink that said, 'She'll be all right. Don't worry.'

But Annie *was* worried. She was worried about many things. Life had changed so much it frightened her. During the war years, the Molloys' livelihood as farmers had been in jeopardy for many reasons – lack of manpower being one and shortage of spare parts for their ageing equipment, another. Then there was always the fear that a German plane on its way home might jettison a spare bomb straight over the Molloy farm following yet another bombing raid on the Belfast shipyards. But they had coped. There had been a sense of purpose then – a determination that the enemy was not going to put them out of business. But these days Eddie always looked worn out, for without Vincey's help and with only Patrick Toner on the permanent staff, and herself and Katy dealing with the milking and feeding the hens and generally helping out, farming 400 acres was proving to be almost impossible. They still had to depend on local school-children for the potato-picking and to bring in the harvest as they had done during the war years. But slowly the men were drifting back. She would speak to Eddie. They needed some more help before he collapsed with the strain.

Katy, however, was Annie's greatest worry. Since Vincey's death she had become moody and angry in turn. Annie was also concerned about the amount of time Katy spent at Vincey's grave. She would have liked her daughter to move on with her life, but realised that after only six months the hurt was still too great. With a sigh she rose and set the kettle to boil on the big blackleaded stove. At least Margaret had persuaded Katy to go to the dance. It was a start.

When Katy and Margaret arrived at the Cashmore Hotel two miles away, it was packed out. Hordes of young people had arrived in taxis and by the busload from as far away as Belfast in the north-east and Castlewellan in the south, and as the girls entered they were surrounded by the masses jostling for space.

'How do I look?' Katy whispered nervously.

She was wearing a powder blue dress with cap sleeves, and a broad white belt which made her small waist look even tinier. Her slim legs were covered with the tanning lotion that everyone used, as nylons were so scarce and she'd applied it evenly, to the envy of Margaret, who always blotched hers. To complete her outfit, she wore a pair of fashionable wedge-heeled shoes.

Margaret whistled in admiration. 'Where did you get the coupons for this lot?'

'Mam doesn't use many of hers and anyway, she makes most of my clothes from dresses she had before the war.'

In spite of Margaret's reassurance, the evening was proving a trial for Katy. At one stage Margaret gave her the weight of her tongue because she had repulsed a young man who had asked her politely if she would like a glass of lemonade.

'You'll never get a fella if you keep giving the boys the high shoulder,' she hissed.

'It's enough that I'm here!' Katy hissed back. 'I only came to stop Mam and you going on about me taking up my life again. I am trying – but I draw the line at being pestered by feckless eejuts who are not fit to tie Vincey's bootlaces.'

'I'm close to giving up on you,' Margaret sighed. 'Now that I am at university I have little time to worry about your affairs. I have my own problems trying to keep up with the load of brainboxes I have joined. But I tell you this, Katy Molloy. You're eighteen years old now, and it's high time you made some decisions about your future. If you're not careful, you'll end up married to a farmer who can't see further than the next furrow, and who will expect you to spend your days tweaking at a poor bloody cow's udders for the milk yield.'

They glared at each other like a pair of gladiators and then burst out laughing. Margaret grabbed Katy's arm. 'Come on. I'll buy you the lemonade myself.'

When they were armed with the cool liquid, Margaret remarked, 'You're so angry all the time, Katy. Why don't you do something positive? Prove to Vincey that the encouragement he gave you hasn't been wasted. Find a job . . . get away . . . become independent.'

'Easier said than done.' Seeing the look of impatience on Margaret's face, Katy added, 'I'm not being defeatist – just realistic. I will start looking soon, I promise.' Margaret was right, she thought. The time *had* come for change.

When they parted later that evening she felt pleased with herself. She had even managed to dance with a fair amount of enthusiasm with Charlie Donoghue, and only once had she felt the familiar anger rise in her when Charlie had remarked innocently but thoughtlessly that it was great to see her at the dance after her recent sorrow. 'After all,' he said, 'life has to go on.' She had wanted to flatten him but had trod heavily on his toe instead. A smile curled her lip now as she settled beneath the sheets. The agony on his face had appeased her. I'm turning into a right sadist, she thought as she drifted into sleep.

She wakened early next morning and lay back against the pillow feeling more relaxed than she had done for a long time. Her sleep, for once, had been dreamless and she let her mind drift to the events of the previous night. She hadn't been kind to Charlie Donoghue, the poor helpless culshie. She sighed. Most of the young men she knew were so dull. They were mostly farmers' sons and she tired of listening to their talk of crops and yields. The man of her dreams was tall, dark and sophisticated with an exciting job – it didn't matter what, so long as it was interesting and didn't have the word 'farmer' in its description.

For a moment she felt a sense of guilt. Farmers were worthy people. Her own father was a treasure . . . but what the hell. This was her dream – she could have who she wanted in it. Her mother's voice sounded in the yard outside. She glanced at the clock and tumbled out of bed. She should have been up and helping long ago. She ran to the tiny bathroom and hastily washed and towelled. She *must* stop indulging herself. She was always wishing for the impossible. No wonder Annie became exasperated with her. What was it she'd said once? Katy paused. 'If wishes were dreams, Katy Molloy, you'd never wake up.' A slow smile spread over her face.

Soon after the dance, Margaret left for Belfast and university, and it was three months before Katy saw her again. She had arranged to meet her in Ballyclinchy and was looking forward to the trip. Ballyclinchy wasn't as interesting as the larger town of Ballynahinch, further on, but there was enough to amuse a girl who lived on a farm two miles from the small village of Bally- nashee, particularly on market days.

Margaret was already waiting at the bus stop when she arrived and they greeted each other joyfully. The older girl did a twirl and asked: 'Have I changed?'

'I think you have,' Katy said slowly. 'I don't quite know how . . . Perhaps it's the new hairstyle and the air of sophistica- tion.'

'Ah, get away with you! I'm still the cucumber who left here six months ago. I have a few more worry lines, that's all. Not surprising when you think of all the studying I have to do. English and English literature are harder at university level.'

They talked non-stop as they walked to the café where they had arranged to lunch, and when they were seated, Margaret asked, 'How have you been since I last saw you?'

'I'm fine.'

There was a finality in her voice which struck Margaret. She wondered if Katy was still not coping, but decided she could do nothing more to help. The waitress arrived to take their order.

'Is it true you've stopped seeing Bernie Hill?' Katy enquired brightly, when the woman had gone. She was anxious to steer Margaret away from personal issues.

'It is indeed. But where did you hear about it?'

'It's goin' the rounds. Bernie got drunk one night and told the whole bar that you had sent him packing and that he was contemplating suicide.'

'Oh! That sounds like Bernie – always prone to exaggeration. He really is the biggest arsehole this side of the Mournes.'

'Margaret!' Katy looked around hurriedly to see if anyone had heard, but there was only one elderly couple by the window and they were both stolidly chewing their way through plates of roast beef and vegetables.

Margaret grinned. 'I'm afraid I've picked up the habit of swearing since I went to university.'

'Why did you send him packing? The man was the biggest catch around. You were the envy of all.'

Margaret shrugged. 'Distance had something to do with it, and the fact that he had not a good word to say about his ex-girlfriends. They had more defects than a clapped-out car and it was always *their* fault that the relationship ended. It was time he had his comeuppance. Besides,' she grinned, 'I got tired of beating him off. His idea of a successful end to an evening was a wrestling match on the ground with me as the potential loser.'

'Maybe he meant no harm – he was just codding around.'

'And Father Connor has a secret love-child,' Margaret scoffed. 'That fella is so devious he could scratch his own back with his elbow. Anyway, as I said – distance had a lot to do with it.'

Katy sighed. 'I wish . . .'

Margaret, ignoring the presence of the waitress who was putting the food on the table, said crisply, 'Stop wishing and make things happen.'

'I'm on my way,' Katy said. 'I've done a lot of thinking about what you said at the dance, and I've decided to look for a job.'

'Will your father mind if you do that?'

'I don't know. Probably. But he has taken on Patrick Toner's son Tom, so I don't think I will be needed quite so much on the farm.'

'That's good news. I always felt you were burying yourself.'

'Farming isn't a bad life,' Katy said defensively, 'but I'm a bit lonely now that you are at Queens – and I've lost touch with most of my other friends since Vincey died, which is another reason why I decided to go job-hunting.'

Relieved that Katy was showing some sense at last, Margararet said, 'You do mean it, don't you?'

'Of course I do. Trust me.'

'I just wondered if you were fobbing me off to stop me nagging you.'

'Not a bit of it. I came to see that I was using the isolation of the farm to stay away from people. I feel safe there.' The old gleam was back in Katy's eyes.

An hour later, she kissed her friend goodbye and leaped on the bus home as it pulled up in the centre of Ballyclinchy. When it moved off, she leaned out of the bus doorway and called out: 'I'll write to you when I've got something going. There has to be someone who needs a shorthand typist.'

The following morning, Annie Molloy stood by the kitchen sink with arms folded, staring thoughtfully out of the window. For too long she had bottled up her sorrows while she coped with Katy's, but now she felt she owed herself a moment or two to chase her own demons away, to let the tears flow. There was no reason to keep them in check, for she was alone. Over the past months, she'd had to be strong – not just for Katy, but for Eddie too. Her husband had taken Vincey's death badly. Now she experienced a great surge of release as tears streamed down her face, blurring her vision, blunting the pain. They dropped on her hands, they tasted salty on her lips, and they cleansed.

At last, with a sigh, she wiped them away. She could go upstairs and sort out Vincey's belongings, now she felt stronger. She would send his clothes to the St Vincent de Paul charity; his other belongings – such as his watch, his fiddle, and various hoarded mementoes and private treasures – she would lock away until she decided what to do with them. With a final dab at her eyes she moved away.

She was halfway up the stairs when she had to lean back against the bannister as Katy tore past her, jumping down two steps at a time, dressed up to the nines in a light jacket and a pair of slacks.

'In the name of God, Katy Molloy, what is going on?'

'Life is, Mam,' Katy laughed. 'As from today I am going to

meet it head on. I am off to the village for a bit of shopping and to have a snack at the café.' She didn't mention that she was anxious to get the weekend paper to see if there were any jobs going.

Once in the café, Katy settled herself at a corner table with a pot of tea and a scone before opening the newspaper to scan the Situations Vacant columns. She sighed in frustration. The only jobs listed were for farmhands, counter assistants, a typist for a paint firm – she'd die of boredom working for a paint firm – and a cleaner for the local school. The rest were for jobs in Belfast, a bit out of her league at the moment. One day, she thought – when she had gained some experience – but for now something of a temporary nature was what she needed to get her started.

She was about to close the paper when her gaze fastened on an advertisement further down the column. It was for a nanny who would be required to live in during the week, and look after a four-year-old girl. The address interested her. Beresford House was only two miles from the Molloys' farm. It was a beautiful house that had been vacant for many years until an English lady had bought it. All that was known of the occupant was that she'd had a baby shortly before she'd moved in, and that her husband had been killed in a bombing raid over Berlin.

Rumours abounded, though. The child was sickly . . . Mrs Sanders was haughty and difficult to work with. She gave wild parties for her English friends who visited often. This last assumption was because Brian Wilson's profits had gone up considerably since her arrival four years ago. Brian Wilson, who owned the only shop in Ballynashee that sold alcohol, was of the opinion that the English were all raving alcoholics. Not that he cared. His business was doing very well, thank you.

The family didn't socialise much with the locals and Mrs Sanders was seen only when she drove her large car into town to do some personal shopping. Katy had seen the child accompanied by a middle-aged woman on several occasions. The latter had seemed rather strict and she'd felt sorry for the tiny tot one day when she'd overheard her being severely chastised for spilling ice cream down her very smart coat.

The only local who worked for the family was Mrs Skelton,

and as she hailed from the larger town of Ballyclinchy she had no close friends in Ballynashee. She was always polite but discreet. The maid who worked and lived at the house was English. She was seldom seen around town but when she did visit, she too was polite but not overly friendly.

Katy re-read the advert. The interviews were to be held at Beresford House. All applications were to be in by 2 April and were to be handwritten. After she had ordered another pot of tea she continued to muse. What the divil did she know about children? She couldn't manage to sort out her own life, never mind try to steer a young child through hers. Still . . .

When the waitress arrived with the tea, Katy smiled at her. 'Have you any children?' she enquired.

Surprised by the question, the waitress replied, 'Yes, I have three.' She glanced over her shoulder before adding confidingly, 'I wouldn't be doing this job if I hadn't. It's hard on the feet and the temper – but the money is useful when you need to feed and clothe them.'

'I don't know a lot about children. Is it difficult looking after them?'

'Take my advice. Don't be in a hurry to settle down and have children. I think the world of mine and I wouldn't be without them, but they keep my hands full.'

'Did you have some know-how about bringing them up before you got married?' Katy grimaced. 'I wouldn't know where to start.'

'Ach away! Ye learn as ye go along. Sure, the children don't know that you are an amateur and by the time they are old enough to catch on, ye've cottoned onto it yourself.' The waitress gave a tinkling laugh. 'I've made my mistakes but I found out the hard way that it's no different from looking after the young animals on a farm. Ye feed them, ye water them, ye cuddle them when they need it – and ye love them. Look! I have to go. Old Sourpuss is giving me a baleful look.'

When she left the café, Katy crossed the square to Macready's to buy a writing pad and envelopes, for she'd made up her mind to apply for the job. The waitress was right: she'd learn as she went along.

Her mother met her at the door when she arrived home. 'I was hoping you would be on the three o'clock bus,' she said. 'Your da would like a bit of help with the milking. He has had to send Tom Toner home. The lad has the mother and father of all colds. He says could you also wash down the milking shed with the hose as Tom has not done it yet.'

'I'll just change,' Kate said. 'Is Tom very ill?'

'Well, he'll live to tell the tale but I have to say that as grey goes, it is definitely not Tom's best colour. With that sandy hair of his and the grey eyes it makes him look like a walking ghost.' She smiled at her daughter. 'Did you have a nice time in town?'

'I didn't meet up with anyone but I had a walk round the shops and tea at Mooney's tea room.' Katy started up the stairs. 'I'd better get changed or I'll be late for the milking.'

'Tom has already brought the cows in so that's done,' Annie called after her. She strolled into the kitchen to continue with her cooking. Her daughter had seemed a bit preoccupied. Had she met a lad? She shook her head. That idea was pure fancy. Katy was too particular. Not one of the lads who had thrown themselves at her head had stood a chance. Katy was waiting for the prince who would never come – not in this area, anyway.

Two miles away, in the drawing room of Beresford House, Sylvia Sanders sat at her desk studying a letter sent to her for her approval from the head of one of the charities with which she was involved. She was a slim and elegant woman who put great store on things being done the right way; it was how she had been brought up. One did not send out begging letters such as this. It was crass in its presentation and too obviously after money.

She frowned. She must bring the matter up at the meeting tomorrow. The letter could not be sent out in its present form. Where was her notebook? Hastily she searched the drawer. Because of her unfortunate habit of forgetting things, she had developed a system of dating and timing everything she had to do. She had always been slightly vague, an annoying characteristic because those who didn't know her well didn't realise that she had a sharp mind.

Putting two delicate fingers to her temple she kneaded it

10

gently, eyes screwed up in pain as the headache she had been trying to shake off increased in intensity. Above her in the nursery her daughter was throwing a tantrum and she felt too fragile to deal with it. Elizabeth had been an absolute trial since Nanny Stevens had left. If she wasn't screaming blue murder because she wasn't getting her own way, she was being bloody-minded for the sheer hell of it. An obstinate child at the best of times, she was worse now that there was no one to control her. Sally, the maid, was too inexperienced, and Mrs Skelton the housekeeper was a bit unsympathetic. Sylvia badly needed someone who understood children, particularly one like Elizabeth, who had the intelligence to manipulate people.

The sound of something crashing to the floor caused her to wince. She rang the bell and the maid entered. 'Sally, I can't stand Elizabeth in this state any longer. Would you take her out for a walk or something and tell Mrs Skelton to make a salad for tonight. I really don't feel well enough to eat a large meal.'

Sylvia was aware from the look on her maid's face that the prospect of dealing with Elizabeth appalled her, but she didn't let this worry her. She lay down on the long sofa and covered her eyes with the black cloth she kept for when she had one of her migraines. Only another two weeks and there should be a new nanny. She'd already received four applications. God! Let the days pass quickly.

It was growing dark when Sylvia woke, her headache gone. She rose gingerly from the couch and switched on the table lamp. The clock showed 7.15 p.m. Startled, she rang the bell and waited. She had slept for over three hours. A stillness and silence lay over the house. The door opened and Mrs Skelton entered, her face still rosy from cooking over the large stove.

'What has happened with Elizabeth?' Sylvia enquired.

'Sally took her out for a long walk and gave her some supper when she returned. I didn't want to disturb you, mam, so I took the decision to have Elizabeth bathed and put to bed. She was tired out after the walk and all the screaming, so she settled down quickly.' Mrs Skelton didn't mention that poor Sally was nursing a bruised shin and was so exhausted herself that she had gone to her room without bothering to eat any supper.

11

'I think I could manage some food now,' Sylvia said. 'No wine though, it might bring on another headache. I'll have a pot of tea with a slice of lemon instead.'

Mrs Skelton was about to shut the door when Sylvia asked, 'Should I go up and kiss Elizabeth goodnight?'

She's wanting me to give her permission not to, Mrs Skelton thought, and said aloud: 'I wouldn't, mam. The poor child has worn herself out. She needs to sleep, and if she feels your touch she might wake up.'

'I'll leave her to sleep then.' Sylvia tried to play down the relief in her voice.

Mrs Skelton withdrew. If madam had taken control of her own child instead of farming her out to a nanny as soon as she was able, she might have had better luck with her, she thought. The child could be a real pet. The fault lay in her being left in the hands of a strict disciplinarian like Nanny Stevens who lacked humour and had a face that would stop a clock. Now, Elizabeth was left rudderless with no one to guide her. Mrs Skelton hoped to God that whoever took the job on this time was young enough to be sympathetic to the child's behaviour but mature enough to cope. She had been pleased when Nanny Stevens had decided to retire.

At the farm Katy was sitting at the table in the big kitchen playing with the food on her plate. At last she put her knife down and said nervously, 'Mam, Da, I have something I'd like to discuss with you.'

Annie and Eddie exchanged glances. She'd been right, Annie thought. Her daughter *had* hidden something from her yesterday.

'Eat up or the meal will get cold. I daresay the discussion can wait without our lives falling apart,' she said calmly.

'Yes, it can wait,' Katy agreed reluctantly.

When they had eaten, she clasped her hands nervously together. Her father and mother sat in silence. Then: 'I have applied for a job!' she burst out.

Eddie was the first to speak. 'Do you need one?' he asked quietly. 'I thought you enjoyed working on the farm.'

'I do enjoy it, Da! But I have been giving a great deal of

thought to my future and I think it is time I went out and did something else. Now that you have Tom Toner working for you as well as his father—'

'Tom will be working for me for a year. He is waiting for a place at agricultural college. I was hoping you would still be around to help out when he is gone.'

'We can always get someone else,' Annie said gently.

Eddie frowned. 'I don't doubt it, but I'd thought . . . I'd hoped . . .' Faded blue eyes looked into hers, revealing his disappointment. He had no son now. He had hoped that his daughter would have been content to learn the workings of the farm. To take over one day. He'd not been keen when she'd chosen to do a business course.

Katy said quickly, 'I might not get the job, but if I did I would only be two miles away.'

'Where did you find an office job around here?' Annie asked.

Katy hesitated. 'I've applied for the post of nanny at Beresford House.'

Eddie stared at his daughter in amazement. 'A nanny? Sure, what do you know about lookin' after babies?'

'I'm sure I'll manage. Besides, I bought a book on rearing children, which I've been studying. It even explains how to cope with medical problems . . . and a friend told me that few mothers know about rearing children in the beginning but they learn as they go along.'

A bubble of laughter rose in Annie's throat.

Katy scowled. 'I hoped you would see my side of things,' she said.

Annie chuckled. 'I do, love. I think you would make a great nanny – and your friend is right in a way. However, this particular mother is paying you money to look after her child and will expect someone who has been trained and will take responsibility for her actions.'

Katy felt deflated. 'You think I shouldn't apply?'

Annie said softly, 'Of course you should apply, but don't expect to have it handed to you. No doubt there will be trained nannies after the job. We aren't many miles from Belfast, and it would be a great job for a girl who wanted to live in the country yet be only a bus ride from the city.'

'Why in the name of God did you choose this and not a job in an office?' asked Eddie. He would never understand children like he did animals. He had spent money on a commercial course for Katy and here was his daughter telling him she was going to be a nanny!

'The only decent secretarial jobs in the paper were in Belfast, and I'm not ready for city life just yet.' Katy looked at him coaxingly. 'I saw the nanny advert further down the page, and when I realised that the address was Beresford House I jumped at the idea.'

Eddie scratched his jaw and looked at his wife. 'What do you think, Annie? Has our Katy a chance of pulling this off?'

'If she gets through the interview then, yes, I think our Katy has the sense to look after a child. I am more concerned that she might find her a handful. I understand she is past the toddler stage.'

'She's four years and a bit,' Katy told her.

'Not a good age to start with. Her habits have already been formed and her personality moulded by someone else's influence. The child may react to having to obey a new set of rules so you will have to go gently.'

'If I was in trouble could I not give you a ring?'

Annie nodded. 'You could, I suppose.' She smiled. 'Sure, why not!'

Katy looked at her father, who looked at his wife and then back at his daughter. 'I'm outnumbered. Life would not be worth living if I didn't give you my blessing. I just hope you listen to your Mam and remember what she tells you. How long have you got?'

'Only a week left. I'll phone tomorrow,' Katy said.

Eddie leaned his arms on the table and said heavily, 'There is one condition.' When Katy started to speak, he held up his hand. 'The mother will be taking you on and paying you a wage in the belief that you know what you are doing. I think the truth should be told.'

'Are you saying that I should tell Mrs Sanders that I have not a clue about children?' Katy gasped.

'I am not! What I am saying is that this lady should be told that you have no qualifications, but that you are confident you can do the job. She can then make up her own mind – then the responsibility lies with her.' Eddie drew on his pipe and continued to regard his daughter.

Katy shrank back in her seat. She loved her da to death but at this moment she felt more like strangling him. It was all right being a man of principle, but a person had to bend the rules occasionally. 'I wouldn't have a chance in hell of getting the job then,' she said rather sulkily.

'I'm afraid that's how it has to be or I won't go along. You have to be honest. If it was yourself who was takin' on a nanny for your child, you would want to know it all. That is my condition.' He rose from the table.

Annie and Katy looked at each other. 'He won't change his mind,' Annie said. 'Now you go ahead and try for it. Sure, there will be nothing lost if you don't get it.'

Beresford House was a red-brick Victorian building which sat elegantly at the end of a long driveway flanked on either side by rhododendron bushes. It faced west, and sometimes the windows took on a pink glow as the setting sun sank towards its nocturnal rest. During the day they were opaque and secretive.

Wide, well-kept lawns stretched away on either side of the house, and the flower beds were filled with colourful plants already burgeoning under the influence of the early April sunshine.

Katy, breathless from running, stopped outside the tall wrought-iron gates for a moment to ease the stitch in her side and stared in awe at the size of the house and grounds. The bus had arrived ten minutes late. Paddy Toomey, the driver, was apologetic; he'd been held up by a large herd of cows two miles down the road. There wasn't a thing he could do about it.

'If I don't get this job because I didn't turn up on time, I'll put the blame at your door, Paddy Toomey,' she'd said, crossly.

Paddy had shrugged. 'Put the blame fairly on me: I will back you up. I can't say fairer than that. Anyway – sure, who around here isn't used to lateness?'

Mrs Sanders, that's who! Katy thought as she swung the gates open and hurried up the long driveway.

The door was opened by a plump grey-haired woman with rosy cheeks. 'You must be Miss Molloy,' she said, smoothing down her apron.

'I'm sorry I'm late,' Katy panted.

'Don't worry. Mrs Sanders is not a great timekeeper and we haven't started interviewing yet. You'll have plenty of time to get your breath back. Everyone is in the little room off the study. I'll show you in.'

'How many applicants are there?' Katy asked.

'Five, now you have arrived.'

As Katy sat down she glanced around. Two young women sitting opposite were dressed in identical smart grey uniforms. Both looked up and smiled briefly before continuing to converse in undertones. Her heart sank. They were obviously trained nannies.

She stole a look towards the other two. The older one looked experienced but she was twisting her hands and glancing anxiously at the two paragons. She's more nervous than I am, Katy thought. The final applicant was slim and smartly dressed. Her red nail varnish and the way she kept touching her hair caused Katy to discount her chances. She decided that her main opposition was the pair in the smart uniforms.

She studied them. Their confidence showed in the way they sat with hands calmly folded over large envelopes. Probably bulging with certificates and references, she decided. Her chances were slim but she must stay cool; they would be completely kiboshed if she acted like an eejut and started stuttering.

She felt her stomach muscles tighten as she eventually entered the interview room. Mrs Sanders was sitting behind a large desk. With a smile, she gestured towards the chair opposite. 'Just give me a few moments,' she said.

Katy watched the slim, pale hand move the fountain pen across the paper beneath it, and hid her own sturdy, well-worked hands as much as she could. In an effort to ease her nervousness she glanced round the room. A fire was lit in a fireplace that had a high mantel. A beautiful Victorian sofa upholstered in red velvet was placed opposite, within toe-warming distance. Above the wainscotting, the walls were faced with a textured wallpaper, and the furniture which was made of mahogany, gave a cosy feel to the room. She was studying the fine prints on the walls when suddenly Mrs Sanders spoke. 'I see from your letter, Miss Molloy, that you live two miles away and that your father is a local farmer.'

Katy nodded.

'What qualifications do you have for the post? Only I couldn't help noticing that you have no papers with you.' Sylvia Sanders was intrigued by this one. She didn't look old enough to meet the criteria yet she appeared calm and in control. She studied the girl shrewdly as she waited for her reply.

Katy's heart was pounding but she forced herself to speak calmly. 'I think common sense and a good relationship with your daughter would be of greater importance than a certificate that says I have done this and passed that. Certificates only tell you that a person has the ability to read and learn and produce results on paper. Putting it into practice is another thing altogether.'

Sylvia nodded. 'Go on.'

'My mam is a sensible woman. If I brought the same standards to this job that she set for me then I would be happy.'

Sylvia's lip curled in amusement. The girl certainly didn't lack nerve. 'Can you back that statement up by telling me, for instance, how you would deal with my daughter's tantrums?'

Katy felt her confidence grow. 'I'm certain at this moment that I couldn't.'

'The others could.'

Katy shook her head. 'I would need to know more about Elizabeth before I answered your question. There's usually a reason why a child throws tantrums. I'd be anxious to know what that reason was.'

Sylvia's lashes lowered, hiding her expression. She sat quietly for a moment, her body relaxed, her hands hidden behind the desk. Eventually, she looked up. 'How did you know my daughter's name was Elizabeth?'

'I asked the housekeeper.'

17

'I see.'

Just as Katy was beginning to feel that she was about to fall apart, Mrs Sanders said, 'Is there anything you would like to ask me before you leave?'

Without hesitation, Katy said, 'Could I meet your daughter?'

Sylvia Sanders' eyebrows rose. 'Why?'

Elizabeth is the most important person in this. It's only fair that she should see me before any decisions are made. After all, we may not like each other and I certainly wouldn't take the job if we didn't. That wouldn't be right for either of us.'

Sylvia pressed the bell, and as they waited she covertly studied the girl before her. She looked sturdy and for one so young she seemed sensible. Sylvia liked her candour and she respected her complete honesty about her inexperience – but was liking enough? The dark-haired qualified nanny seemed efficient, and apart from a slightly irritating habit of continually informing Sylvia of the worth of the academy where she had done her training, she struck her as being competent. She had decided that she was a possibility . . .

'You rang, Mrs Sanders?'

'Yes, Mrs Skelton. Would you show Miss Molloy up to the nursery, please.'

When they had gone, Sylvia leaned back against her chair. She was not one to balk at taking chances by acting on her instincts, but in this particular instance she was wavering. She liked this girl, but . . . Thoughtfully, she drew the reference belonging to the dark-haired nanny towards her and studied it. When she had finished, she nodded. There was one more thing to establish before she made up her mind.

Upstairs, Katy and Mrs Skelton had arrived at the nursery door. Katy smiled at the housekeeper. 'Would you mind if I went in alone?'

'Not at all.' Mrs Skelton gave a slight shrug and turned towards the stairs. Katy quietly opened the door and glanced in. The nursery was a large airy room with shelves full of toys and in the middle of the floor there was a child-sized table and chair at which a small figure sat glumly fingering some sandwiches. A

18

teenaged girl sat on the windowseat casually thumbing through a magazine. Katy's heart went out to the child. She looked so lonely and bored. She was wearing a pink dress under a pinafore. Her hair fell untidily to her shoulders.

When Katy pushed open the door and entered, Elizabeth Sanders turned and regarded her without interest, while the maid threw her an enquiring look. Katy introduced herself before crossing to the table. She looked at Elizabeth. 'Why are you eating alone?' she asked.

The maid, who introduced herself as Sally, looked puzzled. 'She's an only child.'

'She may well be, but no one needs to eat alone when the place is filled with teddy bears and dolls – and clowns with funny faces.' Katy took two teddy bears and one large doll off the shelf and set them down on the other chair. 'Is there room for me as well?' she asked.

The lonely little face lit up and Elizabeth moved over so that Katy could join her on the bench. She offered Katy a biscuit which she took, nibbling on it as she chatted to the slightly bewildered little person with the huge grey eyes.

'Would you like some of my orange squash? I could ask Sally to get another cup. Are you my new nanny?'

'I'm Katy Molloy. Have you some to spare?'

'I have plenty.'

'Then I'm sure your dolly won't mind a bit if I use her cup. Shall we ask?'

Elizabeth giggled as she took the tiny cup from the teaset and handed it to Katy. 'Poppy thinks it will be all right.' She moved closer. 'Have you come to stay?' she asked politely.

Katy looked at the pretty little girl with exquisite table manners. She behaves like a grown up, she thought sadly. 'I'm not sure. We will have to see,' she replied.

Sally looked on as they chatted, until Katy smiled at her and suggested that she should join them; then the three of them ate all the biscuits and shared the squash between them, much to Elizabeth's delight.

When Katy returned to the interview room it was empty. Her nervousness increased as the minutes passed but at last, Sylvia

Sanders entered and sat down to face her.

'I just popped up to have a word with Sally. I understand you got on well with my daughter?'

Kate nodded. 'I liked her very much.'

'She isn't always so lovable. I say that as a mother who loves her to death, but you have been honest with me and I feel I should be just as honest with you.' Sylvia paused. 'I am looking for a nanny who is prepared to live in – with weekends off – on the understanding that occasionally she may have to have her days off during the week if required.'

Katy nodded. 'I normally help out on the farm, particularly at weekends, but I'm certain my parents will not mind.' She rose when Mrs Sanders did. 'I assume I will hear from you when you have made your decision,' she said nervously.

'I can tell you now, Miss Molloy. I'd be very happy for you to take the job.'

Katy gasped. 'The others – I mean – I was expecting you to give the matter some thought before writing to us.'

'I will, of course, write to the other applicants to tell them that the post has been filled – that is, if you want it?'

'Of course I do! I'm delighted.'

'Then let's go into the study and work out what your duties will be, the salary and living conditions. You do understand that the contract in its present form is for one year.' She hesitated. 'I'm taking you on without qualifications, Miss Molloy, so I think that it would be advisable to arrange a one-month probation period. Is that acceptable to you?'

Katy nodded. 'Certainly. I quite understand.'

'Elizabeth will be starting school in September but I would like you to stay until the year is up and we'll go on from there,' Sylvia told her.

As they said goodbye an hour later, Katy couldn't resist asking, 'Why me? I have no qualifications. I had convinced myself that one of the trained nannies would get the position.'

Sylvia smiled. 'You were the only one who asked to see Elizabeth. The others had no interest in knowing how she felt. To them it was just a job. As soon as you asked to meet her, I felt that she would be in good hands. And when I went up to see her she wanted to know if the funny lady would be coming back to have tea with her another time.'

'Tell Elizabeth I would be delighted.'

They shook hands at the door and this time Katy took a leisurely stroll down the driveway, lingering now to admire the beautiful grounds. She felt lighthearted. Her day was made. She had beaten the odds and found herself a job; her bus was not due for another twenty minutes, and the day was sunny. A feeling of euphoria stole over her.

CHAPTER 2

Annie was coming out of the house with a large basket of washing in her arms as Katy arrived home.

'I'll give you a hand, Mam,' she said, her face split by a wide, happy smile.

Annie studied her. 'I get the impression that you have had some good news. You have a smile on you that would light up a room.'

'You never miss a trick,' Katy laughed, as her mother laid the basket down and began to hang up the clothes. She handed the pegs to her. 'I've just landed that job. The pay is six pounds a month.'

'Congratulations,' Annie said, with a mischievous smile. 'Even if it does mean that your da and myself will have to make some new plans now we have lost a valuable helper.'

Katy's smile faded a little. 'I could help out on the farm at weekends.'

'I don't think your father and I will find it too hard to cope,' Annie said. 'I was just teasing. Now that Tom is joining us we will be fine.'

Katy frowned. 'But he'll only be replacing me. You need more help, surely?'

Annie hefted the empty basket and started towards the house. 'Tom will be doing a lot more than you were able to do. He can do more out in the fields for a start. Besides . . .' She stopped for a moment. 'Your da was saying the other day that he is going to advertise for another hand.'

'When I'm earning I can put some money into the kitty,' Katy offered.

They had reached the kitchen. Annie hung the basket on the

hook in the cloakroom and put her arms round her daughter. 'Your da would have a fit if we suggested such a thing,' she said warmly. 'We have a few pounds to spare, my pet. After all, we own one of the more successful farms around. I think he'd want you to save your bit of money for a rainy day.'

'But—'

'But nothing. We don't lack funds, Katy. We lack workers – but now that more men are getting their demob papers I don't think we'll find it too hard to get someone. Now, tell me about the young lassie you will be looking after.'

'She is very sweet – and very lonely.' Katy paused. 'She talks and acts like a child of twelve instead of a four and a half year old.'

When Eddie came in from the fields, Annie told him that Katy had some news for him and he was to be careful what he said.

Eddie settled his large frame into an armchair and rattled the paper. He always enjoyed a good read while Annie was getting supper, and when he was thus absorbed, the rest of the household left him to it and went about their business; so when Katy came down from her room she merely dropped a kiss on his wiry grey hair and joined her mother.

'Have you told m'da yet?' she whispered.

Annie nodded. 'I told him you had news for him, but you know how he is. The house could fall down round his ears but he wouldn't let it interfere with his routine. He'll no doubt ask you about it when we are at the table.'

But it wasn't until after supper, when they were all settled round the big hearth again that Eddie brought up the subject. 'I understand you have news for me?'

'I have indeed. I got the job.'

'I hope you told the poor woman she was takin' on an amateur?' Eddie smiled to soften his words but he was serious.

'I gave her the full picture, Da. There were others there more qualified, but we got on well together and she chose me.'

Eddie put his pipe in his mouth. 'That's it then. I'll say no more. If she is willin' to chance her hand, then who am I to argue? Just make sure you know what you are about, young Katy.' He took up his paper again.

Katy looked perplexed. 'Is that it?'

'Your mother told me I was not to go on about things. We'll see what happens.'

'And you don't mind that I'll be livin' away from home?'

Annie and Katy both jumped as he shot out of his chair. 'You are *what*?'

'It's a live-in job, Da.'

Eddie turned to Annie. 'Why did you not say? I'd never have sanctioned this if I'd known. The deal is off. How do we know what kind of woman this is, or indeed what kind of establishment she runs!'

'Mrs Sanders is a perfectly respectable woman. She is on the committee of several charities—'

'I don't care if she is passing on thousands of pounds to the St Vincent de Paul fund. The woman is not well-known. I need you here on the farm. I have decided.'

Katy blanched. She looked frantically at her mother.

'Eddie Molloy!' Annie said, her voice like a rasp, her face grim. 'You are not going to ruin our Katy's chances. She is *not* cut out for farmwork. Wasn't it yourself who encouraged her to do the secretarial course because you didn't want her slavin' away doing a man's work? You can't cry off now. She will only be two miles down the road. She'll hardly go off the rails livin' that near.'

'She can go there in the mornin' and come home at night like any other body would do.' Eddie stuck his jaw out. Annie was not going to get the better of him. It was true that he had not thought of his daughter as a permanent fixture on the farm, but that was before Vincey . . . He sucked on his pipe with frantic intensity.

Katy, who had been silent up to this moment, started to speak, but Annie gripped her arm and shook her head. She sat down instead.

Annie stood over her husband. 'Now you listen to me, Eddie Molloy. Katy has to leave home one day and this is a good way for all of us to get used to the idea. She has to find her feet – and livin' two miles away is one good way of finding them.' Annie's voice faltered. She had been harbouring some doubts herself about Katy leaving home, but had suppressed them. God knows she would miss her even more than Eddie would, for he was out in the fields most of the day and Katy had been company for her about the house.

Eddie knew when he was beaten, for he'd never seen Annie so adamant. But stubborn to the last, he rattled his paper and clenched his pipe firmly in his mouth. 'I'll give the matter some more thought – but I am not a happy man, I'll have you know that.'

Annie motioned Katy into the kitchen. 'The battle is won,' she whispered. 'Tomorrow he will have worked out the strategy of agreement so that he doesn't come over in a bad light.'

Still Katy looked worried. 'I don't want to fall out with him,' she said bleakly. 'Maybe . . .'

'Maybe nothin',' Annie said fiercely. 'We have to let go. *He* has to let go. Away off to your room and start getting the things together that you are going to take with you.'

Katy's bags were packed. Her father had just arrived upstairs to take them down to the car. Katy watched him as he lifted them and suddenly the realisation that she was leaving her home, perhaps for ever, hit her like a bolt. She ran over to him and clasped him round the neck, burrowing her head against his chest, inhaling the tangy farmy smell that always clung to him . . . feeling the rapid beat of his heart beneath the check shirt he always wore when he was going anywhere important. Her eyes filled with tears.

Eddie dropped the cases and patted her back. Emotional scenes embarrassed him. 'Now, now,' he said gruffly. 'I can't be havin' this display. I'll miss you like I'd miss the daylight if it never came, cusheen, but your ma is right. Sure, you are only the two miles away. It isn't as if you were off to America.'

'Am I doing the right thing, Da?' She was going to strangers and she didn't know if she wanted to, after all.

Eddie held her away from him, desperately longing for his pipe – his great comfort in times of stress – but it was in the rack downstairs. He stroked his daughter's hair with clumsy affection instead and waited for the tears to stop. God almighty! Why did women shed tears so easily? It always threw him when they did

26

that. In their younger days, Annie had been the great one for using this ploy when she wanted him to do something.

Katy gave a watery smile. 'I'm all right now,' she said, and dabbed her eyes.

Annie had deliberately stayed downstairs so that father and daughter could say their farewell in privacy. She knew that Eddie was feeling the sadness of Katy's departure, but also that he would not have wanted anyone, even her, to witness any sentimentality.

When he took the cases out to the car, Annie checked her daughter's appearance. 'You look grand – and very professional,' she nodded, studying the neat, navy blue dress with the white Peter Pan collar and matching white gloves which she had helped Katy to choose. Katy had tied her hair back with a ribbon. 'I still think you should have worn a hat,' she observed mildly.

'Wearing a hat on Sundays is bad enough,' Katy laughed. 'With all this hair that I've got, I can never keep it on for long.' She caught sight of her father coming back and she grabbed her mother for a final hug. 'I'm goin' to miss you both,' she wailed.

Annie returned her hug. 'I'm not goin' to fall apart. I will be seeing you most weekends, for goodness sake.'

When they'd gone, Annie busied herself in the kitchen. Just as Eddie reached for his pipe when he was under pressure so Annie reached for the rolling pin, and soon, the kitchen was filled with delicious smells of baking. Her excuse was that the men would be needing food. She now had four to feed as they had managed to find a new worker to take the pressure off Eddie. She stopped what she was doing for a moment and smiled, remembering how Katy had offered to help pay for an extra hand. Eddie had laughed when he'd heard.

'Tell the girl to save her money. We have no need of it. It will be there for a rainy day.'

'Tell her yourself. It will come better from you,' Annie had advised, and he had done just that.

A fortnight later, Katy was still finding it difficult to settle in at Beresford House, which was so large and elegant in comparison with the cosy farmhouse. Her room with the wide bed and deep-piled carpet and thick curtains had not the same feeling of intimacy as her gingham-curtained room at home. She had never been away from home for more than a few hours until now, and each night she lay in bed suffering wretchedly from homesickness. She had no excuse for feeling as she did, for everyone from Mrs Sanders to the head gardener treated her well.

Mrs Skelton the housekeeper was particularly friendly and helpful. 'Elizabeth has taken well to you, which is the main thing,' she said comfortingly. 'Your homesickness will pass once you have got the routine in the nursery sorted out as you want it.'

Katy knew that what Mrs Skelton said made sense, and chided herself for her spineless attitude. This was her chance to show her parents – and Margaret – that she had the ability to succeed. She sat up in bed. Only two more days and she would be home for the weekend! She would feel better when she'd seen her parents again, and when she returned she would start organising things her way.

The previous nanny had timetables and rules pinned to the wall which Katy had followed in spite of the fact that she found some of them somewhat rigid and harsh. She switched off the lamp and lay deep in thought. A surge of excitement rushed through her. After all, *she* was in charge now. She didn't need to follow someone else's routine.

Elizabeth was delighted when the lists and timetables came down. 'Does that mean I can do what I like, Katy?' she asked, in that precise way she had which saddened her new nanny.

Katy laughed. 'No, it does not, you rapscallion.'

'What is a rap . . . rap . . .'

'It means you are a holy terror. A knave of the first order who would give me a terrible time if I let you get away with it.' Katy lifted the child up in her arms and whirled her round. 'Life is full of rules. There are rules for eating, rules for behaviour, rules for working – there are rules for just about everything, but we'll work it out as we go. We will not hang them on the walls.'

Elizabeth, breathless after being whirled about, and with eyes bright with laughter, cried, 'Again! Again, Katy!' She held her arms up. 'Nanny Stevens never gave me swings. I like it.'

Katy looked at her watch. 'It's only three o'clock. How would you like to go for a walk along the riverbank instead?'

'Yes! Oh yes! Mummy won't mind.'

'We'd better let her know, though.'

Sylvia was in the drawing room. She was putting fresh flowers into a tall vase, picking each one up delicately from the trug which she had placed on the coffee table. She looked up as Katy knocked on the door and entered with Elizabeth.

Elizabeth ran across to her mother. 'Mamma, Katy is taking me for a walk along the riverbank.'

Sylvia frowned. 'I'm sorry, poppet. Veronica is coming over and she will be bringing David with her. He'll want you to play with him.'

'I don't want to play with David. He is horrid. I want to go along the riverbank with Katy.' Elizabeth's tiny mouth pursed.

'Elizabeth, go to your room! I want to have a word with Katy.'

'I won't! I won't!'

Sylvia, her face pink with exasperation, grabbed her daughter's arm and marched her towards the door. 'To your room, at once!'

She returned to Katy. 'I think that in future it would be better to let me know of your plans before you mention them to Elizabeth. This could have been avoided if you had spoken to me first.' Slim pale fingers went to her forehead as the sound of the door being kicked and the screams of Elizabeth could be heard through the panelling.

Katy could barely hide her amazement. The scene could have been avoided if Sylvia had been more tactful! 'I had no idea you had invited a little friend over. I wouldn't have minded taking him along as well.'

Sylvia waved her arm. 'I can't go back on what I've said. Take Elizabeth upstairs now and try to pacify her before my visitors arrive.'

As Katy left the room following Sylvia's imperious wave of the hand, she was thoughtful. She could now understand why the villagers referred to her employer as 'that haughty one'. Until now, Katy had found her friendly and very amenable to suggestions, and this outburst really surprised her. She frowned. And what of the 'wild parties' Sylvia was supposed to give? Since she had arrived at Beresford House, the nearest thing to a wild party she'd seen was the committee gathering two weeks ago, when the sherry, it is true, had flowed freely.

Katy scooped the struggling Elizabeth up in her arms and made her way upstairs. The force of the child's frustration was so great that loud sobs were wracking the small form. The tantrum was out of all proportion to the situation. Katy tried holding her close the way her own mother had held her when she was 'putting it on' as her father called it, but this child's state was beyond any *she* had ever got into.

When they reached the room, she put Elizabeth down but she immediately ran to the door and kicked it hard. Katy acted instinctively. She opened the toy cupboard and hauled out the enormous cardboard box that held rejected toys. Emptying them onto the floor, she placed the box by the bed and took Elizabeth in her arms again. 'If you must have a tantrum, then jump on this. It will be more fun than kicking a door,' she pleaded. 'Besides, if you don't stop I think your Mam might tell me I am no good at my job and I'll be asked to leave.'

Katy didn't think the child had heard her, so loud was the crying and hiccuping, but the little face registered surprise. Katy lifted the struggling form onto the bed and pointed to the big carton. 'Jump!' she ordered.

Elizabeth stopped and looked at the box. 'No!'

'Go on, jump!' commanded Katy. 'You might as well have some fun while you're making a fuss.'

She took hold of the small hand and Elizabeth launched herself off the bed onto the two-foot-high box. Tantrum forgotten, still hiccuping, she laughed with pure delight as the box crumpled slightly beneath her.

'Again!' Elizabeth laughed. 'Again!' Katy sighed with relief.

There was a knock on the door and Sally entered with some orange squash and biscuits for Elizabeth and a cup of tea for her.

Sally raised her eyebrows. 'How did you get her to stop?' she whispered. 'A tantrum usually lasts for about an hour till she has nearly choked herself.'

'Call it divine assistance. I was desperate and asked Himself up there for help. I suddenly thought of the trick with the box.' Katy nodded towards the now-flattened carton lying on the floor.

'Who could keep up a tantrum when it's more fun jumping onto a helpless box?'

Sally laughed. 'I wish I'd thought of that. Many a time since Nanny Stevens left I've been nearly at my wit's end when she had one of those. She can be a right little rip when she likes.' She looked towards Elizabeth, who was now quietly sipping her drink. 'Now look at her. She has the face of an angel.'

Katy whispered, 'Has Mrs Sanders' friend arrived?'

Sally nodded and grimaced. 'Thanks to Missie Two Shoes here, *I've* got to take him out for a walk round the grounds.'

As the weeks passed, Katy grew very fond of the bright, eager little girl. They developed a respect for each other and a bond of trust was forged between them. But once when Katy left the nursery while Elizabeth was absorbed in painting, she had, on her return, surprised a look on the little face which had troubled her. Elizabeth had been staring out of the window, the paintbrush still in her hand, and Katy had sensed a loneliness in the droop of the lips and the prolonged stare. She had taken the child into her arms and cuddled her and had been rewarded with a smile.

Today, they were going into town with Sylvia. Elizabeth was excited. A ride into town with her mother was a rare event.

'Will we be allowed to go round the market and look at all the animals?' she asked her mother.

Sylvia smiled, her finely chiselled face hardly creasing in its perfection. She lifted grey suede gloves from the table and slowly and elegantly slid them onto her hands. 'If Katy doesn't mind. I think it would be a good idea. We can meet for tea and cakes at the tea rooms at four o'clock.' She looked at her watch and then at Katy, her eyebrows arched.

'We'll have a lovely time. I'll look after her,' Katy promised.

Sylvia said, 'I have no worry about that, my dear. How glad I've been since your arrival I cannot fully put into words. Elizabeth is a different child since you came.'

Katy glowed with pleasure.

'Well, let's not linger,' said Sylvia, and swung Elizabeth up into her arms. 'I shall regret this later,' she whispered. 'She weighs a ton and I'm not very strong.'

Elizabeth, however, was delighted to be in her mother's arms and grinned at Katy over her shoulder as she was carried to the car.

During the course of the afternoon, Elizabeth had stroked the hindquarters of most of the animals in the pens. Her hands reeked of hot animal flesh and she kept pushing them towards Katy and saying, 'Smell my hands. They smell of dung.'

'God save us. Your mam will kill me if I bring you into the tea room with those hands. Could you not be contented just looking? Let's get you into the cloakroom before she arrives.'

Watching Elizabeth's animated face in the washroom mirror as she puddled her hands in the soapy water, Katy smiled. Of all the things they had seen and done this day, the one thing that would remain in Elizabeth's memory would be the joy of stroking the cows and the sheep and feeling their warm skin against her own. Her eyes had not stopped swivelling the whole time they were touring the market place, and Katy had difficulty keeping up as the small figure darted here and there, anxious not to miss a single thing. She had watched and listened in fascination as the auctioneer rattled off his high-speed jargon, and had sighed with envy when a particularly pretty pony was sold.

That evening, a tired Elizabeth was tucked into bed, the prayers she said each night under Katy's watchful gaze, being missed, for she could hardly keep her eyes open. Within minutes she was asleep.

Katy tiptoed out. She would inform Sylvia there was no point in her going up to kiss Elizabeth goodnight. She was well gone.

Sylvia was in the act of putting the phone down when Katy knocked and entered. The young girl noticed the smile playing round her employer's lips and as she crossed the room the smile widened.

'I've just had the most wonderful news! My brother Charles will be coming to stay. He will arrive in two days' time.'

'You've never mentioned you had a brother, Mrs Sanders,' Katy observed

'I don't suppose I did.' There was a pause. 'By the way, I'd like you to call me Sylvia.'

The words, spoken so casually, startled Katy. She wasn't sure what she was expected to say.

'I must arrange for his room to be prepared,' Sylvia continued, her mind now on the impending visit. 'He will be spending the summer with us. I must inform Mrs Skelton. Please excuse me.'

When she'd gone, Katy realised she had forgotten to warn Sylvia that Elizabeth was fast asleep. Still, she didn't suppose it mattered as Sylvia now had other things on her mind.

'I'm tired of playing with my toys.' Elizabeth looked appealingly at Katy.

'Would you like me to tell you a story?' Katy asked.

Elizabeth looked at her in awe. 'Can you make up stories? Nanny Stevens only read them out of books.'

'It's much more fun to write your own stories,' Katy smiled. 'That way, you can make all the people in them do what *you* want them to do. I used to sit in my special tree and invent stories, and then in the evening I went up to my bedroom and wrote them out. I have an exercise book filled with them.'

Katy laid down her sewing and joined Elizabeth on the floor where she sat with her dolls among the large floppy cushions. 'I shall have to get your drink and biscuits soon so it will have to be quick.'

Elizabeth cuddled up against her and Katy put an arm round her. For such a young child, Elizabeth had a quick, enquiring mind. Already, she could write simple words and add a few numbers together and was a practised questioner. No one escaped. Katy didn't think that this time it would be any different. 'I'll tell you the story of the deely bobber,' she said.

'What's a deely bobber?'

Katy smiled. She'd been right. 'Well, a deely bobber is a bit like a leprechaun but different.'

'How can he be like him and be different?'

'Because a leprechaun wears a suit of red and green, whereas a deely bobber wears a suit of green and red – do you see the difference?'

'Of course!' said Elizabeth, looking wise.

'Whatever the leprechauns do, the deely bobbers do the exact opposite and that really makes the leprechauns angry because they see themselves as being very important,' Katy went on, enjoying herself.

'What exactly *does* a leprechaun do?' Elizabeth folded her arms excitedly.

'A leprechaun is the great one for dishing out advice,' Katy informed her. He thinks he knows it all. He sits up on a toadstool hammering away at mending shoes, and when he throws the shoes onto the ground to be collected, the deely bobber who is sitting *under* the toadstool, collects the shoes and takes all the nails out again. He also undoes all the advice given by the leprechaun.'

'That isn't very nice.'

'I suppose not,' Katy said. 'On the other hand, as the deely bobber sees it, people should be encouraged to make their own decisions and shouldn't be told what to do by an elf squattin' on a toadstool. He thinks that if all the decisions in life are made for us, our brains will shrivel.'

Elizabeth looked uncertain. 'But why do they take the nails out of the shoes when the poor leprechaun has hammered them in?'

'The deely bobber removes the nails so that the shoes have to be mended again and again, otherwise the leprechaun would be out of a job. You see, it's the only job he ever does.'

'Why doesn't the deely bobber explain that to the leprechaun?'

'What, and ruin his pride? He has more sense.'

They both started at the sound of a chuckle. Katy turned swiftly. A tall man was leaning against the doorframe looking at them, his eyes crinkled up in laughter.

Elizabeth scrambled to her feet. 'Uncle Charles! Uncle Charles!' She flung herself at him, causing him to stumble slightly.

'Whoa! What a missile you are. I nearly fell over.' Charles gave his niece a big hug.

Katy had time to study him. So this was Sylvia's brother, Charles. He was much taller than his sister and whereas Sylvia's hair was fair, his was a deep chestnut. But it was his eyes that made Katy's heart jump. He was gazing straight at her with eyes that were deep brown and fathomless. Eyes that could hold secrets. To her annoyance, she felt herself blush.

'Come and meet Katy. She's my best friend.' Elizabeth pulled him forward.

Katy was suddenly aware that she was still sprawled across the cushions. She scrambled to her feet. The man must think she was mad, telling an intelligent child like Elizabeth such a load of tarradiddle.

'Hello there. My name's Charles Gilbert – and you must be Katy Molloy. Please to meet you. Loved the story,' he grinned as he shook her outstretched hand.

Katy eyed him warily. Was he codding her?

'Do we get to hear the rest?' he asked pleasantly.

'It wasn't a story as such,' she told him, trying to extricate herself. 'I was encouraging Elizabeth to question and discuss.'

'I see!' said Uncle Charles, his lip curling in amusement.

Katy said with a trace of asperity, 'Would you like some tea? I was just about to fetch Elizabeth's snack.'

When she returned, they were both leaning out of the open window arguing about whether the tiny green shoots were flower shoots or just grass. It had been a harsh winter and nature was struggling to produce. Flowers were slow to bloom; streams were sluggish. Katy noticed that his face, in profile, had a look of strength about it. Not a man to tangle with, she thought. Suddenly, he turned towards her and it was as though she'd had an electric shock as his eyes looked into hers. The curve of his mouth as he smiled at her set her heart racing.

'Tea!' Charles shouted, as he swung his niece in his arms.

'And orangeade,' said Elizabeth, and added excitedly: 'Uncle Charles will be staying all summer, Katy.'

'That will be grand for you.' Katy handed Charles his cup.

'Please don't be cross with me for teasing you,' he said. 'It was a lovely story.'

'It was a daft story,' she said crisply, 'but Katy liked it – that's what counts.'

When she'd finished her snack, Elizabeth became absorbed in undressing her 'children' for bed, her little tongue protruding from the corner of her mouth in concentration, her small body relaxed as she pushed her hair from her face.

Charles watched his niece for a second before turning to Katy. 'Does she ever mention her father?' he asked quietly.

'She knows he went to heaven and she keeps his photo by her bed. Apparently she asked her mother why did her friend David have a daddy and she didn't, so Sylvia explained as much as she could and asked her if she would like a photo of him. She tells people her daddy is an angel.'

Charles nodded. He was intrigued by this girl with the rosy cheeks and kind eyes. 'You are very young for such a responsible position,' he ventured.

Katy stiffened. 'Your sister didn't think it was a problem.'

'I didn't mean to imply that it might be. I just wondered why one so young should wish to take on the responsibility.'

'I actually did a secretarial course but there aren't many jobs like that being tossed into the pot in this area, so when I saw the advertisement for a nanny, I went for it.' She smiled shyly. 'It's my first tentative step towards independence. Eventually, I hope to work in the city.'

'Do you dine with us tonight?' Charles enquired.

Katy frowned. 'I haven't been told otherwise. Sylvia and I usually dine together as she doesn't like eating alone, but when she dines out I take a tray to my room.'

Charles hesitated. 'How has she been? Sylvia, I mean.'

'I didn't know her before I came here so I can't compare.'

'Does she still paint?'

'Paint? I've never seen her do any, and certainly she hasn't mentioned that she was interested in painting.'

'She's very talented. Before she met her husband Bertie it was what she did. She made a lot of money from her paintings. When he was killed she put all her equipment away and refused to touch a brush.'

'How strange! And sad, too. I would have thought that painting would have been an excellent way of taking her mind off things.'

Charles shook his head. 'On the contrary. Sylvia said it gave her too much time to think and remember.'

'She certainly keeps busy with all her committees,' Katy mused.

'It's one of the reasons why she decided to employ a nanny. Haven't you been in touch?'

'Yes, of course, but lately I've been away a lot. However, I'll be working at the airport in Belfast now, supervising the extension of the runways and the building project which my firm has designed. That's why I was able to make this visit.'

Elizabeth had put her dolls to bed, and now she came over. 'Katy, can we go down to the brook and look at the fishes?'

Katy smiled at Charles. 'Speaking of jobs, this is one I have to do. I'll see you at dinner.'

Later, as she idly watched Elizabeth crouching by the brook stabbing with her net in an effort to catch the tiny fish, she wondered if Charles had a girlfriend. He had spoken of his latest project and how glad he was to be in Ireland again, and how much his niece had grown since he last saw her six months ago . . . but no mention of any girlfriend. Katy thought he was too attractive not to have someone in his life. She leaned forward to stare at her reflection in the water. At another time, the grotesque sight of her face changing in form in the rippling stream would have made her laugh, but now she felt irritated. Her cheekbones were non-existent, hidden as they were under plump rosy flesh. She took a twig and stirred the water in frustration.

Elizabeth turned. 'You look so cross, Katy – just like Mummy does sometimes. I don't like it when Mummy looks cross.'

Katy hugged her. 'I'm not really cross. I was just giving myself a good talking to.' She loved this dark-haired bundle of mischief who was a terror if roused, and her intelligence made working with her interesting. 'I think we had better get back. It's time for your supper. Would you like me to ask Uncle Charles to come up and kiss you goodnight before you go to sleep?'

'He always does when he's here,' said Elizabeth and skipped away.

By the time she had settled Elizabeth for the night and tidied up the mess of toys, Katy felt drained, so it was with a sigh of relief that she settled down into a hot bath and allowed herself to relax. It was such a lovely bathroom compared with the one at the farm, which was more functional than decorative. Years ago, her father had the bathroom installed in what had once been a small bedroom, at the same time as the telephone was put in. Her mother laughed as she told Katy how her father had moaned about 'these ugly pylons crossing the countryside', but she had told Eddie that if it meant she didn't have to do the milking by lamplight on a dark evening, she didn't care if there was one stuck in their own backyard!

Dinner that evening was a jolly meal. Brother and sister, pleased to see each again, had a lot to catch up on. They didn't neglect Katy though, and she discovered as she listened to them that they both had the same droll sense of humour. She hadn't heard Sylvia laugh so much since she'd known her. When they moved into the drawing room after the meal, Katy excused herself. 'I'll just go up and check on Elizabeth and then I'll take a stroll round the grounds.'

Later, when she made her way downstairs, Charles was waiting in the hall.

'Do you mind if I walk with you?' he asked.

Katy hid her surprise. 'Not at all.'

'Good! My system could do with a dash of cold, crisp air.'

They walked in silence for some time before Charles spoke again. 'Sylvia appears happy. I think having you around has been good for her – the last nanny was older and rather severe.' He paused. 'How are you coping with my niece?'

'Looking after Elizabeth is more fun than work.'

'Even when she has one of her famous tantrums?'

'Why shouldn't a child let out her frustrations?'

Charles laughed. 'No wonder Sylvia thinks you are wonderful. Are you always this tolerant?'

'God, no! You should hear me when I'm not gettin' my own way at home. My mother says that when I was younger, I invented the tantrum and put it to good use. I was a holy terror.'

'So that's why you understand Elizabeth when she gets one. Sylvia says that you have all but cured her.'

'And the devil has lost his horns,' Katy scoffed. 'I'm sure she'll find time for another one.'

They had stopped by the spinney at the edge of the grounds. Charles said, 'Let's walk on. In spite of the chill the evening is so beautiful I'd like to go a little further before it gets really dark.'

Katy didn't give a toss if the night grew to be inky black. A man of culture and experience was holding her arm and talking to her as though she possessed a brain.

Annie took lunch down to the field where the men were doing the ploughing. In spite of the May sunshine there was still a slight chill in the air following the recent harsh winter. Hedges which should have been heavy with bud were only just showing signs of life; the may blossom was the sparsest she had seen it. She laid the wicker basket on the ground, called to the four workers and sat down to wait. Annie always felt happy when Katy came home for the weekend, even if she did spend most of it working on the farm. The house seemed empty without her presence.

Katy was laughing at young Tom Toner. They made a fine couple, and she wouldn't mind at all if Katy came in one day and said she was going to marry the lad, for he was respectable and a hard worker. Unlike his father, who was small and wiry, Tom was a tall lad with strong shoulders. He had a quick mind and a ready wit and, like his father, there was little he didn't know about farming. Annie had hopes for him and Katy – not that her daughter had shown much interest, but there would be even less chance of anything happening if he went off to college. When they were all lounging on their elbows scoffing the food she had brought, Annie asked him outright why he thought it necessary to go to college.

'Farming, as we know it, is passing,' Tom began. 'To get ahead and to make money, farmers will have to be more educated—'

'Jaysus, man. One trip over to England on a plane and you know it all.'

'Don't climb on your high horse, Eddie.' Patrick Toner spoke soothingly. 'The lad is young and has a long way to go yet – God willing – and it has to be admitted that since the war ended Britain is rarin' to go. You and meself are too long in the tooth to make so many changes; our day is done, but even we can listen and learn or go down the plug-hole with the sewage.'

'Have you seen the film on at the picture house, Katy?'

Katy looked at her mother in surprise. It was unusual for Annie to be interested in what was on. 'No, but I'm meeting Margaret tonight. We might go.'

Annie hid her disappointment. Another time, she thought, and gathered up the rug and the hamper.

That evening, Katy listened as Margaret rattled on about her life at the university, and of her evenings spent with the group she belonged to in the cafés and the student bar. There was no stigma attached to girls having a drink as there was in public bars but it all seemed very decadent to Katy and she said so. Margaret grinned. 'Most of us stick to lemonade or orangeade. Anyway, here I am chattering on about my life. How is *your* life going along these days?'

'What life?' Katy made a face. 'I look after Elizabeth all week and then at weekends I help out on the farm.'

'Why don't you go out more? I'm not your only friend, Katy Molloy. I know a couple of lads who would pull their eye-teeth for a date with you, and I saw Molly McCabe in Belfast last week and she says they never see you these days.'

'To tell you the truth, Margaret, I feel I've left Mam and Da in the lurch so I like to help out when I come home. Patrick Toner and Tom help, but Tom will be going to college at the end of the year and when he goes, my da will need someone else in his place now I'm gone.'

'Katy, I'm sure your mam and da don't expect you to devote your entire life to the farm. Why else did they send you to college to do that shorthand and typing course?'

Katy chuckled suddenly. 'I suspect Mam has plans for me and Tom.'

'How so?'

'Yesterday, when she brought lunch down to us in the far field, she made a remark about the pictures and asked if I'd seen what was on. I've just realised that she was hoping Tom would take the hint. I hope to God he didn't realise what my mother was getting at.'

The waitress came to take their order. When she had gone, Margaret, her eyes dancing with devilment, said, 'Every girl in the area fancies Tom. You sound as though the idea would be worse than death.'

'Tom and I are great friends,' Katy objected. 'I value his friendship. Compared to some of the lads we went to school with, he is a gem and he will make someone a wonderful husband – but I don't think of him in that respect. He is more like a brother to me. Besides, he has never asked me out or shown any sign of it. Do you want me to be bold and forward?'

'He likes you, I know that for a fact. The poor lad is afraid of rejection. You are considered a "catch", you know.'

'*Me?*'

'Yes, you eejut. *You!* Your father has one of the most successful farms for miles. You have had all your orders since you were born. You always wore the best clothes and you made the rest of us feel like we were on poor relief when you came waltzing into school with your leather music case and your shiny shoes. The boys were always wary of you because they didn't want to appear to be sucking up.'

'Lord! I thought it was because I wasn't pretty enough. Only Freddy O'Connor ever gave me a second look, and he had as much fascination as a frog.'

'He was the only one who could match up to your way of life. I can't believe you have spent all these years thinking that you weren't good enough.'

'Neither can I – now!' said Katy. God, the hours she had spent moping in her bedroom because no boy would ever look at her. She had always thought that the friends she had were more Margaret's than hers. Margaret had taken her under her wing.

'Would you go out with Tom if he asked you?' Margaret spoke through a mouthful of food.

Katy paused as she lifted her fork. 'I'm very fond of Tom and I would go out with him as a friend, but that's as far as it goes.'

'There isn't anyone else, is there?'

Katy hesitated.

'Well?' Margaret persisted.

'No, and I've just burnt the tongue off myself with all the chatter,' Katy cried. 'Can we not eat up and then get on with the rest of our day?'

Margaret looked at Katy with more interest. There was something going on here. She would find out eventually for she was adept at winkling out secrets, just as Katy was at keeping them.

CHAPTER 3

As she walked up the drive on Monday, Katy was looking
forward to seeing Charles Gilbert again. Also, she missed Elizabeth – she always did when she returned home to the farm. They
had fun together and Katy felt a sense of loss when she was back
among a group of adults whose prime aim was to get the
workload done and who had little time for being silly and
looking at life from a child's angle. And who could blame them?
Farming was a chancy business, and a bad winter or a summer's
drought could affect their livelihood.

Upstairs in the big house, Elizabeth ran towards her, her tiny
face alight with joy. 'You're back, Katy! I do wish you didn't have
to go away. I missed you. Uncle Charles and Mummy were
fighting and I don't like it when they do that.'

Katy folded the child in her arms and swung her round. 'I
missed you too. I'm pleased to be back.' She placed her tiny
charge on the shelf where her toys were. 'Sit up here with your
teddies and then we can look at each other. Now! Tell me why
you think Mummy and Uncle Charles were fighting – I'm sure
they weren't.'

'They were! They were! Mummy doesn't want Uncle Charles
to invite Pamela over here. Mummy says that Pamela will stay
too long.'

Who was Pamela? Katy wondered. A girlfriend of Charles'?
She hugged Elizabeth and said, 'Grown ups do row occasionally.
I expect they are friends again by now.'

Elizabeth shook her head. 'Uncle Charles went away again.'

Katy's heart sank. 'Where did he go?'

'I think he went back to London.'

Katy helped Elizabeth down and said swiftly, 'It will all blow over. You get your paints out and I'll go down and ask Mummy if we can take the bus into Ballynashee after lunch for a wander round. We'll stop off at Cahey's for ice cream.'

Sylvia wasn't around, so she strolled into the kitchen, still curious about the row that had upset Elizabeth.

Sally, busy polishing silver, informed her that Mrs Sanders was at a meeting over at Farthing Lodge and wouldn't be in for lunch. Katy looked into the pantry. Mrs Skelton was nowhere to be seen.

She frowned. 'Why was Elizabeth left upstairs alone?' she asked.

Sally bridled, her normally cheerful expression replaced by one of annoyance. 'She went upstairs to get one of her toys. Mrs Skelton gave her permission but told her to come back as soon as she'd got it. I heard you come in and I knew you were with her because of the racket you were both making.'

Katy apologised. 'It's just that she is upset. She seems to think that her mother and her uncle had a big row.'

Sally laughed. 'It wasn't a big one – I heard raised voices but it was soon over.'

'Where is Mr Gilbert now?'

Sally shrugged. 'I'm not sure, but I think he has gone on a trip to see a friend. I heard him tell Mrs Sanders that he might be away overnight.'

So he hadn't returned to London, Katy thought, relieved. 'If Mrs Sanders doesn't come back before I go, will you tell her that I have taken Elizabeth for a bus ride into Ballynashee?' she instructed. At that moment, Mrs Skelton walked in with a basket full with vegetables and fruit.

She glanced at Katy. 'Are you staying for lunch?'

Katy nodded. 'Yes. Then I'm taking Elizabeth to Ballynashee for the afternoon. I was just asking Sally to let Mrs Sanders know.'

After a lunch of soup and soda bread spread with lashings of salty butter, Katy sat back in her chair and looked at Sally. 'How long have you known Mrs Sanders, Sally?' she asked curiously, glancing over at Elizabeth, who was playing with her dolls by the door.

'I was with her for two years before we came here. I started working for her a short time after she married.'

'You didn't mind leaving England and all your friends to come over here?'

Sally shook her head. 'Most of my friends were either married or courting, and I was fed up ducking and diving during the bombing raids so I felt I had little to lose and all to gain by coming.'

'You did gain by it!' Mrs Skelton turned to Katy. 'She's courtin' Fred Finney's son. He's the gamekeeper for Mr Thompson the other side of Ballyclinchy.'

'So that's what you get up to of an evening,' said Katy with a grin.

Sally blushed and returned the grin. 'I can't believe that I am likely to be settling down here. I thought living in Ireland would be like living in a foreign country. I was here months before I could understand half of what people said to me, and when I started going out with Davy I wasn't the most popular girl around. Everyone thought that because I was English I was "stuck up" and they didn't care for me pinching one of their men.'

Katy patted her shoulder. 'Take not a bit of notice – now I must get Elizabeth ready for our outing.'

When they arrived in Ballynashee it was packed with people. Katy had forgotten that there was a fair on just outside the small town, but Elizabeth was delirious with excitement at the news.

'*Plee-eese.* I've never been to a fair. Please let's go.'

Katy gave in. 'All right, young madam. But no jumping around. It will be very crowded so you must hold my hand tightly.'

It was indeed very packed and she had to lift Elizabeth up several times because of the press of bodies trying to progress along the paths between the stalls. The queues of people waiting to go on the rides added to the problem, but they joined one so that Elizabeth could have a couple of turns on the roundabout before moving onto other things. By the late afternoon Katy was exhausted. Fortunately, Elizabeth was also beginning to tire so she coaxed her away from the other attractions with the promise of an ice cream.

Katy groaned when they eventually found the ice-cream van; the queue here was just as long as the others. She was now feeling even more irritated by the continuous jostling and she had the beginning of a headache. Elizabeth having caught sight of some swings wanted to go on them.

'You can't go on the swings *and* have ice cream,' Katy said firmly. 'You'll be sick.'

'I'm never sick, I promise.'

'No!' Katy's voice was sharper than she had intended, but her one great desire at the moment was to find a quiet peaceful spot away from the crush and the noise, and she was finding Elizabeth's demands irksome. The sound of the music blaring out from the loudspeakers was pounding in her head. God! She had lived on a farm for too long. Elderly ladies felt like this. Not eighteen-year-old girls.

Wearily, she placed Elizabeth against the guy ropes of the tent next to the ice-cream kiosk and fumbled in her purse for money as the cones were being filled.

'Haven't you got any change?' the ice-cream seller called over the noise.

Katy fumbled again and shook her head. Sullenly the grumpy vendor took the note she proffered and handed over the change. Balancing two cones in her hand and trying to hold her clutch bag under her arm, she took it and turned towards the side where she'd left Elizabeth leaning against the ropes. To her horror she wasn't there. She whirled around frantically, her eyes searching, searching. Throwing the ice-cream cones down in panic, Katy grabbed an arm. 'Please! Have you seen a little girl in a blue coat?'

Several heads shook. Katy ran into the tent next door where it seemed as though half the county was trying to get hoops round objects on a table. Desperate, she pushed through. God! She was so little. She'd never find her in the crowd. Her heart was pumping with fear. Her breathing was coming in a series of gulps and she knew she looked wild.

Still she tore around asking the question: 'Have you seen a little girl wearing a blue coat?'

Sympathetically they all shook their heads until at last a tall man with the bluest eyes she'd ever seen said he had.

'Where? Oh, where?' Katy clutched his arm.

He pointed. 'Over there by those guy ropes by the ice-cream stall.'

Katy said faintly, 'That was where I left her.' She realised she was still clutching his arm. He looked down at her and took her by the shoulder to steady her.

'Look, I'll give you a hand. The name's Terence. Terence Coleman. Why don't we use the tannoy? God knows it will give us a rest from the racket that's belching out of it at the moment.' He smiled reassuringly at her. 'Calm! That's the way to do it. No good going round like a headless chicken – doesn't do a blind bit of good.'

They made their way towards the sound system area and Katy waited restlessly whilst Terence explained the situation. She felt a tremendous relief to be able to leave the decisions to someone else. When he came back she looked anxiously at him.

'They are going to make an announcement and we are to make our way to the large tent in the centre with the blue flag on it. Lost children are taken there.'

They found it. The first announcement had already been made. They waited for fifteen minutes. Two children were brought in sobbing. Katy was now so frightened she was unable to stand up. She sat down and lowered her head to try and stop the nausea which threatened to overcome her, and jumped as another announcement came over the tannoy.

Terence gripped her arm. 'Hold on. It'll be all right. Someone is sure to find her.'

'Oh God! Poor Elizabeth, she'll be so frightened. And how can I tell her mother?'

'She isn't your little girl?' Terence asked, in surprise.

'I'd be about thirteen years old when she was born . . .' Katy suddenly shot up. 'Oh! Elizabeth! Elizabeth!' She raced across to the entrance and clasped the small figure to her. Terence Coleman followed more slowly. Now that the panic was over he studied the girl with the jet black curly hair and the long-lashed eyes. She was even prettier than he'd first thought, which pleased him. Terence Coleman didn't go in much for rescuing women, and plain ones had not a chance in hell.

'I got lost, Katy. I was scared,' Elizabeth was sobbing. 'I went to watch the funny men dancing on big tall poles and I forgot where I'd left you.'

Terence listened with feigned interest. He wasn't interested in kids either, but this one did seem to have some class.

Katy held Elizabeth close. 'Shh-sh. You're back with me now. It has been an adventure.' She looked up at Terence. 'I can't thank you enough,' she said gratefully. 'This could have been a nightmare but for you.'

Terence grinned. 'Why don't we get out of here? I'll treat you both to an ice cream. How does that sound, young lady?'

Elizabeth gave one last hiccup. 'Ye-e-s, please.'

Terence lifted her onto his shoulder. 'Now you can see over everyone's head.' He glanced at Katy. 'Tea for us, I think, don't you?'

Katy nodded gratefully. 'My treat. To thank you for your help.'

'Well, if it will make you feel better,' he agreed.

Halfway through her ice cream, Elizabeth suddenly spoke. 'Katy, do we have to tell Mummy that I got losted?'

Katy looked at Terence and then back at Elizabeth. 'I think we should mention it. Perhaps we can make it sound less horrible though.'

Terence nodded. 'That's about right. No point in worrying your mam.'

Later, when they said goodbye, Katy confessed with a blush that she felt embarrassed about the whole thing. 'You must have wondered how anyone with sense could entrust their daughter to such a person.'

'It happens. No need to feel bad about it. The situation ended well. Be thankful for that and just put it behind you.' He shook her hand. 'I'm off back to Belfast tomorrow. I hope all goes well.'

'Thanks, Terence. I don't know how I would have managed without you.'

When Katy settled into her seat on the bus, Elizabeth fell sleepily against her. She felt her own lids growing heavy, and as she relaxed into a half-doze, she began to wonder about Terence

Coleman. Where did he live? What did he do for a living? She had been too distraught to notice much at the time, but later in the café she had been struck by his kindness and the way he had handled Elizabeth. She smiled. He was also a good-looking young man.

Charles arrived back on Wednesday while Katy and Elizabeth were down at the swimming pool watching it being filled. She caught sight of his car going up the drive towards the house and a feeling of pleasure ran through her – a feeling that mildly disturbed her. Nearby, Elizabeth was jumping around in delight because she would be able to swim once the pool had warmed up, now that the sun was at last beginning to throw out some heat.

'Elizabeth, stop jumping around.' Katy grabbed the child by the arm. 'There isn't enough water in there yet to break your fall if you go over the edge.' She could see that the men who were filling the pool were worried by her antics. 'I saw Uncle Charles drive up. Let's go to the house and meet him.'

Elizabeth ran ahead. Katy followed more slowly. She was relieved that the good weather was now upon them as Elizabeth loved being outdoors. It was several weeks now since she had last thrown a tantrum and Katy hoped that, barring any major upset, they would soon be a thing of the past. She stopped as she saw Charles and Elizabeth coming towards her.

'I'm going to be shown the swimming pool,' Charles grinned. 'I have no choice, I'm afraid, so I hope you won't mind retracing your steps.'

'You don't need me. You go ahead. Just deliver Elizabeth to me when you're done.'

'I'm afraid you don't get off so easily.' Charles creased his eyes against the glare of the sun. 'The girlchild wishes you to walk with us.' He turned to his niece. 'Is that not so?'

'Yes! We are then going for a walk in the woods. Mummy isn't home and Uncle Charles says he needs to stretch his legs and—'

Katy threw up her hands. 'All right! All right! But we must be back in time for your lunch.'

'Can't we bring it with us? It won't take long to put a few things in a basket, and I'm sure Mrs Skelton will be pleased to have the house to herself for a while.' Charles smiled coaxingly at her and Katy's heart beat faster under his gaze.

'In that case, you two go see the pool and I'll arrange for a cold lunch to be packed. I'll meet you in fifteen minutes by the elm tree down at the gate,' she said, trying to sound brisk.

When she returned, Charles was sitting with his back against an ornamental tree a few feet from the pool, his face turned up towards the sun, while Elizabeth crouched nearby examining some small detail on the ground. As Katy approached, he rose hastily to relieve her of the heavy basket. Elizabeth looked up briefly before returning to her scrutiny.

'What is Elizabeth doing?' Katy asked curiously.

'She's making a bed of leaves for a slug she has found,' Charles informed her. 'She wanted me to hold the slimy creature while she made the bed, but I declined.' He took the rug from her and called Elizabeth's name. She rose to her feet.

Thrusting the rug towards her, he winked at her. 'We can't ask Katy to carry everything. She isn't strong enough.'

Elizabeth pouted as Katy put a warm cardigan on her, for there was still a slight chill in the air in spite of the sun. 'I'm not cold. I don't want this on.' Katy's heart quailed. Elizabeth was wearing the mulish look that usually preceded a 'paddy'.

She looked sternly at her. 'If I had suspected for one moment that you were going to misbehave and spoil a lovely outing then I would have said "No" to it,' she said firmly.

'I'm not cold!' Elizabeth insisted.

'You will be when we get into the woods. When we find a clearing where the sun can shine through, you may take it off if you like.' Elizabeth continued to glare. 'It's a fair bargain,' Katy coaxed.

'I second that,' said Charles.

Elizabeth looked from one to the other. 'All right,' she said grudgingly, to Katy's relief. The last thing she needed was a scene in front of Charles.

A short distance into the woods they found a pretty glade where the trees had been culled. Here, the faint musky smell of damp leaves was less pervasive and the sun was still high enough to shed its light and warmth into the area. They found a patch of mossy grass just by a large tree. Charles laid the rug down and leaned against its trunk while Katy unpacked the hamper and laid the food on the small tablecloth she'd packed with it.

'I'm hungry!' Elizabeth volunteered.

'You can take your cardigan off now if you like,' Katy replied and handed her a thinly sliced ham sandwich.

Elizabeth shook her head. 'I'm a bit cold.'

Katy and Charles smiled at each other, and as she handed him his sandwich she surprised a wistful expression in his eyes. What cherished memory had come into his mind to produce such a look? She withdrew her gaze hurriedly and busied herself with drinks and cups, drawing the woody scented air into her lungs as she did so. It was none of her business. Folding an arm protectively around Elizabeth, she bit into her own sandwich, enjoying the sensation of sitting here with these two people who had come into her life.

Elizabeth was now contentedly munching an apple while poking through leaves with a stick she had found. She chattered away happily to herself in the way that nearly five year olds do, unaware of the adults as they sat in silence, both occupied with their own thoughts.

Charles was the first to speak. He looked at Katy from beneath half-closed lids, his voice lazy and soft. 'I understand your parents own a farm a short distance from here. Wouldn't you have preferred to work on the land and tend the animals rather than cope with my fiend of a niece?'

'Not in this world!' Katie said vehemently. 'I want something more than milking cows and feeding chickens and breaking my back stooking hay.'

'You tell a rollicking good story. Have you thought of becoming a writer?'

Katy laughed. 'I've thought of it – but it was *only* a thought.' She nodded towards Elizabeth who was curled up asleep against a tree. 'I think you will have to carry our friend.'

The sun had moved behind some clouds and the air had cooled, and as they walked along Katy's thoughts were busy. Charles hadn't mentioned that his girlfriend was coming to stay shortly – and she also wondered why Sylvia didn't want her to

51

come. According to Sally, Pamela was an old friend of the family and an old schoolfriend of Sylvia's

Each Sunday after Mass, the Molloy family visited Vincey's grave. Katy always stood aside. She couldn't share the moment – not even with her parents. She'd stand there, head bowed. Apart. Then when they had walked away, she would linger for a moment to touch the headstone, tracing her hand across his name etched into the marble, trying to breach the infinity between them.

Today she spoke quietly into the nothingness that surrounded them both. 'I'm going to get on with my life, Vincey,' she whispered. 'I know that you will understand. You always did. I miss your spoiling and your laughter, and I sometimes crave to hear your footsteps clomping up the path when you would whirl me in your arms and tell me I was beautiful. It wasn't true – I know that – but you always made me feel special and I will never pass through a day without thinking of you . . .' She stopped as her father called to her. 'I'm away now, Vincey. I'll be back again.'

Eddie Molloy watched his daughter walk towards him. Annie had sauntered on down the road with her friend Rosie McGrath so he stood alone. His eyes softened with pity. The expression in his daughter's eyes was naked in her sorrow. He took her arm and gently propelled her from the churchyard. He had a sudden desire to hold her and tell her that he understood but he couldn't find the courage or the words – he was a farmer, not a philosopher – but there were moments such as this when he wished he was more articulate.

After lunch, he settled himself in his armchair in front of the big range to read his paper whilst Katy and Annie washed the dishes.

'He'll never make it beyond the fourth line,' Annie whispered, smiling. 'Not that I could blame him. He works hard, and by the end of this day he'll have done more work than some would do in two – Sunday or no Sunday.'

'Do you ever wish you weren't a farmer's wife, Mam?' Katy folded the cloth she was holding and leaned against the huge stone sink.

Annie pulled the kettle over the heat. 'We'll take our tea out into the porch. We don't want to disturb him.'

They settled themselves on the bench beneath the window and Katy waited for her mother to speak.

Annie took a sip of the tea. 'That's better!' she said. 'I like a good strong cup of tea – one that you could stand a spoon up in – none of that weak stuff with the faint perfumed flavour which is enough to turn a body's stomach.'

Katy smiled. 'Are you goin' to answer my question?'

Annie's eyes misted over with nostalgia as she stared into the distance and fingered the bun of hair at the back of her neck for a moment as her mind travelled backwards in time. She sighed.

'If I had my time over I wouldn't change a thing. Your father was the love of my life, but I have to say that I wish to God he had been anything other than a farmer, for I was a young lass with all my life before me. I had my pick of the fellas.' She looked at Katy and grinned. 'You wouldn't know it by looking at me now, but I wasn't bad-looking. I had more than one proposal of marriage. John Foley, who was studying accountancy, was head over heels in love with me and I was sorely tempted but there, you can't stop nature and you can't stem love. I had eyes for no one but Eddie Molloy so I gave up all thought of the easy life and settled down to be a farmer's wife.' Annie set her cup down.

'What became of John Foley the accountant?'

'He became Foley the keeper of the graveyard.'

Katy choked. 'Not old bent-over Foley with the grey beard and the shock of white hair that doesn't look as if it ever said hello to a comb?'

'The very one,' said Annie with sadness in her voice. 'And don't you go by what he looks like now. Those blue eyes of his could tear the heart out of a girl just by smiling at her.'

'But what happened to him? He looks years older than my da.'

'What happened was that he lost his wife and his only child in an accident many years ago and it tore him to pieces. He had his own accountancy business at the time but he took to the drink and it all went downhill. He was bought out by a firm called Briggs and Son from Belfast. He sold his house and bought a damp hell of a cottage along the road between Ballynashee and

53

Ballyclinchy and there he lives to this day.'

'Why is he so stooped?'

'He is crippled with arthritis. He has it in his shoulders and he finds it hard to hold himself upright. It was all that damp in the cottage.' Annie paused. 'I hear your da stirring. We'd better get inside. He'll want you to help with the milking.'

Later as she lay in bed, Katy thought about what her mother had told her. Up till then, she had never thought of Annie as ever being young and desirable. She was just her plump, capable mam who could bake and cook with the ability of a trained chef. In the early photographs she had been snapped while haymaking dressed in dungarees with her hair bound tightly in a scarf or, as in her wedding photograph, she stared at the camera with a stiff smile pinned to her face. Katy was intrigued by the revelation that her mam had once been young and carefree. It was a chastening thought that *her* children might one day have the same difficulty imagining that she had once been pretty and desirable.

When she arrived at Beresford House next morning, she found the place a hive of industry. The spring cleaning had started. Mrs Skelton said everyone had to pull their weight, so wondered if Katy could deal with the cupboards in the nursery as the toys had been all over the place when Sally had gone up to clean down the walls and take the curtains down for washing.

She was on her way upstairs to see Elizabeth and to get away from the feverish busyness downstairs, when she met Charles on his way down. She said, 'Good morning,' and was about to pass when he touched her arm.

'I hope you don't mind, but I told Elizabeth that I would take her on a trip to Newcastle. My sister tells me it's a pretty little seaside town. I have a great desire to get away from all this activity.'

'Of course I don't mind,' Katy said, 'although I'd already arranged to take her into town with me.'

'Splendid. Then you can keep your promise. Come to Newcastle with us, instead.'

Katy said doubtfully, 'Elizabeth has to clear her toy cupboard out. If she refuses then I fear she can't go. She hates doing it, you see, but she knows the rules. No clean cupboard – no treat.'

Charles carried on downstairs. 'Let me know the outcome,' he called out cheerily.

Elizabeth ran to meet Katy as she opened the nursery door. 'I wish you didn't have to go home at weekends,' she said, as she hugged her. 'Couldn't I come with you next time? Please!'

'Then what would Uncle Charles do without *you*?' Katy said fondly.

'I don't see Uncle Charles very much. I only see Sally. He doesn't come up when she's here, only when you are, and Mummy has been out all weekend.'

Katy felt pleasure at the words but she hid her expression. Then: 'You remember we said that one day soon you would be asked to tidy your toy cupboard?'

'Ye-es.' Elizabeth looked mulishly at her.

'Today is the time,' Katy said gently.

'But Katy! Uncle Charles is taking me on a trip to the seaside!'

'I know,' she answered. 'So the sooner it is done the better, wouldn't you say? Now I will pop downstairs to get your morning milk, and when I've gone you can tidy up – it won't take long.' Before Elizabeth could argue, Katy left the room.

Mrs Skelton looked up as she entered the kitchen. She was cleaning out the range and her face was smudged. 'How did you get on?'

'By the time I bring her mid-morning snack to her, Elizabeth will have finished tidying her cupboard.'

Sally walked in. 'There are toys flying everywhere. I hope you're right. As I passed the nursery I could hear things hitting the cupboard door at the rate of knots.' She put an armful of curtains down.

Mrs Skelton scolded her. 'Never mind what is happening in the nursery, my girl, you have work to do. Get that boiler on and start the washing. We have no time for worrying about another's domain and responsibilities.' She looked pointedly at Katy.

'It's all under control,' Katy said. 'I just came down to get the milk and biscuits.'

As she entered the hall Charles emerged from the drawing

room. 'I can't stand this bustle,' he sighed. 'Everyone is tearing around madly. Sylvia has distanced herself from the chaos. She should have warned me. Look, could you hurry this tidy cupboard business? I'd like to get away as soon as possible.'

'I've done it! I've done it, Katy.' Elizabeth came puffing down the stairs. 'Can we go now, Uncle Charles?'

He raised an eyebrow at Katy.

'I just want to inspect,' she whispered. She ran up the stairs to the nursery where, to her surprise, not a single toy was lying around. She opened the cupboard and jumped back as several teddies fell out followed by dolls and games tumbling out with gathering momentum. She frowned. Now what!

She stood thoughtfully at the top of the stairs for a moment before calling out, 'Elizabeth! I'm afraid your toy cupboard has just been violently sick. Could you come up here?'

There was the sound of feet and Elizabeth hurtled into the room, followed almost immediately by a bemused Charles. She stared at the toys lying all over the floor. 'How can a cupboard be sick?' she cried, looking at Katy in amazement.

Katy glanced sternly at Charles, whose lips were quivering. 'Do you remember the day you and I went into Ballyclinchy to the market and you were sick because you stuffed yourself with too much ice cream?'

'Ye-es.'

'Well, the same thing has happened with your cupboard. It had too many toys stuffed into it at too fast a rate, and when I opened the door it sent them all flying out again.'

'Oh dear!' said Elizabeth. They both looked round at Charles as a suspicious sound came from his direction. 'I shall make it better,' the little girl sighed.

'Perhaps Uncle Charles could help you,' suggested Katy. 'Remember, if the job isn't done properly, the trip to Newcastle is off. While you are doing it, I'll be in my bedroom.' She studiously avoided his eyes as she passed him.

Half an hour later, the job done, they bundled into the large car. For Katy, riding in it was a dream. Her father's car was a Standard 10, and although functional and reliable, it couldn't beat the Wolseley for comfort. She leaned back against the soft upholstery to enjoy the scenery. Ahead, outlined across the skyline were the Mountains of Mourne, looking purple and mysterious with distance. There were times when they looked ominous and looming when there was little sun and the mist swirled, but today they were friendly. The miles passed quickly as the big car sped effortlessly along. There was only one short delay as they rounded a corner to find a farmer standing perilously in the middle of a narrow road with his back to them, shepherding sheep into a field.

Katy had suggested a picnic on the sands but Charles shuddered. 'I loathe sand and paste sandwiches. It makes me remember the ghastly trips Sylvia and I made to Brighton with our parents. Our teeth remained gritty most of the day. We will have lunch at a hotel I found on my first visit.'

After lunch they wandered down Newcastle main street towards the harbour at the other end. The street was virtually straight and looked as though it would go right through the mountains sweeping down to the edge of the sea, breathtaking in their beauty, but it was an optical illusion as in fact, the road eased its way round the foot of the hills, with the harbour and the sea on the left. The three sat on the harbour wall to watch the fishermen emptying their cargoes of fish from the tiny boats and sniffed the sharp salt-laden air with enjoyment.

When they tired of that, they made their way back towards the station, following the waiter's instructions to, 'Go past the station and round to the links by the Slieve Donard Hotel. The highest sand dunes are there and the sandy beach is less crowded than the main one.' Looking directly at Charles, he added, 'And the golf course is of a high standard if you should wish to play a round or two, sir.' Charles thanked him.

A train whistle blew and Elizabeth let out a shriek as steam suddenly belched from the train's funnel. They laughed and Charles lifted the child onto his shoulder so that she could count the green carriages as they walked along beside the station fence.

As it was still too cold for swimming, they paddled and helped Elizabeth to build a sandcastle, searching for shells to adorn it. Once she had her pile of shells and smooth stones near her, the little girl knelt in contentment to decorate it and Katy and

Charles settled down on the rug to enjoy the spectacular view around the coastline. Katy pointed out the distant sands of Dundrum Bay to the east. Charles suggested a trip there on another occasion and she smiled with pleasure.

They were so comfortable in each other's company, the desire to make conversation lapsed and they lay side by side, their eyes closed against the glare of the sun. Occasionally Katy opened hers to glance across to where Elizabeth continued to be absorbed in her task, before settling down again to her thoughts. Today she had sensed a subtle shift in the relationship between Charles and herself which pleased her.

Charles, too, lay with his eyes closed until the sun caused them to feel hot beneath his lids. He sat up and leaned on his elbows to stare down at the girl by his side. Her hair, shining and vibrant, was spread across the rug and once again he was struck by her freshness and vitality. 'Your hair is very beautiful,' he murmured.

Startled, Katy's eyes flicked open. Charles was staring down at her with a gentle smile just lifting his lips. She blushed and scrambled hastily to her feet. 'How about that cream tea you promised us?' She called to Elizabeth. 'Leave the decorating, little one. Uncle Charles is taking us to tea.'

Charles grinned. 'The boss has spoken, Lizzie.'

Elizabeth scowled. 'Don't call me that name, Uncle Charles.'

'Sorry, Lady Elizabeth.' Charles swung his niece up and tramped off across the sand. Katy hastily folded the rug into the bag, gathered up the rest of the stuff lying about, and followed. Her heart was beating fast. She mustn't put too much store by the look in his eyes. He had probably just been paying her a simple compliment.

She caught up with him and they walked along in silence. Elizabeth, head drooping with tiredness, was now being held in his arms. 'I think we have worn the girlchild out,' he whispered. He smiled at Katy conspiratorially and again she felt that little surge of pleasure.

Sylvia seemed mildly distracted at dinner. She was toying with her food and spoke very little. Katy quietly got on with her own meal until suddenly her employer put down her spoon and said,

'Katy, regarding Pamela, the friend of ours who is coming to stay . . . I do realise that this is an imposition on my part but . . . should Charles and I be busy with meetings, could you possibly entertain her for me?'

'Oh dear.' Katy immediately panicked. 'I'm not very good at entertaining, Sylvia. I don't know what your friend would expect . . .'

'Please say you will. I am sure that Charles will take some time off. It will only apply on those occasions when we are both unavailable.'

Katy sighed. 'I'll do my best.' She hesitated for a moment. 'What about meal-times? Would you prefer me to eat with Mrs Skelton and Sally when your friend comes to stay?'

Sylvia paused with her spoon halfway towards her mouth. 'What on earth for?'

'I thought that as you were entertaining . . .'

'For heaven's sake, Katy, you are not just my daughter's nanny – you are also my companion. You know I hate to dine alone. We made an arrangement.'

Katy smiled. 'I needed to have the situation clarified.'

Sylvia rose. 'Well, now you know!' She took her coffee and went into the drawing room. Katy followed, wishing Charles was here: Sylvia sounded tetchy.

'I understand you have known Pamela a long time.'

Sylvia smiled. 'We were at school together. We never agreed on anything – our interests always clashed. Pamela was keen on boys – I was more interested in art – and invariably we ended up being thoroughly beastly to each other, but as our parents were close friends, we were always making exchange visits to each other's houses. When Pamela came to ours she tended to go around with Charles, thank goodness, so I was left in peace to do what I wanted. Charles was younger than Pamela but he was a very serious young man who always seemed older than he was.' Sylvia crossed her elegant legs and leaned back. 'Actually, I haven't seen Pamela for ages – the visit was Charles' idea. Apparently Pamela is getting over some affair or other and needs time to recover.' She paused. 'My old schoolchum has a capacity for making men fall in love with her.'

Katy's heart sank. 'Is she clever as well as beautiful?'

Sylvia's expression was wry. 'She *is* clever, but she didn't make full use of her abilities.' She looked curiously at Katy. 'I've often wondered why you haven't gone to university, my dear.'

Katy was startled by the change of direction. 'I suppose I could have done,' she said.

'What would you have read at university?' Sylvia probed. 'What is your particular interest? I understand from my daughter than you tell wonderful stories.'

Katy laughed fondly. 'I'm mad about books. I love anything to do with them,' she confided. 'There was a time when I thought I might study Literature at Queens – my friend Margaret is reading English there – but,' her voice quivered, 'things happened. My brother died suddenly . . . I lost my confidence. And I was needed on the farm.'

The other woman looked thoughtful. 'I have commissioned an expert to set up a library here. My husband had an extensive collection of books which at the moment are in storage. There are some valuable books among them and some first editions. He was an avid collector. How would you feel about giving a hand now and again to the work? It would add some interest to your stay here.'

Katy gasped. 'I'd love that, but when would I find the time?'

'I'm sure we could arrange to have Sally take Elizabeth off your hands sometimes, and there is the occasional weekend.'

The idea of handling precious first editions and helping to catalogue a library appealed strongly to Katy. She could ask her mam and da if they could manage without her for a while . . . The phone rang. Katy waited as Sylvia rose to answer it.

'We'll make arrangements about your involvement tomorrow,' Sylvia said.

As Katy left the room she saw the other woman prop herself on the edge of the chair and whisper into the phone, her dainty foot swinging while she twisted the cord round and round her fingers.

She's behaving coyly, she thought in amazement. Like a young girl in love. It was obvious she was talking to a man.

CHAPTER 4

For Charles Gilbert, the return to conventional architecture after three years as a fighter pilot had been a depressing experience, and the fact that he was a partner in the successful firm of Peter Greenway & Associates didn't help in the least. He had become increasingly restless and bored, and was on the point of getting out when an exciting new project had come to his attention. Tenders were being sought for the further expansion of the airport in Belfast, to accommodate the newest jet-propelled planes. A former aerodrome, the airport now required longer runways and larger buildings. His firm submitted his designs, and following weeks of nailbiting tension, the telephone finally rang to say they'd got the contract.

Charles immediately made arrangements to fly to Ireland, and within a month had set up the operation. He had expected difficulties to arise as work progressed, and as they did, so they were ironed out. He had always enjoyed a challenge, had confidence in his ability to meet problems head on and solve them – until now. Now, a big one had cropped up which had already caused him hours of worry, with no prospect of a resolution. Meetings had been called, but even with the combined efforts of his team, no headway was made.

Today, at the end of the latest meeting, Charles looked round at his stretching, yawning colleagues. The matter under discussion had still not been resolved and he felt irritated and disheartened. He threw his pencil onto the wide table, flexed his own aching shoulders, finished the water in his glass, gathered up his papers and stood up. Catching Keiron Moore's glance, he motioned him over.

61

Keiron looked Charles in the eye. 'You are not a happy man – anyone can see that – but what more can I do to make that old bastard budge?' The 'old bastard' in question was Barney Fogarty, whose cottage sat on land that was essential for a runway.

'You could offer him more money,' Charles suggested. 'Having to re-site a runway will cost a damn sight more than any extra you offered the old coot. I need that land. *We* need that land. If this airport is to succeed then we must be able to grow. Planes are now bigger and faster . . .'

'Jaysus, man, you don't need to tell me,' the other man objected. 'I was in on the first design for the gas turbines when I was an apprentice, and I'm well aware that when the jet propulsion gets going this place hasn't a chance in hell of accommodating the speeds the planes will reach when taking off. But Barney Fogarty has lived in that cottage on that land for the last seventy years – as did his ancestors before him – and at his age sure, what the hell does he care about speed and the necessity to lengthen the runways. As he told us to our faces, the noise from the existing planes is bad enough without him having a bloody jet tearing hell for leather over his home.'

'If he moves then he won't have that problem,' Charles said irritably.

'Ach! it isn't just that – Barney is as deaf as a post, anyway. The point is that he doesn't want to die anywhere else but where he has lived and breathed all his life. Sure, you can't blame the man. An Irishman's home is precious to him – just as yours is.'

'Offer him another two hundred pounds.'

'You heard the vote – we aren't to offer any more. He has already been offered twice what the place is worth. We are to play a waiting game.'

'The committee needn't know,' Charles insisted. 'Just test him out once more – there's a good chap.'

Keiron shook his head. 'I think we should leave it for the month that the committee has decreed – to allow Barney a final decision.' He gave a wry smile. 'Maybe you should have stuck to conventional architecture and not got into aviation. There will always be a Barney Fogarty unwilling to play ball. Well, I'm away off home.'

Charles was thoughtful. Keiron was right – but he was determined he wouldn't fall at the first hurdle. This was the first big project he had won, and he had won it because of his wartime job as a fighter pilot – the chairman of the interview panel had told him so – and he was not about to let an old man scupper his dreams. Not without a fight. Besides, he loved it here and intended to stay for quite a while yet.

He glanced at his watch and swore under his breath. Pamela's plane must have landed by now. Grabbing his briefcase he rushed from the room, briefly acknowledging the small group still standing by the bar.

Pamela was waiting at the arrivals hall looking tall and elegant in an expensive charcoal-grey suit with a cute red pill-box hat perched precariously on her blonde hair. She looked every inch the model she was, and Charles watched in amusement as a small group of men ogled her. She stood there like a bright flower seemingly unaware of the appreciative stares directed at her.

'I'm sorry I'm late. I got held up at a meeting.' He kissed her lightly on the cheek and stooped to grab her luggage.

Pamela Goodman, who had been perfectly aware of the interest she had stirred among the group of young men, wasn't pleased by the lighthearted kiss. She would have preferred it if Charles had swung her into his arms and given her a proper one. His size and the strong handsome face had caused two passing girls to turn and look in admiration and she felt that a more exuberant greeting would have given her the edge on them.

'It's been quite an uncomfortable fifteen minutes waiting for you to arrive,' she pouted. 'Those men have been ogling me and I was anxious to move away but I was afraid we'd miss each other.' She smiled seductively into his eyes as she took his arm. 'It is lovely to see you again, darling. I've been too busy just lately to have a holiday so I'm really looking forward to having a good rest and getting to know you again. I have missed you so much.'

Charles grinned. Pamela would never be short of escorts, and he didn't think for one moment that she had missed him as badly as she intimated. 'That's nice,' he said. He played her games and he did it from habit. A smile curled his lips. He doubted he would ever be able to play such social games with Katy Molloy. That young miss would see through him at once, and he had a feeling that she would lose respect for him if she thought for a moment that he was being insincere.

They reached his car and Charles settled Pamela into the front seat while he put her assorted luggage in the boot. Judging by the amount she had brought, she intended to make her stay a long one. He groaned. Sylvia and Pamela were old sparring partners who couldn't spend much time together before they began to irritate each other. Already Sylvia had made it quite clear to him that as he'd encouraged Pamela's visit, he was to be responsible for her entertainment; she herself had too much on at the moment. He had important things afoot himself, so God knows what Pamela would do with her time. He hoped young Katy wouldn't mind taking her on the occasional sightseeing trip. He would have a word with her.

Pamela was quiet during most of the journey, staring out of the window at the scenery, and it wasn't until they were on the outskirts of Ballynashee that she spoke again. 'Charles, darling, is this *it*?'

Charles' lips quirked as he glanced quickly at her. 'Yes, this is *it*. What did you expect?'

'Aren't there any towns?' Pamela's voice rose on a squeak. 'So far, all I've seen are fields and cows and sheep.'

'We've just passed through two – Ballynahinch and Bally-clinchy – and the one we are passing through now is Ballynashee, which is only two miles from home.'

'But there isn't anything going *on-n-n*. I'll die of boredom!'

Charles stopped the car for a moment and turned to her. His eyes softened. She looked so elegant – so regal – and so out of place with that ridiculous perky hat and the grey kid gloves resting on her lap. 'There is Newcastle, of course,' he said. 'I understand it is seething with holidaymakers all summer. It boasts a couple of good hotels – the largest of which has an excellent golf course.'

'What about entertainment?'

'There is a bandstand and I believe there is a show once a day on the pier . . .'

'You're making fun of me!' Pamela's pretty face looked cross.

Charles laughed. 'Pamela, darling. You came over here to recover from a broken romance. I thought you were going to relax and recharge your batteries – that is what you told me when you asked me to suggest to Sylvia that you should come.'

'On the other hand, if it is too boring and I have nothing to amuse me, I will have too much time to think – which will make me feel worse.'

'I'll take you into Belfast on occasions to dine and visit the opera house,' Charles promised, adding, 'but on the whole, you will have to make your own arrangements. I am working on a very important project at the moment and we have hit a rather sticky patch which has to be resolved – and quickly.' He restarted the engine. 'You will love it here, I'm certain, and we do have a swimming pool at the house.'

Katy, standing at the window as the car drew up, scrutinised the woman who stepped out. As she had expected, Pamela was beautiful and she noted how Charles took her by the arm to lead her up the few steps to the front door and the way she turned her face up to his. She sighed and moved away to join Elizabeth, concerned by the thoughts running through her mind. She had actually felt resentful of Charles' attention to his companion and she had no right to do so.

'Your mother's friend has just arrived, Elizabeth.'

The little girl looked up. 'Pamela?'

'Yes. Uncle Charles has just taken her cases into the house.'

'Is Uncle Charles home? Hooray! We can go down to the pool.'

'I don't think so. It's rather late.'

'Will Uncle Charles come to see me before I go to bed?'

'I'm sure he will. He might bring his friend up to see you as well.'

Elizabeth turned back to her painting without replying so Katy made her way downstairs to prepare her tea tray. She had noted the child's lack of interest in their guest.

'How well do Elizabeth and Pamela Goodman know each other?' she asked Sally.

The girl shrugged. 'It's hard to say. I think as far as Elizabeth is concerned, she can take her or leave her. When Miss Pamela is in a good mood then Elizabeth is happy in her company, but she steers clear if she is in a bad mood. Of course, it works the other way as well – they both have the same mental age if you ask me.'

'Sally!'

'I mean it,' the maid grinned. 'You ask Mrs Skelton. She has only met Miss Pamela once and she couldn't believe how she bickered with Elizabeth, who was only three and a half years old at the time.'

After tea, while Elizabeth was having her special hour with her mother, Katy ran a bath. For one precious hour she could relax, although irritatingly, today she found thoughts of Charles and Pamela intruding. She wondered just how deep their relationship was at the present time. Sylvia had mentioned that she had thought at one time she might have Pamela as a sister-in-law, but then Charles became caught up in the war and the relationship had faltered. She leaned back, chiding herself for the tiny stab of jealousy that ran through her.

Katy made a special effort when she dressed for dinner that evening. She wore the new dress she had bought three weeks ago which, the assistant assured her, made her brown eyes look dark and mysterious. Furling her thick curly hair up into a roll she pushed a large comb into it. There was a chance it might fall down with the weight of it, but with careful head turning and a prayer, it would stay the distance.

She looked into Elizabeth's room to check on her and found her fast asleep. She wouldn't see her again until after her weekend at home. Indeed, under normal circumstances she would have been on her way this evening, but she had accepted Sylvia's invitation to dine. 'Wish me luck, Lady Elizabeth,' she whispered, and made her way downstairs.

Outside the dining-room door she drew her shoulders back, took a deep breath and put her hand on the door knob. She was about to turn it when she heard a tinkly laugh and then a voice spoke.

'You mean the *nanny* will be dining with us? Very democratic of you, Sylvia. I can't remember our nannies being afforded that privilege.'

'Don't sneer, Pamela. Things are different here. And anyway, the girl is also my companion. She keeps me company – I hate dining alone.'

Katy hesitated, a flush staining her cheeks, her confidence eroded. She felt a hand on her shoulder and turned quickly to find Charles smiling at her. 'Are you going to turn that handle, or are you just polishing it?'

He hadn't heard the exchange, Katy thought. She looked into the friendly eyes and stiffened her shoulders. Why should she let a stranger with a laugh like a row of Tibetan prayer bells – and without manners – upset her? Sylvia was the hostess. If she wanted her to dine with them, then dine with them she would.

Charles quirked his eyebrow. 'Well?'

'I was taking a deep breath. I haven't met your friend so I am a bit nervous.' But still she stood there, looking at him.

She had a melancholy sort of beauty tonight, thought Charles. Huge brown eyes stared trustfully into his and her voice, with its soft Irish burr, was soothing to his ear. He smiled gently at her and nodded encouragingly. She opened the door.

Charles ushered her towards Pamela and made the introductions. Katy held out her hand and Pamela touched it, nodded briefly and turned to smile coaxingly at Charles. 'Darling! Sylvia tells me that there is a golf tournament at the Links in Newcastle. Is there a chance we might go? You can't be busy all the time.'

'It starts next week. I'll see what I can do,' he promised.

When they were seated, Pamela turned to Katy. 'Have you been nannying for long? You don't look old enough to have had much experience.'

Before Katy could reply, Pamela turned away with a shudder. 'Sylvia, do you remember our nannies? Mine had whiskers and yours looked a hundred years old.' She gave another tinkly laugh.

Katy lapsed into silence. Pamela leaned towards Charles. 'Darling! Do you remember the day you put the frog in Miss Sassie's bed and she made you and Sylvia stay in – and wouldn't take you to the park for days to teach you a lesson?'

Charles smiled and nodded. He explained to Katy that Miss Sassie's name was actually Sassington, but neither he nor Sylvia could pronounce it. At that moment Sally entered with the food.

Sylvia asked Charles to pour the wine.

Katy was grateful for the interruption. She wondered if she was only imagining that Pamela was trying to exclude her from the conversation. The others hadn't seemed to notice. Charles was smiling as Pamela continued to reminisce about their childhood, and Sylvia seemed lost in thought.

However, when they retired to the drawing room for coffee, Charles took Katy's arm and said softly, 'You've been very quiet.'

'I was interested in hearing about your and Sylvia's childhood.'

'Sorry about that.' Charles grinned. 'Pamela does rather like to hark back to those days and she is a bit of a chatterbox. I hope you didn't feel too left out.'

As the evening progressed, Katy desperately tried to stifle a yawn. Sylvia and Pamela continued to talk about a time of which she had no knowledge, and although Charles attempted to change the theme he had little success. He winked at Katy and with a tiny shrug, leaned back with her to listen. There was a touch of conspiracy in his action and Katy was pleased, but as soon as she could do so politely, she excused herself.

When Charles woke the following morning, he did so with a headache and a vague feeling that something had gone wrong with the previous evening. He lay back against his pillow and gently massaged his skull, trying to bring his thoughts into focus. He remembered feeling annoyed with Pamela because she had babbled on so. He should have done more to include Katy, but he had given in. Too much brandy had made him lethargic. He glanced at his watch. It was eleven o'clock. Katy would be at the farm now. He had a sudden desire to see her – and why not? The day was his own as Sylvia and Pamela had taken Elizabeth to Newcastle, and a two-mile walk to clear his head seemed like a good idea.

Less than an hour later, Charles knocked on the weathered door of the farmhouse. It opened and a plump woman in a flowered pinny, clutching a carton of Rinso in her hand, surveyed him. 'I was doin' the washin',' she said, as he glanced at it. 'Can I help you?'

'You must be Katy's mother,' he smiled. 'I wonder . . . could you tell me where I could find her? My name is Charles Gilbert. Katy works for my sister – Sylvia Sanders.'

Annie shook his hand as a feeling of shock ran through her. Katy had not mentioned that he was so good-looking and with such an air of sophistication. And so tall, too. She quickly recovered and smiled back. 'Katy is helping with the haymaking down in the far field. Would you like a cup of tea before you make your way there?'

'Another time,' Charles said. 'Right now I would like to have a word with Katy.'

Annie pointed towards the distant fields. 'Go round the back of the barn and climb the stile into the top field. Follow the smell of hay and three fields away you'll catch sight of the harvester and hear the noise.'

Charles thanked her. He sensed that she had continued to stand at the door to watch his departure, but he kept his gaze ahead as he rounded the large creosoted barn and, as promised, caught the smell of the fresh-cut hay drifting on the soft breeze. The sun was warm on his face as he climbed the stile and made his way towards the distant sound of activity.

As he drew near, he saw Katy riding on top of a cart filled with hay which was being driven towards the edge of the field where he stood. He watched as the driver stopped near a line of stooks some distance away. There was a young man with her. They were laughing as they tumbled off the hay cart. He caught her in his arms and for a moment the laughter ceased as they stared at each other. He was young like her, with the same air of innocence. We travel along a different path, Charles thought, and stood for a further moment to observe them, surprised at the tinge of jealousy he felt as he watched the interaction between the two young people.

Katy had caught sight of him and waved. He strode towards them, the stubble crunching beneath his feet, the harsher stalks pricking his ankles.

'What are you doing here?' Katy asked, breathless. The young man by her side looked on, his arm still draped casually across her shoulder.

'I needed to take a long walk to clear my head,' Charles

grinned. 'I thought it would be an idea to find the farm and see if you would like to join me – however, I now see it wasn't such a good idea. I hadn't realised that you would be working on your weekend off.'

'It's all hands to the fore at harvest-time,' Katy laughed.

'I thought haymaking began in June?' Charles said.

'It depends on the weather,' Tom explained. 'April and May had a fair amount of sun and some of the hay in the low fields is ready.'

Katy hastily introduced Tom Toner. 'You are welcome to join us for lunch,' she added. 'Mam will be down with the basket of food very shortly.'

Charles shook his head. 'I couldn't impose – but thanks.'

'If you are worried about takin' the bread from our mouths then don't,' she grinned. 'There are no food shortages here at the farm, not like in England. And I'll bet you a farthing that my mam has put in extra, knowing you are here – that is, if you called at the house first.'

'Yes, I met your mother. She directed me here.'

'Are you two goin' to be there gassin' all day? We are catching you up, you pair of articles. Get those stooks onto the cart.' The voice came from the cabin of the enormous harvesting machine edging its way along.

Katy turned and waved. 'Right away, Da.' Turning to Charles, she said, 'Please stay.' She pointed towards a tree at the far side of the field. 'Make your way there and we'll join you shortly.'

Tom Toner added his plea. 'Come away on, man! The rest and the crack will do you good before you set off again.'

Charles smiled. 'All right.' He watched them as they hurried away towards the middle of the field then made his way to the tree.

As Katy had predicted, her mother arrived with enough food for them all, and so they sat or lounged by the tree and shared the contents of the hamper. Charles felt relaxed and content. Katy's father had a great sense of humour with an ability to tell a good story, and he laughed along with the others as Eddie recounted some choice tales. He now knew where Katy had acquired her skill.

He found Patrick Toner, with his blunt uncompromising manner, rather harder to like, and realised that the other man was watching him warily as his son Tom spoke of his ambitions for a future in farming. Charles suspected that Tom's father had expectations where Katy and his son were concerned. It was evident in the way he bracketed their names when speaking of events. Charles listened as the two young people teased each other with an ease that spoke of familiarity, and his heart sank. Tom was a nice enough lad and he would make an excellent farmer if his plans worked out, but the idea that Katy would ever be his soulmate he found disquieting.

The following day, after supper, Eddie Molloy lit his pipe and informed his family that he was off down to the brook. 'It's no wonder the pair of ye are always complaining about the size of your hips,' he observed. 'You won't burn off the fat if you tumble into a chair as soon as the meal is down.'

Annie watched him walk away, and when he was well out of hearing she turned to Katy. 'Rather my big hips than look like the scrag end of mutton,' she said, in amusement. 'If your da was any thinner he'd go through the eye of a needle. Sure, there is nothin' of him. The only thing that can be said for him these days is that he is wiry and strong for all of it. The man never stops. He is like a herring on a hot griddle – always on the go.'

She thinks the world of m'da, Katy thought, and hoped that one day she would find an understated love as fast and as true as the one that existed between her parents.

They lay back in their chairs and there was silence till Annie said, 'Do you want the wireless on?'

Katy opened her eyes. 'Not really. I'm enjoying the peace and quite, trying not to think about going back this evening.'

Annie looked startled. 'Are you not happy working at Beresford House?'

Katy, realising she had spoken without thinking, said hastily, 'No, no! I love working there. It's just . . . well, a friend of Sylvia and Charles has come to stay for a while . . .' She rose and stood by the fireplace. 'Mam, it's difficult to explain. It isn't anything she has done or indeed, said. It's just that she acts so grand and

71

her attitude makes me feel as though she regards me as some-thing less than nothing.'

Without moving from her position in the chair, Annie stared straight at her child. 'You are the respected daughter of Eddie and Annie Molloy and the sister of Vincey Molloy – and there is not a better thing to be. I will not listen while you start with that caper. You've just been through a bad patch and are beginning to make something of your life – I'll not see you go under again. Where is your pride, Katy? You don't have to wear clothes costing a fortune or have all the trappings of wealth to be someone of worth. What is inside you is what you are.' Annie closed her eyes. The subject was finished with.

Her mother was right, Katy thought. Everyone was important to someone somewhere, and she had momentarily let the haughty Pamela make her forget that. She leaned down and dropped a kiss on her mother's forehead. 'I'm off to the pictures with Tom.'

She could barely concentrate on what was happening on the screen because her mind was still focused on Charles and Pamela. What were they doing now? Were they out together having fun? She bet they weren't sitting in a dark cinema like her and Tom – they were probably dining at some top-class hotel. She gave herself a mental shake. This was not doing any good. She stared at the screen, forcing her mind to concentrate on Henry Fonda's on-off romance with June Allyson and eventually the action and the plot took over and the evening passed off well.

When Katy arrived at Beresford House the following morning, she met Charles coming through the main gates. He was walking with head bent, a frown creasing his forehead. 'Good morning, Charles. Did you oversleep or have you been sacked? You are usually long gone by the time I arrive back after the weekend at home,' she joked.

Charles' expression eased and he grinned. 'They wouldn't get rid of me *that* easily. There's a problem which is holding the work up so I've decided to take a couple of weeks off in the hope that by the time I get back, it will be resolved and things can get moving again.'

'Shouldn't you be there resolving it?' She reddened. 'God! Sure, it isn't any of my business. I'm sorry.'

'It isn't actually *my* problem but it affects my input,' Charles explained, not taking offence. 'I thought I'd go for a walk and see if there was a way round it. Later, I'm taking Pamela for a shopping trip to Belfast.'

He looked so rueful, Katy laughed. 'That should be fun on a beautiful day like this.'

Charles studied her. 'What will you be doing today?'

'This morning I am meeting the expert who is going to catalogue Sylvia's library. She has asked me to assist him when he begins shortly.' She could barely keep the excitement from her voice.

'I'm impressed,' Charles said truthfully. 'What about the Lady Elizabeth?'

'Sally is taking her out until lunch – I'm on duty later. By the way,' she added, 'did you enjoy your short time at the farm?'

'I certainly did. It's a whole new world.'

Katy smiled. 'I hope you enjoy your shopping trip to Belfast as much.'

'I will not, you evil girl!' Charles walked on and then stopped. 'Katy?'

She turned.

'Do you fancy an evening stroll in the woods after dinner?'

'I hardly think . . .'

'Yes or no?'

'Yes.'

He went off whistling and Katy, feeling suddenly lighthearted, ran up to the house. The chances of them getting away for a walk without the delectable Pamela were very slim. But the great thing was that he had wanted to. Just the two of them!

That evening they did manage to slip away, however. Sylvia and Pamela were once more in heated discussion, arguing amiably about the best way to advance Pamela's modelling career. They decided to go up and try on the new outfits Pamela had bought that day, bemoaning the depletion in their clothing coupons allowance, and when they had left the room, Charles turned to Katy. 'How about that stroll?' He grabbed her by the hand and whirled her out of the house and down the driveway towards the river.

They strolled along without speaking until they came to a grassy bank where the reeds had thinned out and Charles motioned for Katy to sit down.

Katy was curious. He had never shown any inclination to be alone with her before. 'Why are we here?' she asked.

Charles didn't answer directly; instead he posed a question of his own. 'At the farm the other day, when your friend Tom was talking about his plans and the way farming of the future would be moving, I noticed that you put forward a good many salient points to endorse his argument when your father questioned his views. How did you come to know so much about the new methods?'

'I've been listening to Tom for some time and I'm an avid reader of the farming magazines – and I do have a brain, you know,' she said teasingly. 'Now! What do you want of me?'

Charles told her all about Barney Fogarty and his refusal to sell his cottage so they could build a runway. 'As I listened to you putting forward your arguments to Tom and your father, I wondered if I could make use of your knowledge of the Irish way of thinking to try and make sense of Barney's refusal to cooperate.'

'Can't you build the runway elsewhere?'

'For various reasons, no.'

'I suppose you can't blame the man if what you say is true – that he was born in his cottage and has lived there all his life,' Katy said reflectively.

Charles nodded. 'But Barney wouldn't lose out. In fact, he would be better off – I can assure you.'

Katy looked thoughtfully at him for a moment before saying, 'My da once told me that sometimes people only hear what they expect to hear, although, if they listened carefully, another meaning is there altogether. I wonder, could you find out what Barney Fogarty actually said?'

Charles nodded. 'I'll phone Keiron Moore as soon as I get back.' His hunch had been right. This girl with her untrammelled mind could see more clearly than the rest of them put together, and she was intelligent.

When he spoke to Keiron later, he got straight to the point.

'Keiron, when you spoke to Fogarty, can you remember exactly what he said?'

There was a pause. 'Yes, I can remember the exact words. He told me he wasn't having any of it. He said he had lived in his cottage since the day he was born, as had his forebears, and he had no intention of dyin' anywhere else.'

Charles frowned. 'You're sure he didn't say anything more than that?'

'No. He shut the door in my face.'

'Look, I'm going to give this some thought. I'll contact you tomorrow.' Charles glanced at his watch – he needed to talk to Katy but she'd already retired for the night. He could hear the murmur of voices coming from the drawing room which meant that Sylvia and Pamela were still on friendly terms. He hesitated then ran silently up the stairs and knocked softly on her bedroom door.

When she opened it, doing up her dressing-gown, he said quietly, 'I need to talk to you.'

Katy hesitated. 'Come into the nursery for a moment.'

'I've just had a word with Keiron Moore – the colleague who spoke to Barney Fogarty. He says that Barney told him that he had been born and bred in that cottage, as had his ancestors before him, and he intended to die there.'

Katy had settled herself on the window seat. She stared out into the night for a long time, then turned to Charles and said thoughtfully, 'To an Irishman of Barney's years, his home is the one thing he has left that has been consistent in his life. It wouldn't matter if it was on the moon or in the middle of the desert. Every stone, every nook and cranny, every bit of wind that whistles down the chimney in a certain way, is all part of the familiarity that binds him to it. If you were to offer him a mansion with every gadget to make life easier for him, he would not give you so much as a thank you for it. He has lived with the inconveniences and the sounds when the storms pass over, and these are the things he would miss – the things that he has lived with all his life and wants to live with till the day they put him in his box and carry him to the graveyard.'

'And the land? What about the land?' Charles asked urgently.

'I don't think Barney Fogarty would give a toss about a piece of land. His home is what he cherishes. I could be wrong – very wrong – but if I were you I would ask Barney which matters most, the land or the house.' Katy rose. 'Can I go to my bed, now?'

Charles nodded absently, his mind already busy deciding what action he would take tomorrow. There was the sound of a door closing, and realising that Sylvia and Pamela were on their way upstairs, he hastily entered his own bedroom.

By nine o'clock the following morning, he was on his way to his meeting with Keiron. There was a knot of excitement building up inside him. He had a feeling that things were going to work for him at last. If they did, then he had Katy to thank for it. He glanced at his watch and wondered idly what she was doing now. She hadn't been in the dining room when he had slipped in for a quick cup of tea and slice of toast earlier. Nor had she been in the kitchen, where she usually prepared Elizabeth's breakfast tray.

In fact, at that moment Katy was gathering together all the things that Elizabeth insisted she wanted to take down to the pool with her. Katy had promised her that she would teach her how to swim if she ate up all her breakfast. She was removing toys from the window seat when she caught sight of Charles getting into his car. She frowned, puzzled. Yesterday evening she had heard him tell Pamela that he would take her to lunch in Newcastle today. If he had forgotten, then he was in trouble. She would not take kindly to being let down.

Katy turned away. 'Have you finished chewing that piece of toast?' Elizabeth was sneakily hiding the crusts underneath the rim of the plate. She ignored the action. A row over a couple of paltry crusts was not the way to start a lovely sunny day and she could see by the mutinous look on Elizabeth's face that it would not take much to set her off. Instead, she continued to pack the capacious bag.

When Sylvia and Pamela joined them later, Pamela complained that the sun was not very hot and Sylvia remarked crisply that she should get into the heated water then and stop moaning. She should be thankful that it was not raining.

Pamela pulled a face and, throwing off her towelling robe she did a perfect dive into the water. Katy watched enviously as she swam the length of the pool with effortless grace, the long slim legs propelling her along, hardly disturbing the water in her wake. Her blonde hair was encased in a rubber bathing cap and still she managed to look beautiful.

Sylvia settled herself into her seat and drew her straw hat down over her eyes. 'I'll swim another time. I just feel like relaxing.' She had noticed the look on Katy's face and smiled to herself. Pamela always had that effect on women.

When she had tired of swimming, Pamela pulled herself out of the pool and began to towel herself dry, her pretty face creased into a frown as she listened to Katy and Elizabeth discuss arm movements. Elizabeth was fidgeting with impatience because she wanted to get straight in, to start practising.

'Would you mind taking Elizabeth to the shallow end of the pool?' Pamela asked. 'I want to relax after my swim and she does tend to be a bit of a nuisance.'

Katy felt anger rise at the curt authoritative tone, but she asked Elizabeth to gather up her towel and inflatable ring and take them to the shallow end. She forced herself to remember that Pamela came from a class where nannies were expendable and not under normal circumstances treated as one of the family.

However, as she gathered up her own towels, Katy leaned towards Pamela and said quietly so as not to wake Sylvia, 'It's a pity you find Elizabeth's presence irksome. She is such a sweet child when you get to know her.'

Pamela flushed. 'I don't find her presence irksome,' she whispered fiercely and glanced hastily at the sleeping Sylvia. 'It's a reasonable request since I want to lie back and relax.' Pamela wasn't keen on children but she valued Charles and Sylvia's friendship too much to risk offending them.

Katy and Elizabeth were still splashing about in the pool when Charles drove up later, so they didn't witness his arrival. Pamela had, however, and she sat up and began to push her hair into place. She removed the light covering she was wearing over her shoulders and pushed it down behind the cushions as she waited for him, relieved that Charles hadn't forgotten they were going out to lunch. When she had discovered that he had gone into a meeting, she was furious and had ripped the explanatory note into small pieces after reading it.

Katy was only aware of his return when he joined Pamela, and as she watched Pamela hold her face up for the light kiss he planted on her cheek, she wondered if he had spoken to his friend Keiron about the situation with Barney. She tried to still the tiny surge of envy that hit her as she watched the kiss; begrudging them their intimacy and feeling ashamed because of it.

It seemed ages before Charles started walking towards them. Katy hoisted herself up onto the side of the pool and at the same time, Elizabeth saw him and climbed out and ran to him. 'Uncle Charles!'

Charles swept the tiny wet figure up into his arms and carried on towards Katy. He put Elizabeth gently down. 'What are you doing down at this end?'

'Elizabeth was getting a bit noisy. Sylvia had fallen asleep and Pamela wanted to rest. It seemed sensible to bring her down here.'

Charles nodded and then smiled. 'I have great news – Barney Fogarty has agreed to sell us his land! You were right. He didn't care where he moved to, within reason, so long as his cottage went with him. If we move every brick and rebuild a few miles down the road, he'll be a happy man. He will then be nearer the general stores and can meet up with his friends more easily as they all live in the village.'

'That'll be Ballacraig.'

'I have no idea. Keiron did the negotiating and reported back.' Charles smiled. 'I would like to invite you out to lunch to say thank you.'

Katy's eyes widened in surprise. 'There really is no need. Sure, all I did was figure how the mind of an Irishman would work.'

'Keiron Moore is as Irish as you can get, and *he* didn't read the signs. Shall we say Saturday? I'll call for you at the farm about midday.' He glanced towards the other end of the pool. 'I'll be in trouble if I don't get back to Pamela. She is a bit cross because I'm late. She thought I'd forgotten our lunch date.'

Katy's gaze followed his. She very much doubted that he would be in trouble, but *she* might be if the glare Pamela was throwing this way was anything to go by. She sank into a deck-chair and watched Charles walk back to the other girl, her mind already on the delightful knowledge that on Saturday it would be her turn to lunch with him.

CHAPTER 5

The following days were difficult ones for Katy. The weather became suddenly hotter and the heat seemed to be affecting everyone. Sally in particular was walking around with a sulky expression because Pamela had complained loudly about the dust in her room.

'If it isn't the dust then she'll find something else. The woman should be shunted out of the place,' Sally hissed. No one could lift her spirits.

Mrs Skelton didn't escape. 'Does madam think my cooking is not good enough!' she remarked sharply, slamming the dishes down on the table one evening. 'A crow takes more sustenance.'

Katy tried to placate her. 'She is a model, Mrs Skelton,' she said. 'Sure, models live on fresh air at times so they can keep their figure. She isn't casting aspersions on your cooking. There is not a better or a lighter hand than yours – and well you know it.'

Mrs Skelton, however, was not to be mollified. 'When does she go, that's what I want to know. She's a troublemaker, that one.'

Katy forebore to answer. It was true that Pamela was getting under everyone's skin; she too had found herself biting on a retort when Pamela had given her yet another subtle reminder that she was only Elizabeth's nanny. In the company of Sylvia and Charles, however, Pamela was perfectly sweet and at these times Katy could see why they liked her. She was bright and witty and treated Charles to cajoling looks out of wide blue eyes, causing him to smile and tease her.

When Katy arrived at the farm on Friday evening, it was with a sigh of relief that she flopped into her da's armchair while her mam made the inevitable pot of tea. 'The panacea for all ills,' she said gratefully, as she sipped the strong brew.

'You look tired,' Annie remarked. 'Is Elizabeth being difficult?'

'It's the heat, mostly,' Katy yawned. 'I haven't been doing much with Elizabeth for the past two days. I've been helping Arthur Foster to sort out the books for the library. He has been so helpful, Mam. He wears thick glasses and peers a lot and knows *everything* about literature.'

'Are there so many books that a man has to be employed to do this?' Annie asked in amazement.

'There are – but mainly it's the fact that there are also many rare books. Sylvia's late husband's family collected them over many years and now Sylvia feels a responsibility to carry on caring for them.' Katy put her empty cup down and rose. 'Mam, I feel bad about saying this in view of the fact that I only see you and Da at weekends, but Charles has invited me to lunch in Newcastle tomorrow. Will you mind very much?'

Annie smiled. 'Certainly not. Your father won't either.' She looked at her daughter worriedly. 'In fact, I don't want to see you do a thing on the farm this weekend.'

'But Mam, I don't mind.'

'We have enough help at the moment. The hay is in and the rest of the work can be done by the lads. I want to hear no more. Away and enjoy yourself – do some shopping – mollycoddle yourself for a change. Spend some of that money you are earning,' Annie said firmly.

'I still think I should pay you and Da some of my wages.'

'Don't bring that up in front of your father,' Annie warned. 'He wants you to have a bit past you for leaner times. Don't forget that this job is not permanent so you will need a bit for when you are job-hunting again.'

Later that night as she lay in bed, Katy mulled over what her mother had said. There was some wisdom in it. She was happy in her present position, but as Annie had pointed out, it wasn't permanent and there was no guarantee that she would find another job so easily. She huddled into the blanket and let her thoughts go. What would it be like to live in Belfast and hold down a job . . . and what job would she settle for in the end . . . and would she be able to cope with independence? It was different for Margaret. She had her student friends and all of them were housed, fed and watered at reduced rates. She, on the other hand, might find herself alone and trying to cope. A surge of excitement ran through her. It would certainly be a challenge for the Katy she had now become, who was determined to push through life and not sit dreaming and hoping up in a tree and doing nothing to make it happen.

Next morning, following a good night's sleep, Katy felt so refreshed she took the bus into Ballyclinchy to look for a pretty dress. Belfast would have been better, she thought, but Ballyclinchy was more familiar – and it was nearer. She found a pink flowered cotton sundress with broad shoulder straps and treated herself to a pair of strappy white sandals to go with it. She reached home with just enough time to prepare for Charles' arrival.

They dined at a small hotel near the harbour and Katy glowed with pride as the waiter showed them to a table situated in a window alcove looking out to sea. Charles was taller than most of the men already there, and it didn't escape her notice that they were catching the eyes of some of the other women. The waiter held the chair for her and she sat down and looked out of the window and then at Charles, trying to hide her excitement.

Charles, seeing the look in her eyes, felt suddenly protective towards her. She looked sweet and vulnerable and nervous. 'Have you been here before?' he asked, and snapped the white napkin from its folds.

Katy laughed. 'A farmer's daughter rarely gets such a treat. My friend Margaret and I have taken the odd trip to Belfast and dined at the cafeteria at Gordon's, the big department store, but for the most part it's the tea rooms in Ballynashee.'

'Then one evening you must let me take you to dinner in my favourite restaurant in Belfast,' Charles said cheerfully. 'We'll pull out all the stops.'

The rest of the afternoon was spent driving along the coast road, round to the more rugged areas of the Mournes and on to Warrenpoint where they sat on the wall and licked ice-cream cones and stared out across the water. It was a day that Katy would store in her mind for those times when she felt blue.

When he dropped her off at the farm, Charles smiled and touched her face with his finger – trailing it along her chin – telling her that she was beautiful and unspoilt and that one day some young man would fall in love with her. She wanted that man to be him, but the odds were stacked against her. She sighed as she settled down to sleep. What had a raw Irish girl got to offer a man like him? Charles was just a lovely fantasy. Tomorrow she would visit Vincey's grave and for the first time she would not feel guilty because she had enjoyed herself – which was progress of a kind.

On Thursday, she collected Elizabeth and took her along to say goodbye to her mother. Some time ago she had promised the little girl that they would spend a day on the farm and today, with Elizabeth bursting with excitement, they were catching the bus for the two-mile trip.

Sylvia kissed her daughter. 'Behave yourself. Do as Katy tells you,' she warned.

Elizabeth hugged her mother tightly. 'I will, I promise. I'm going to be allowed to sit up in the Wishing Tree if I'm good. I'll make a wish for you, Mamma.'

Sylvia's eyebrows rose. She looked at Katy as Elizabeth ran off excitedly to tell the others in the kitchen where she was going.

'It's just an ordinary tree,' Katy said with a grin. 'I used to spend hours up in the special tree wishing my life away. Elizabeth has convinced herself that if she makes a wish it will come true, so I will have to do some detective work. I would hate to spoil her illusions.'

Once again Sylvia realised that she had made a good choice when she'd given Katy the job of looking after her daughter. She now regarded her as one of the family. It was disappointing that Pamela had difficulty in accepting Katy's position, but it was understandable. Pamela was used to a nanny being one of the household staff.

Sylvia drew in a deep breath and with slightly flushed cheeks said, 'Look, I've been meaning for some time to invite a friend of mine to dinner. His name is Robert. I've got to know him pretty well, and I'd like him to meet my family and I wondered – I thought . . . I'd like you to be there.' She waited for Katy's reply, feeling tense and for her, unusually nervous.

Katy smiled to herself. Sylvia *had* been talking to a man that night. Aloud she said, 'Thank you, I'd like to come.'

Sylvia relaxed. She'd gone through agonies preparing to tell everyone about Robert, but it was now five years since her husband had died. She'd fallen in love with Robert within two weeks of meeting him at a charity function. He had been kind and understanding with her, and had made her feel like the girl she was before her husband's death. 'I've been trying to pluck up courage to tell Charles,' she said now.

'I'm sure he will be delighted,' Katy said gently. 'I'd better go and collect Elizabeth or we'll miss the bus.' Now she understood why Sylvia had been quieter than usual during the past fortnight.

They only just made it. The bus was rounding the corner as they reached the stop. Joe Cummings, the driver, slid the window across and called down: 'The pair of ye will have a heart attack, racing along like that. You know I always wait a minute or two in case Mrs Skelton is on the way. That woman is always late. How are you, Katy?'

'I'm fine! Are you goin' to open the doors or are we to pass through like a pair of spirits?' Katy gasped, holding her side.

'It's not my job. Collie Green is the door operator. Since when has the driver had to act as conductor, you article?' The doors opened as though on cue. Collie Green grinned down at them.

'I was havin' a snooze at the back. There isn't a soul on board so ye's have the place to yourselves.' He hoisted a delighted Elizabeth onto the bus and plonked her on a seat.

When they arrived at the farm, Annie met them at the door. Katy pushed Elizabeth forward. 'This is Miss Elizabeth Sanders. Elizabeth, this is my mam.'

Annie took the small hand into hers. 'I'm very pleased to meet a friend of my daughter's.' She smiled, adding, 'I've made a picnic basket up for you because I thought you would prefer that to sitting at a large table with an old woman. It's much more fun to eat outdoors. We'll talk when you come back.'

As they walked across the yard, Lazarus the enormous lazy cat who sat on the roof of the cowshed for most of the day, climbed down to greet them. 'A great honour,' Katy informed the excited child. 'He never bothers to greet anyone.'

'Why do you call your cat Lazarus?' Elizabeth asked curiously, as they climbed the last stile to the big meadow.

'Because he is always begging for food, like the man of the same name in the Bible.'

'He is very fat,' commented the little girl.

'That's the trouble. The fatter he gets, the more food he needs, and he never takes any exercise.'

When they arrived at the tree Elizabeth gazed at it in awe. 'It's so big, Katy. Can we really climb it?' she asked doubtfully.

Katy thought, This is how it affected me when I first saw it. I too was scared and awed by the sheer size of it, and Vincey had to help me up into the first fork of branches . . . Suddenly she wanted to tell Elizabeth that it was too high for a small child to climb, to pull her away, to suggest they go down to see the men picking the early potatoes instead, for up till now she had jealously guarded her retreat and now she was on the brink of sharing it and suddenly she wasn't certain . . .

'The Wishing Tree,' breathed Elizabeth. 'Your very own Wishing Tree. I'd love to have a tree like this.'

'You have a swimming pool – isn't that better?'

'No!' said Elizabeth. 'Anyone can have a swimming pool, Katy. But you have your own private, special tree.'

Yes, I do! thought Katy, suddenly aware how privileged she had been. She'd been surrounded by a lot of love and had been allowed the freedom to tear around the place. There was never anyone to harm her – not that anyone would have dared – not while Vincey Molloy was around. Even at the age of ten, he was built like a house. She'd had a childhood that this little girl with all her wealth had cause to envy. Here in this tree she had looked out over the farm and beyond, and in this private place she had made plans and wished and dreamed. She stooped to lift the tiny figure onto the lowest branch.

They sat there for a long time, listening to the sounds of farm life around them. The clink of the chains two fields away as the horses pulled the harrow along . . . the click-click sound Patrick Toner made with his tongue to encourage them to move on . . . the animal noises drifting on the quiet summer day, from the farm itself. Elizabeth was enchanted, her eyes bright with enjoyment as they tried to identify them.

Eventually Katy said, 'We must get down soon and have our picnic. Why don't you make one last wish before we go.' She smiled at the concentration on the little face and was glad she had let Elizabeth use her tree after all.

'Now, don't expect your wish to come true immediately. The Wishing Tree doesn't work that way – you have to be patient,' she warned.

When they arrived back at Beresford House, and for days afterwards, Elizabeth spoke endlessly about her wonderful afternoon sitting up in the tree until, on the third day, Pamela put her hands over her ears and said she'd had enough of the blessed thing. It was only a tree, for God's sake. Elizabeth looked at her with pity. Pamela wouldn't know about such things. She threw Katy a secret look and they smiled at each other.

June continued hot and they were all sitting by the pool trying to cool off when Sylvia decided that it was all too much; she went back to the house to have a cool bath and lie down in her shaded room. Katy and Elizabeth made their way to the shallow end so Elizabeth could practise her swimming.

When they had gone, Charles and Pamela continued to converse in low voices. He had just told Pamela that he had to go to England on business shortly, and she was annoyed because it meant that she would be stuck here when she would actually prefer to be at her weekend cottage in Hove. She was only here because of him. She hid her annoyance, however, and said cajolingly, 'Can't someone else do the work? After all, you are the boss.'

'Which is precisely why I have to go. We need some extra funding for this project and I am the one who is responsible for finding investors. I am arranging a meeting with some high fliers and have hopes of getting a contract to open some businesses within the airport.'

Pamela bit her lip. She never had any difficulty in finding men to wine and dine her, but when it came to marriage, Charles was the one she wanted. Unfortunately, since his demob from the Air

Force he had been busy building up his bloody business and her dream had eluded her. When she'd heard through the social grapevine that he was going to stay with his sister in Ireland for a time, she had made plans to follow him. Just lately she felt that her hopes were close to being realised, although his interest in the nanny had been a complication. Her eyes narrowed. She would not be beaten now.

Charles, having firmly explained the situation, waved to the others to join them, but Pamela, her beautiful face tight with annoyance, took her camera from her bag and went off to take photographs and ponder on how to turn the new situation to her advantage. She couldn't be too blatantly obvious by following him, but something had to be done.

'I've upset Pamela's plans,' Charles said ruefully, as Katy settled into the deck-chair beside him. 'I told her that I am off to England on business in a few days' time. She wanted to take a trip to Dublin next week and was hoping we could spend the day together. I am definitely out of favour at the moment.'

'Couldn't she wait till you got back?'

'Seems not!' Charles sighed. 'But I'm afraid it can't be helped. I have some work that I left unfinished and there is a very important meeting to set up. The trouble is, Pamela has always been able to charm people into giving her what she wants, and she gets a trifle miffed if things don't work out the way she expects.' He brightened. 'The good thing is she doesn't sulk for long.'

Katy lowered her gaze. It was obvious that Charles saw a Pamela that others did not.

Charles rose suddenly. 'I've just remembered that I have a telephone call to make. I won't be long.'

He had hardly reached the rose arbour when Katy suddenly became aware that Elizabeth was crying and stamping around. She started up from her seat and ran towards her. Two angry wasps were buzzing round Elizabeth's face and she was fast becoming hysterical. Katy flapped her hand in an effort to chase them off as Elizabeth backed away. 'Keep still,' she cried, 'and they won't harm you. Do keep still!' The wasps were persistent so Katy continued to flap her hand, and this time they flew off just as Elizabeth stepped back in terror, only to lose her footing and fall with a loud scream into the water.

Charles heard the commotion and raced back in time to see what had happened. He dived into the water just as Elizabeth went under, her arms flailing helplessly. When she resurfaced, the tiny arms began to use a swimming action and he grabbed her and steered her towards the side. Pamela was nowhere in sight.

Katy reached for Elizabeth and Charles climbed from the pool. 'She'll be all right. By the time I got into the water she was already starting to use her arms correctly. What on earth happened?'

Katy explained, while she comforted the crying child and wrapped her in a large towel. Charles, towelling himself dry, nodded. 'She is terrified of the things. She was stung badly as a toddler.'

Elizabeth had stopped coughing and was clinging to Katy. 'Those naughty, horrid wasps!' she cried. Suddenly her eyes lit up. 'I did swim in the deep end, Uncle Charles, didn't I?'

'You did very well under the circumstances, darling. I'm very proud of you. I knew it wouldn't be long before you learned.'

Katy said, 'We'd better get back to the house,' and added practically, to Charles' amusement, 'It's just as well we were all in our swimming gear.'

'Please don't tell Mamma.' Elizabeth grabbed Charles by the hand. 'Don't let Katy tell. I won't be allowed to go into the pool again.'

Charles looked at Katy. 'Need we? The child is fine now. She really was beginning to lose her fear and she's right. Sylvia is always on tenterhooks when Elizabeth is in the water. If she knows about this little episode she might ban her altogether till she is very much older. You may have noticed that Sylvia rarely goes in herself.'

Katy looked thoughtful. Elizabeth was a very bright little girl for her age and it would be a shame if she had her swimming curtailed when it gave her such pleasure. She looked anxiously at her. 'Are you certain you feel all right? You must say if there is anything that bothers you. It was quite a frightening moment – did you swallow much water?'

'I didn't! I didn't! I was more scared by the horrid wasps. Please don't tell Mamma,' Elizabeth pleaded.

Charles raised his eyebrows. 'Well?'

'All right, but you must tell me immediately if you feel sick or anything.'

Elizabeth nodded frantically. 'I will, Katy, I promise.' She skipped ahead.

As they followed, Katy said to Charles, 'I'm not entirely happy about this. I feel that Sylvia should know all that happens to her daughter.'

Charles stopped. 'If you feel very strongly about it, then of course you must do what you think is right, but I'll be happy to explain to my sister should she ever find out. After all, you can't go to her with every little drama that occurs in Elizabeth's life.'

Katy sighed. 'I suppose you're right. She *is* my responsibility.'

At the moment they reached the house, Pamela, having witnessed the whole scene, was emerging from the spinney, a smile just edging towards her mouth. She had found a neat way of putting Miss Nanny Molloy in her place. From her vantage point she had quickly realised what was happening and having put her camera to her eye to record the event, she had made the discovery that from the angle she was taking the photograph, it looked as though Katy was slapping Elizabeth. She smirked. As soon as Charles had gone and her film was developed, that girl was going to have some explaining to do and Charles would not be here to help her.

On Saturday, Katy took the bus into Belfast to meet Margaret. It was some weeks since they'd met as Margaret had been studying hard for her end-of-year exams and hadn't been able to get home.

'It's what we all do,' she explained when she phoned to apologise for not coming home so often. 'We tend to leave it all to the last minute and then it's a mad scramble to fill our minds with the relevant facts.'

The exams were now over and Margaret suggested having lunch at a reasonably priced restaurant she knew, after which they could do some shopping as the end of summer Ball was coming up and she was on the lookout for a dress to wear. She wanted Katy to vet it for her.

Katy agreed eagerly. Trips to Belfast were not on her normal calendar and there was no way she was turning down this offer – although she suspected that she wouldn't be much help in approving the suitability and style of whatever kind of outfit Margaret bought. She was usually startled by some of the outfits she wore. She'd never have the nerve to wear them herself, although on Margaret they looked great.

When they had greeted each other she stood back and surveyed her friend. Margaret had grown her hair longer and it softened the lines of her face so that she looked less assertive than she normally did. 'The hair suits you,' Katy said, and watched in amazement as a slow flush crept over Margaret's cheeks.

'My boyfriend Michael persuaded me to grow it. He likes long hair – says it's more feminine than the short style.'

Katy grinned and took her arm as they walked along. 'A boyfriend! I never thought I would see the day that my friend Margaret Kelly would bow to a man's will.'

Margaret stopped. 'Nor have I!' she said with mock severity. 'I just went along with the experiment because I also like change.'

'That part is true,' Katy agreed. 'I've seen you through more changes of style and opinions than I can count.'

The restaurant was at the end of one of the many little streets in the area known as The Entries. As they waited for service Margaret rattled on about her life at the university. 'I'll never be able to settle back in Ballyclinchy now I have tasted the evils and the joys of living in the metropolis,' she said, with a sigh. 'Life here is more spartan than I was used to at home, but there is such freedom.'

'I can understand that,' Katy agreed. 'I've got so used to my own bit of independence since going to live at Beresford House I find myself getting impatient with all the coddling when I go home to visit the parents.'

'Did I tell you that I'm now living out of residence?'

'I'm not sure what that means,' said Katy, puzzled.

'It means I'm not livin' at the university. I'm dossing with some other students.'

'Dossing? What kind of a word is that?'

Margaret put her knife and fork down on her empty plate. 'You really are a holy innocent, Katy,' she laughed. 'You seriously need to get out into the world and preferably the city where there is not a cow or a sheep in sight. Dossing is what we students do when we all tip in together in one house.'

'But I thought . . .'

'Five of us who got on well together decided to live outside the university as we found it a bit restrictive. It took some doing but eventually we found a fairly decent house that had been vacated by a cousin of one of our lot. Frank, knowing that his cousin was leaving, offered him a bribe – to which we all contributed. We moved in two weeks ago. It needed a lot of cleaning done but it's ours now.'

'Frank?' Katy squeaked. 'You are telling me you share the house with lads? What would your mother say if she knew? And come to that, what possesses you to live in a house that is a tip?'

'It's called "Freedom", Katy. We have very strict rules. There are three lads and two girls. The lads have their sleeping accommodation upstairs. Norah and I have the two rooms off the living room – and comfort is the last thing on our minds.'

'I still think it's a chancy thing to do – I mean, living in the same house as lads.'

'It's done, Katy. Since the war people have become less stuffy. A lot of things happened then that knocked morality off its pedestal. Nevertheless it is not that way with us and I'm hurt that you should think that either Norah or I . . .' Margaret suddenly collapsed into laughter. 'If you knew Norah, such a thought would never enter your mind. Norah behaves as if she is second cousin to the Virgin Mary.'

'But Margaret . . .'

'Eat up. We have a dress to buy and I am not going to justify myself a moment longer.'

Margaret proved easy to please. They found a lovely dress in the second store they shopped in and while they waited for it to be parcelled up, Margaret had an idea.

'Why don't *you* come to the Ball?' she asked.

'What?'

'Of course, you would need to go in on someone's ticket because it is for students and their guests, but that wouldn't be a problem,' Margaret said thoughtfully. 'I know one or two lads who aren't taking partners.'

'Oh no, Margaret. You aren't going to land some poor lad with someone he doesn't know and may not take to – it would be embarrassing for both of us.'

'We'll be in a group. You don't have to bid him the time of day if you don't want to. I promise you – it will only be a name on a ticket. Say you'll come?'

Katy was thoughtful as Margaret paid for the dress, gabbing away to the assistant as though she had known her all her life. When she rejoined her, Katy gave a shaky laugh. 'I'll come. I'm no dancer and if you leave me alone for more than two minutes, I'll kill you stone dead when the Ball has finished.'

Margaret laughed. 'Get yourself a decent dress so that you can make a good impression. Tell your mam you will be staying with me overnight and that you will be safe enough. Let me know for certain sometime in the next few days so that we have time to go shopping.'

While her mother was finishing the preparations for the Sunday lunch, Katy joined her father in the sitting room. It was a rule, on Sundays, that they were barred from the kitchen until the meal was on the table because Annie had her own system for doing things and it bothered her if anyone interfered with it. She didn't mind the help with the washing up, but too many bodies in the kitchen held her back.

Katy broached the subject of the university dance. 'Would you mind if I went, Da? It would mean staying overnight with Margaret though, because it doesn't end till the early hours . . .' Katy's voice trailed away as he stared at her over his paper.

'What do you mean by "the early hours"?'

'It isn't over till around two o'clock in the morning. There won't be a bus back at that time of night.'

'And what about Mass on Sunday?'

'Margaret goes to Mass at St Malachy's near the City Hall. I'll be goin' with her . . .'

Annie called from the kitchen to say the lunch was on the table.

'We'll discuss this after the meal – see what your mam has to say.'

Annie said it was fine by her. If they couldn't trust their daughter to behave herself, then what chance was there? She looked severely at Eddie. 'You are not goin' to play the heavy father, are you?'

'She is eighteen years old. I am still responsible for her – and I do trust her. It's the others I don't trust.'

'Da! These are students we are talkin' about – not mass murderers.'

'Don't take a blind bit of notice, Katy.' Annie looked at Eddie. 'Well?'

'Why do ye's bother to ask? What say have I in anything?'

Annie winked at Katy. 'He knows fine well that his life would be hell on earth if he didn't agree.' She kissed Eddie on top of his head. 'You make all the big decisions. This is only a minor one,' she consoled him.

When Katy arrived at Beresford House the following morning, she had an uneasy feeling that something strange was in the air. Mrs Skelton looked strained and ill at ease, and she didn't offer Katy a cup of tea which she normally did before she went up to the nursery to take over from Sally.

'No tea this morning, Mrs Skelton?' Katy asked, and felt more alarm bells ring as Mrs Skelton turned away and said, 'Not this morning, Katy, for Mrs Sanders wants to see you in the drawing room shortly. She had to pop out for a moment.'

Katy frowned. Sylvia never 'popped out' anywhere. She had servants to do that. When Sylvia went out it was for a reason. 'In that case I'll away upstairs and take over from Sally then.'

'She isn't upstairs – nor is Elizabeth. Sally was cleaning up the mess down at the pool following last night's party when Mrs Sanders asked her to leave what she was doing and take Elizabeth over to play at young David's house.'

Katy was bewildered. 'Party? Sylvia didn't mention she was having a party.'

'It was a spur-of-the-moment decision. We were told on Saturday afternoon and Sally had to go shopping in a hurry. About a dozen people came. It was Miss Pamela's idea.' Mrs Skelton turned and began to fuss with the big kitchen range.

'Have you any idea why Sylvia wants to see me?'

Mrs Skelton continued to scrape away at the fire and said over her shoulder, 'No. She just left word that she wanted to see you as soon as you arrived.'

'I get the oddest feeling that something is wrong. I also get the feeling that whatever has happened involves me, and that you have been asked not to discuss the matter with me.'

Mrs Skelton straightened and moved towards the sink. 'Katy, love, I will have to be honest with you. I think there is a problem – as you guessed – and it does involve you but I honestly don't know what it is. I only know that Sally overheard Miss Pamela and Mrs Sanders having words and your name kept coming up. The last thing she heard was Mrs Sanders saying that she would have a word with you as soon as you arrived on Monday morning.'

'About what?'

'I have no idea. I was to tell you to see Mrs Sanders in the drawing room as soon as she rang the bell . . .'

The bell rang with a ferocity that made them both jump. 'Merciful God!' Mrs Skelton held her hand to her bosom. 'That thing scares the divil out of me.'

Katy went off to answer the call, more puzzled than concerned. She entered the drawing room to find Sylvia standing by the tall fireplace looking stiff and composed and with an air of determination about her that made Katy feel uneasy.

Her employer came straight to the point. 'Katy, I'm going to ask you a question and I would like you to give me an honest answer.'

'I would never be anything else,' Katy replied in bewilderment.

'I'm sorry to have to ask you this, but I've got to.' Sylvia was desperately hoping that the girl would have an explanation. Katy was good at her job and she had become very fond of her. She looked sternly at her. 'Have you at any time laid hands on Elizabeth in anger?'

Katy paled. 'Not in anger – never in anger – but yes, I have had occasion to tap her on the hands when she has been particularly unmanageable. In the early days when she was really naughty it was sometimes necessary, but it was always just an admonitory tap. You surely don't think . . .'

Sylvia's shoulders drooped. She sighed. 'I trusted you, Katy. I had no idea you used these methods. I thought you had a different system.'

Katy stared at her. 'I've never smacked Elizabeth – for God's sake, I would never do that. It was never more than a tap. We were laughing or playing games within minutes. Elizabeth would soon have let you know if I'd ever hit her. How could you possibly believe such a thing of me? How could you, Sylvia?'

Sylvia's voice, usually drawling and soft, sounded tired and held a note of disappointment in it. 'I have proof, that's why. I have proof and I was hoping that you could give an explanation.'

Katy's heart began to beat fast. She would keep calm. There had to be some dreadful mistake here. 'What do you mean, you have proof?'

'I'm afraid I can't say what proof. I have given my word not to involve anyone in this, but I can assure you, Katy, that there is irrefutable evidence that you hit Elizabeth.'

Katy went whiter still. 'I told you that I only smacked her hand – not hard – just enough to make the point. Why don't you ask Elizabeth? Examine her for bruises, if you must!'

'I have no intention of traumatising my daughter. However, I did ask her if she had done anything naughty that might make someone angry,' Sylvia said sadly. 'She immediately ran off crying, saying that she would never trust you again. You do see that I have no alternative but to ask you to leave. I will of course give you severance pay, and to make things easier for Elizabeth I will tell her that you have gone on holiday. Should I find that I have made a mistake . . .'

Katy's face was ashen. 'I could never work for someone who could think such a thing of me, Sylvia.' The depth of the pain she felt showed by the way her voice quivered. 'I need trust as much as you require loyalty, and I think I have a right to know what this evidence is and who supplied it.' A spark of anger tinged her words. Then she turned on her heel and quietly left the room.

When Katy closed the door behind her, Sylvia sank into the large settee and covered her eyes with her hands. It was all so distasteful but she had been given proof and there could be no second chance. Why, oh why had Katy allowed Elizabeth to rile her to the point where she had given into temptation and smacked her so hard that Elizabeth had been left with a large bruise on her cheek?

Seeing Katy's face, Mrs Skelton took her by the arm and steered her towards a chair in the kitchen. 'Come and tell us all about it. I bet that Miss Pamela had something to do with this business.' She poured out a mug of tea and handed it to Katy. 'What was the summons all about? I can see by the state of you that it was serious.'

'Very serious. Sylvia has evidence that says I hit Elizabeth . . .' Katy's voice broke. She took a gulp of the tea.

Sally, who had just entered the kitchen, looked at Mrs Skelton. 'What!' they cried together.

Katy stood up in agitation. 'I really don't feel I can stay in this house any longer,' she said.

'You can't leave like this,' Sally objected. 'You wouldn't lay a hand on that child. She adores you.'

Katy said, 'Look, I'm grateful for your support, but I must go. I'll contact you soon, when I have calmed down. At the moment I'm so upset I could do something silly.' She knew she would start crying any minute.

'But your job? What about Elizabeth?'

'The job is not important – I can always find another one – but I'm very worried about Elizabeth. She will be so confused about this. Could you tell her that I will try to get in touch sometime?'

'Away you go!' Seeing the girl's distress cut the heart out of Mrs Skelton. 'When Mr Charles comes home I intend to have a word with him,' she promised. 'He'll soon sort things out.'

On her way down the driveway, Katy caught sight of Pamela reclining in a deck-chair by the poolside. Suddenly she had no doubt in her mind that this woman was involved somehow. She was devious enough, and Mrs Skelton said she had been whispering with Sylvia. She set off towards the pool.

On seeing her approach, Pamela stood up, casually placing her book down on the vacant seat.

Katy watched the smile that spread over her face and knew that she had not been mistaken.

'Have you been telling lies about me?' she asked baldly.

Pamela made no pretence that she didn't know what Katy was talking about. 'I saw you swipe Elizabeth, causing her to fall into the pool. If it hadn't been for Charles she might have drowned.'

'You bad-hearted article!' Katy cried. 'You weren't even there!'

'I was watching from the spinney. Charles had his back to you at the time, and as I was the only witness I felt it was my duty to tell Sylvia. It won't do any good to pretend to her that Charles saw what happened. He only came running when he heard the child scream.'

'Why did you wait till now to tell your tale?' Katy asked, maintaining her calm.

I had to wait for the film to be developed, you Irish peasant, Sylvia thought, but said aloud: 'I had to search my conscience. After all, I might have been mistaken in what I'd seen.'

Katy took an involuntary step forward and stopped. 'Why do you dislike me so much?' she asked quietly. She was determined to retain her dignity. She would not let this woman incite her to anger. She watched Pamela turn her back on her and she drew in a breath. She had the greatest desire to throw the noxious woman into the pool but common sense prevailed. Instead, turning on her heel, she strode off down the path.

CHAPTER 6

Eddie Molloy was not a man of violence – to him all life was sacred – but at this moment in his heart and mind he felt murderous as he stared at the body of Lopper. He had to turn away as Patrick Toner stooped, lifted the body of the old dog, and placed it in his arms. Without looking at him, he began to walk from the spot.

Patrick scuffed some soil over the bloodstained area where the dog had lain, and followed. Just recently there had been a spate of sheep deaths, which was bad enough, but Patrick knew that this was a particularly terrible blow for Eddie; Lopper had been Vincey's dog, and now his last tie with the lad had gone.

'I'll carry on with the ditch-building, Eddie. You go on home and deal with things.'

Eddie shook his head. 'I'll lay him in the shugh by the side of the field while we get the work done, then I'll take him home and bury him. We are nearly done, anyway.' He gave a deep shuddering sigh.

Patrick nodded and they walked in silence towards the loose stone wall where Eddie laid the dog in the shugh that ran along the bottom before resuming their work. Patrick had known Eddie all his life. The pair of them, as boys, were always getting into mischief and then, as they reached manhood, they got into scrapes of a different kind. There were good times and some bad but in all the years he had known him, Patrick had never seen such devastation in his friend's eyes – not even when Vincey had been buried. Eddie had been stricken by his son's death, there was no doubt about that, but Vincey's death had followed on after an illness, whereas this looked like a callous killing. He stole a look at Eddie, whose face was grey and drawn, but held his tongue. The man should be allowed to work out his grief in the manner he desired. Later, he would help Eddie to bury the old fellow. There was little else he could do.

Eddie was standing in the kitchen when Katy walked in. He had just told Annie the bad news about Lopper and Annie, white-faced with shock, was handing him a mug of hot tea. He turned in surprise at the sight of Katy. 'What are you doing home?' he enquired, his tone sharper than usual.

Trying to still her trembling, Katy walked to the rack and took down a cup. This was going to be even harder than she'd thought. The palms of her hands were wet and the words wouldn't come out. She looked from one to the other.

Annie put her cup down and waited. Something was wrong.

Katy suddenly burst out: 'I've been sacked for smacking Elizabeth!' She stared at her da and swallowed nervously. The words had come out all wrong. She should have spoken quietly and reasonably. Instead, she had managed to condemn herself.

Eddie was only half-listening, his mind still on the tragedy he had just witnessed. Losing a job was of no consequence in the light of that terrible discovery. He wanted to shout at the pair of them that Lopper was dead, and he was all he had left of his son. Now that he was gone, all he had left of Vincey was his memories . . . but he was a bad communicator – always had been – and for too long he had held his worries and his sorrows close to him, easing his grief by working harder on the farm.

'I said you were not experienced enough for the job,' he sighed.

Katy stepped back in horror. 'You believe I am capable of doing this? You, my da, are willing to condemn me?'

'What are you on about! I'm not condemning you. You are out of a job – it isn't the end of the world. You must have done something to offend.'

'You weren't listening to me.' Katy's anger surfaced, finding a new source for outlet – a new victim. 'You are condemning me without knowing my side of things.'

Eddie's face turned red. 'Don't you speak to me like that, my girl. I think as your father I am entitled to some respect.' More angry words tumbled out as father and daughter squared up to each other.

Annie stood, transfixed, looking from one to the other. She was suddenly frightened at the torrent of abuse issuing from her daughter. All the darker memories came flooding back. The childish tantrums ... the stubborn mulishness of the young face ... the sound of breaking glass as a toy hit the mirror, followed by the panic in the young eyes She felt helpless as she listened to the two people she loved most hurting each other. She made a tentative move towards Eddie, but he shook his head.

'No daughter of mine will speak to me like this,' he was saying.

'I'm not staying in a house where there is no trust,' Katy cried. Her face crumpled in despair. Oh God! How had things got this far?

'You will go nowhere without my permission, my girl.'

Katy pushed past her father and ran upstairs. Annie tried to follow but Eddie stopped her. 'Leave her to reflect,' he ordered, and strode angrily out of the house.

Annie slumped into the big armchair by the blackleaded range. How quickly it had all happened. One unfortunate sentence ... a twisted interpretation ... and whoosh – a family in turmoil. She was still wondering if she should follow Katy to her room, when the phone rang. It was Margaret Kelly for Katy.

'I'll get her for you,' Annie said. She knocked on Katy's door and entered. 'Margaret Kelly is on the phone; if you don't feel up to it I can ask her to ring back.'

Katy shook her head and dabbed swollen eyelids. 'Talking to Margaret will take my mind off all this.'

Annie busied herself in the kitchen as she awaited Katy's return. She and her daughter needed to talk, and while Eddie was out seemed the best time. Once she had the whole picture she might be able to make them both see sense. Poor Eddie had been distraught over Lopper's death and Katy's news had been the last straw. She should tell Katy of Lopper's death so that she would understand, but on reflection she decided against doing so. Her daughter had enough on her plate just now.

Katy put her head round the door. 'Can we talk, Mam?'

Annie was thankful to see that Katy was now more controlled.

'We can,' she said cheerfully. 'Sit down and tell me properly what has happened.'

While Katy spoke of the scenes at Beresford House, Annie listened in silence, her face registering her horror. 'I think Mrs Sanders owed you more of an explanation than that!' she said, outraged.

Katy sighed. 'Sylvia was loth to discuss it in detail. She said she had evidence, and that something Elizabeth said further convinced her.' She frowned. 'I can't understand that, but Sylvia was quite definite about it.'

'She must know how much you loved that child,' Annie said.

Katy rose. 'I only had another month to go before my contract finished so I'm not going to let it spoil my life. After all, *I* know the truth. I'm more worried about the effect this will have on Elizabeth. It's fortunate she knew I would possibly leave when she goes to school in September.

'You were enjoying your work in the library, too. You'll miss that,' Annie pointed out.

Katy sighed. 'I've loved handling those rare editions.' She sat down again. 'Mam, I forgot to say . . . Margaret was ringing to ask if I was going to come to the Ball. I told her about my being sacked and the row with m'da, and she asked if I'd like to stay for a week till things calm down. I'm to ring her back if I can come.'

'You mean – today?' Annie cried. 'Oh Katy, darlin', I'm not sure if . . .'

'You can make it all right with Da. Please, Mam. I can't face him at the moment so it seems a good move to let tempers cool. I was going to ask you if I could stay a couple of days after the Ball anyway.'

'All right,' Annie said. 'I'll square it with your da – you know he loves you, Katy,' she added. 'He had a worry on his mind and I think he was only half-listening to what you were saying.'

An hour passed before Eddie arrived back. Katy had already gone and Annie was sitting on the porch with a buttered farl and a bowl of homemade soup. She rose as he reached her. 'I'll fetch your lunch; sit down and rest for a bit.' She'd had time to think since Katy left and she had it all planned as to what she was going to say.

She returned with a fresh bowl of soup and set it down on the table and took up her spoon again. They ate in silence until Eddie said, 'Where is the girl? Why is she not eatin' with us?'

'Margaret rang shortly after you left. She wanted to know if Katy would be going to the university Ball and if so, when was she coming to Belfast to buy the dress.'

'Annie! Stop chuntering on about dresses. Where is Katy? I don't like her sulking. Call her down here for a bite to eat.'

Annie took a deep breath. 'That's what I'm tryin' to tell you. She is on her way to Belfast to stay with Margaret.' She raised her hand as Eddie started to speak. 'I thought it best in the circumstances to let her have a week – or even two – away from us. The girl is in a terrible state, as much about the row she had with you as the fact that she has been dismissed from her post. Staying with a friend like Margaret and being able to talk it over with her, will help her get things sorted out in her mind. I said I would explain the situation to you and let her know if you approve.'

'I'll give the matter some thought,' Eddie said curtly, but he was already wondering if it would not be for the best. Life would be unbearable if he and Katy were waltzing round each other like a pair of boxers all the time. He needed peace and comfort in his own house after a hard day's work. He drew heavily on his pipe, staring thoughtfully into the distance while Annie went into the house to wash the bowls and tidy up. Maybe it was best to let Katy go until the situation eased.

He joined Annie in the kitchen. 'I'm willin' to go along with your plan,' he said. 'It's not a bad thing for Katy to have a bit of independence, and I'd rather she was with Margaret than on her own, but I want to know what has been happening. I wasn't myself when she came in . . .'

Margaret was waiting at the bus stop near Queen Victoria's statue at the City Hall when Katy arrived. As she stepped down onto the pavement a frisson of excitement shot through her. The place was teeming with people. Young people with knapsacks sat around on the steps and any bit of grass available. Pedestrians were jostling each other along the pavements up and down the Donegal Road while queues formed for the buses and trams. Overlooking the scene was the City Hall itself – a large Victorian building of white Portland stone which was now milky grey with age. It was a building which echoed various architectual styles with its turrets and domes and scrolls.

Margaret laughed as she staggered back under the onslaught as Katy threw her arms round her. 'In the name of God will you behave.'

'I can't help it! I'm just so excited to be here. Do you realise that the only thing I've done when I've come to the city is walk round shops. I want to see everything.' Katy's spirits had lifted so much she was able to put the past few hours to the back of her mind. The thoughts, the worries and despair would surface again, but for now she felt elated and – yes – reckless.

Margaret folded her arm into Katy's. 'Our place is a twenty-minute walk but you'll pass the Opera House – it's worth a look, being such a beautiful ornate building. Another day you can have a stroll around when you get settled – and you must take a bus along to the Queens Bridge Road and look over the River Lagan and marvel at the massive riggings that are the cranes of Harland and Wolff's shipyard – but for now you will have to be content with a walk to the house.'

Katy was impressed when she saw the house. It was situated in a narrow cobbled street in one of the older housing areas, and was sandwiched between two rows of similar buildings. It had a red brick frontage with long, deep windows.

They entered a narrow hallway and Margaret led her into the small living room. She introduced her to the occupants. There was Donal Bannon, her ticket partner, whom Margaret said preferred food and drink to girls and who was going to be a chemist; the tall beefy second-year medical student, Frank McGrady, who could drink the Lagan dry; and Mickey, who seemed kind and was the first one to say, 'Welcome to the ranch, Katy.' Like Margaret, he was reading English.

'Norah isn't here at the moment. She had a couple of days at home to put in some quiet study.'

Katy looked round at the small group. They were all so friendly. She knew she was going to enjoy this fortnight.

She was given a tour by Margaret, who reminded her that the men's sleeping quarters were upstairs. The girls slept in two converted rooms off the living room with a bathroom nearby. Furniture was sparse and obviously second-hand, but Katy felt excited by it all. There was an air of casual decadence about the place that she found somehow heartening.

It was the night of the Ball. Katy felt excitement bubble up inside her as she stood in the centre of the group watching the goings-on. Donal Bannon had gone to find out what time the food hall would be opened. The whole exercise had been meticulously planned from the beginning. Donal, being the one with a high regard for his stomach, had been assigned this chore. 'Otherwise,' warned Frank – who, being in his second year was experienced in such matters – 'the whole shebang will fall apart for us, for the queue stretches half a mile and by the time the last fifty poor unfortunates get to the tables there is little left but the jellies and the odd curled-up sandwich.'

Already their group had increased in size, and to Katy's amusement she noticed that there were several men hovering around Margaret, who looked colourful and very glamorous in an emerald-green satin ball gown. Slightly off the shoulder and with an enormous sash, it was the most startling dress in the room. Katy, having been warned not to buy anything that clashed with the colour, had laughingly remarked that Margaret was insane to make such a proviso, as at some time or other she would be certain to have someone standing nearby in a clashy dress. 'Not everyone has been alerted to the fact that Margaret Kelly will be be wearing a lurid emerald-green satin dress,' she'd teased.

Margaret had laughed good-naturedly. 'Cheeky article! I can always move away from them, but I don't want the pair of us to be waltzing away to opposite ends of the room all evening.'

Katy had therefore settled for a demure cream dress in fine wool which sported cap sleeves and was loosely draped but plain. 'I hope no one hands me a candle to hold,' she giggled when she and Margaret chose it. 'I'll look like the Statue of Liberty.'

She leaned close to Margaret now, and whispered, 'You're doin' all right for yourself. I'm glad I'm with you – I can mop up the overflow.' Margaret clicked her teeth and winked before continuing her conversation with the fellow opposite. His companion, seeing that Katy was laughing, smiled.

'Remember me? The name is Terence Coleman.'

Katy studied him shyly. His eyes, thick-lashed and bright blue, gazed into hers. He looked vaguely familiar and yet . . . ?

'Cast your mind back. A fair . . . a lost child . . . oodles of ice cream?'

Katy gasped. 'Now I recognise you – but only just. You have longer hair and you seem taller and – oh, how rude of me.'

Terence shrugged pleasantly. 'I can understand your difficulty. The penguin suit makes me look taller and my hair has been bleached by sun as I've just been abroad for two weeks. Also, I wore sunglasses the day we met.'

Katy felt excited. His look was so intense, his face so finely chiselled, with high cheekbones and a sensuous mouth which curved to one side . . . a bit Errol Flynn-ish. She dragged her gaze away as Donal dashed back.

'Rumour has it – in the form of the head chef – that food is about to be served, so get your pert bums along to the front hall.' He grabbed Katy by the hand and pulled her along. She looked over her shoulder and surprised a look of annoyance on Terence Coleman's face. She sighed inwardly. She probably wouldn't see him again this evening.

She was wrong. When the dancing restarted, he was at her side. 'May I – before your boyfriend returns?'

Katy smiled to herself. She'd lived with the group for a week and already she had realised that Margaret's appraisal of Donal was spot-on. The likelihood of that skite Donal asking her onto the floor was extremely low. He really had only come for the food and drink. She let Terence lead her onto the floor for a waltz.

He said, 'You dance very well.'

'I do indeed,' she agreed, as he whirled her into a turn. 'I've been well taught.'

'And I admire your modesty,' he grinned.

Katy, supercharged with the novelty and excitement of this new experience, laughed in delight. 'It's my first Ball,' she said. 'The only regular dancing I've done is Irish dancing, and for that I had two left feet. After that, ballroom dancing was a dream.' She was breathless with effort by now.

'Shall we sit the next one out?' Terence asked, as they left the floor. They found a quiet corner and set about getting to know each other.

Katy discovered that he was older than most of the other students. He'd had to interrupt his education, he explained, when he was called up in the latter stages of the war.

'Just like my brother,' said Katy. 'What are you studying?'

'Engineering – following in Father's footsteps, so to speak.' He cocked his head on one side. 'My very favourite dance.' He held out his arms and Katy moved into them for the quickstep, her mind already on the possibility that when the Ball was over he might ask to meet her again.

Terence Coleman was having similar thoughts. He was jaded by the girls he usually went out with. They were all much the same. Well-educated, well-dressed, well-stacked in the right places and with plenty of money. This one would be a novelty. Already he was her hero because of the incident at the fair. She was such an innocent. He had met her on one of his good days when he was feeling generous. It was those eyes of hers that had done it. He had shocked himself when he had offered to help her find the kid, but for once his heart had ruled his head. Christ! He'd even eaten ice cream with the pair of them. He hated ice cream.

'It was a great evening. Was it not a great evening?' Frank McGrady, slurring his words, was draped across the settee. He had been dumped there by Donal and Mickey Flynn – the other male in the group. Norah Byrne, the quiet studious girl who had been introduced previously to Katy, had volunteered to make some strong coffee, and before she left the room she remarked that it was a wonder that Frank McGrady hadn't succumbed to alcohol poisoning by now, in view of the amount he threw down his throat on such occasions.

They were all feeling happy, even if they hadn't been able to match Frank's capacity. Katy, who had taken quite a liking to the Pimms she had tasted for the first time, was feeling a bit giddy. It could have been worse, she reflected. The drink had tasted like lemonade with a slight kick, and all that fruit floating around made it look so innocent. If it hadn't been for the eagle eye of Margaret, she too might have been in a similar position to Frank, but for the latter part of the evening Margaret had encouraged her to drink orange juice.

'It's been a great gas altogether!' Katy exclaimed, and meant it. It was the first time since the altercation with her da that she had truly been able to enjoy herself, and the chance to put the unpleasantness of the manner of her sacking to the back of her mind was a bonus. Her heart began to pump. What would Charles think about it all when he returned?

'I noticed you were dancing a lot with Terence Coleman,' Donal remarked.

Katy started, and brought her mind back to the present.

'Be careful how you go with that fella. He has an eye for a pretty girl.'

'Haven't we all,' Frank slurred. 'The darlin' Katy being prettier than mosh-sht.'

'This may not be the time to bring it up,' said Margaret, 'but how would you feel about Katy coming to live with us?'

Katy gave a gasp. 'What?'

'Why not?' Margaret countered. 'What is there at home for you? You could stay with us and look for a job. It's what you were going to do anyway, at one time, so your da won't make a fuss, will he?'

'I suppose not, but I would still need his permission.'

'That's fine,' said Margaret. 'Meanwhile, could you all give it some thought, so that Katy will know how she stands?'

Frank gave a huge snore. 'That's him well away!' sniggered Donal. He shrugged. 'I'm happy. Anything that helps cut down cost is fine by me. I'm in a terminal state of financial embarrassment.'

Mickey Flynn nodded. He liked Katy. She was quiet and she seemed a sympathetic person. 'Same here,' he said.

There was only Norah left. As soon as she placed the tray down on the table Margaret posed the question to her.

'I'm not deaf. The kitchen is only a few feet away – remember that, you lot, when you are swearing. Yes, I'm happy about it. It means the rota will work out better.'

'The rota?' Katy asked.

'Never mind that now – Norah looks after it and we can discuss it another time. The main thing is that we are all in agreement about Katy staying. She can pay her way so we have no worries there, but what about Frank? He is too drunk at the moment to cast a vote.'

'Arrah, don't give it a thought. We can all swear blind that he cast his vote. Sure, he'll never remember and anyway, he's too good-natured to refuse.'

Margaret put down her cup. 'I don't know about the rest of you, but I'm away to bed. It's now four o'clock in the morning and if I'm to attend ten o'clock Mass tomorrow I'll need some sleep.' She pulled Katy up. 'Your truckle bed awaits you.'

Next morning after Mass, Frank, now sporting a hang-dog expression and holding a wet flannel to his forehead, accepted the idea that Katy should become one of them. They were all sitting round the table eating a late breakfast, except for Frank who couldn't face the idea of watching them all scoff 'bloody porridge and burnt toast'. He lay slumped in an armchair.

'Have you got a job?' Donal enquired.

Katy reddened. 'No, I haven't, but my savings will keep me going until I find one.'

Norah, whom Katy had now established was the most domesticated member of the group, for she seemed to be the one who did the cooking, came back after making a fresh pot of tea. 'I think it might be a good idea to fill Katy in on how we run things.'

'That's your job, Norah.' Margaret explained that Norah, who was studying mathematics, was the one who dealt with rotas and sorted out the finances.

Norah poured herself a cup of tea and began to explain the system. 'We all chip in with our share of the rent, and put a certain sum in the kitty for gas and electricity and food. If there is any left at the end of the month, it is put in a special pot marked "keep your thieving hands out of my insides" and this is used for emergencies.'

'How do you manage to possess a phone?' Katy asked anxiously.

'That's thanks to Donal's da. He worries about the lad and likes to keep in touch. But we take more calls than we make.'

'There isn't often much money in the pot,' Frank cut in, and groaned as a pain shot through his skull.

'It might happen more often if Katy joins us. The rent will be split six ways for a start,' said Norah before continuing. 'There is also another arrangement whereby we don't all swan off home to our parents on the same weekend . . .'

'Why?' Katy asked.

Frank spoke up. 'If we did, then we would all come back laden with food at the same time and because bread doesn't keep and butter goes off quite quickly, we could end up starving in our garret till the next sortie.'

'*Who* is supposed to be explaining the system?' asked Norah, throwing Frank a black look. 'Anyway, you should be suffering in silence to atone for your overindulgence, so shut up.'

'Have you not got a refrigerator?' Katy asked. She was used to seeing one at home, in which some of the farm produce was kept.

'We are students, not millionaires. Sure, where would we find the money?' Margaret laughed. 'Lord, Katy, you're in for a shock. If you've never had to eat rancid butter on toast, or steamed hard bread over the kettle so you could cut it – you haven't lived.'

Katy was thoughtful as Norah chuntered on about how she 'kept the books' and how everyone had to get a receipt for any purchase made that wasn't directly related to the domestic arrangements.

'We could buy a refrigerator,' Katy said suddenly.

'How? We haven't two pennies to rub together,' Donal scoffed. 'And who do we know who has a refrigerator?'

Katy explained: 'If I'm here as an extra body, then I'll buy one – and until it's been paid for I won't pay rent. I will, of course, pay my way towards the food bill.'

Norah sat forward and she and Margaret looked at each other. 'Do you have enough saved up?' Norah asked, slightly amazed.

Katy nodded. 'I had a well-paid job and when I left it, I was given severance pay and two weeks' holiday money.'

'God, what a brilliant idea. We wouldn't have to take turns to go home on our scavenging missions,' said Mickey, who hated being away from Margaret.

'Within reason,' Norah said cautiously. 'The bread can still go mouldy, and it will be a *small* refrigerator of course, but we can be a *bit* more lenient. We shall still have to use the meat safe at times.'

Margaret spoke directly to Katy. 'Tackle your parents about it when you get home, but be discreet. They may not like the idea of you living here with those three cahouns sleeping upstairs.' She grinned over at the three men and continued: 'I know I said that since the war people are more tolerant of this kind of thing – but it doesn't apply to all parents.'

'Speaking of men, where is this boyfriend Michael you spoke of?' Katy asked later when she and Margaret were in the privacy of her friend's bedroom.

'He's upstairs. You spent some of the last few hours in his company.'

'You mean Mickey is the Michael you spoke of?'

'Sounds daft when said like that, but yes – Mickey is the Michael I spoke of.'

'But you flirted all evening with other fellas . . . did he not mind?'

'Students do that. Mickey did his fair share. Everyone had a good time without it getting out of hand. After all, who wants a pair of sweethearts gazing soulfully at each other all evening! By the way, I noticed that you were spending a lot of time with Terence Coleman.'

'He was charming,' Katy said.

Margaret frowned. 'Be careful. He has a reputation for—'

'Just what I'm looking for,' Katy broke in with a grin. 'I'm out to further my education.' Seeing Margaret's look of concern, she said seriously, 'I know what I'm about, Margaret. All I'm doing is catching up on life. I can handle things.'

111

'You aren't dealing with a Tom Toner here. This man has seen it all. He is much older than the rest of us, and he has been through the last two years of the war – seen fighting . . .'

'I may be a simple country girl, but I'm not daft – so stop worrying.'

'Just you be careful, Katy Molloy,' Margaret replied.

Katy stared out of the window. She had every intention of being careful but she had a lot to learn and she was going to take any opportunity to advance her knowledge of men and relationships. God knows she had managed to botch a few up just recently.

Later that week, Katy took the bus home to Ballynashee. She was so nervous she felt her heart pumping away inside. It was going to be difficult seeing her da for the first time since their acrimonious parting.

But Eddie wasn't back from the fields when she arrived home. Her mother was preparing supper. Katy hugged her. 'How have things been since I went away?' she asked anxiously.

Annie checked the saucepans and moved them from the heat before sitting down. She still hadn't mentioned to her daughter that Lopper had died. Each time Katy had phoned in the past two weeks her nerve had failed, for Katy had loved the big shaggy dog almost as much as Eddie and for the same reason – because he had been Vincey's dog. She sighed. Now that her daughter was home it couldn't be hidden any longer.

Katy looked nervously at her mother. Something was wrong; she could see it by Annie's expression. 'Is m'da . . .'

'Your da is all right, but he isn't himself at the moment.' Annie paused. 'It's hard to have to tell you this, Katy . . .'

'Oh God! Is he ill? It's my fault – I should never have had that row with him.' Katy had never known her father to be seriously ill. The nearest Eddie got to sickness was the occasional sniffly cold.

Annie put up her hand. 'There is nothin' physically wrong with him, so stop with the panic. He is just not himself. He goes round doing the chores on the farm with head bent and a lost look about him. At home here he says little, other than to answer when I speak to him.'

'Why? What has brought this on then if it has nothing to do with our row?' Katy asked, puzzled and alarmed.

Annie sighed. 'The day you came home and told us that you had been sacked, your da had just found Lopper dead in the far field. The poor old creature had been shot. We thought at first it was deliberate, but it turned out that Jack Murray shot the dog by accident when he was chasing after that rogue fox that was killing the hens around the area.

Katy stared at her mother in horror, tears forming behind her lids. 'And I behaved so badly to him – oh, Mam!'

They had both been at fault, Annie thought. Katy for her defiance and Eddie for turning in on his emotions and then taking his sorrow out on his daughter. Before she could reply, there was the sound of scraping feet at the door and Eddie walked in.

Katy went to him. 'I've just heard about Lopper. I'm so sorry Da.'

Eddie nodded. 'It's over. Life moves on. If it had been any other animal than Lopper I'd have been fine, but he was special.' His voice was soft but with a deadness to it that pierced Katy's heart. She watched him sit down in his armchair. The spirit was knocked out of him, as her mother had said.

After supper, Eddie tapped his pipe out on the hearth and began the process of filling and lighting it, his thoughts heavy with guilt. He had spoken harshly and without thought to Katy at their last meeting, and for the past two weeks he had been unable to get it out of his mind. He had since gone about like a man stricken, aware that he should have supported his daughter – not castigated her. He needed to make amends.

With a sigh he threw the match into the empty grate and turned to her. 'I want to apologise for what happened last time we were together.' He lifted his hand as Katy started to speak. 'I have helped to raise you and I have taught you how to behave, and I should have shown more faith in you. When your mother explained what had happened, I wanted to go to Beresford House and have it out with Mrs Sanders but she convinced me I should not. Just say the word . . .'

'No, Da!' Katy gasped. 'I want to forget it. I'm still not certain

113

how Sylvia got the idea that I had been smacking Elizabeth, but it no longer matters – I am moving on.' She rose and knelt by her father. 'I am just thankful that we are friends again.'

'That's settled then,' said Annie crisply. 'Now, tell us – how did the Ball go? Did you have a good time?'

Katy told them how enjoyable it had been and how much fun she'd had living with Margaret and her friends.

'You don't mind the bustle and noise of the city, then?' Annie observed.

'I loved it, Mam.' Katy told them proudly how she made her own way round the city, and how she had taken a bus down Donegal Street and had then gone to the Queens Bridge to look at the River Lagan, and how fascinating it was to watch the enormously high cranes of the Harland & Wolff shipyard weaving about the skyline as they carried equipment overhead. All the while, Eddie smoked his pipe and was silent.

'Do you still want to work there?' asked Annie, shrewdly guessing that Katy wanted just that.

Katy glanced nervously at her da. He hadn't moved other than to put his pipe to his lips. 'I do. Margaret says I can share her room for as long as I need to while I look for a job. There is a groups of five living in the house and I got on well with them and they said they wouldn't mind if I stayed.'

Annie spoke to Eddie. 'What do you think?'

Eddie didn't answer. Annie repeated her question more loudly and he reluctantly turned to her. 'Think about what?'

'Our Katy finding a job in Belfast and living with Margaret Kelly?'

Eddie rose. 'I'll give the matter some thought while I'm mucking out.' He knew he would give in, if only because he felt he owed Katy something for his doubting her, but for all that, he couldn't be seen to be too soft.

When he'd gone, Annie said, 'You can pack your bags. If your father had any objections they would have been given just then – and don't you worry about him. He was worse than this a week ago. I think he is on the mend, thank God.'

Charles was glad to be back. In spite of the stress he had been

114

under when the Barney Fogarty thing was going on, he had enjoyed his first few months in Ireland. He put his case down by the telephone table and went into the kitchen to see if Mrs Skelton would be able to stretch the evening meal to include him.

She could and she would, she said, adding that she was sorry there had been no one around to greet him. Sally was out with Elizabeth and Mrs Sanders was at a meeting.

'Is Miss Pamela around?'

Mrs Skelton's lips pursed. 'Miss Pamela has gone out for the day. I understand she has gone to Belfast to stay overnight with a friend who is visiting – which is why Sally is out with Elizabeth.'

Charles frowned. 'It's Monday. Shouldn't Katy be here by now?' He glanced at his watch. It was ten o'clock in the morning.

'Katy doesn't work here any more.'

Charles leaned against the heavy kitchen table and regarded Mrs Skelton curiously. Something was wrong. 'Why?'

'You will have to ask Mrs Sanders about that.' Mrs Skelton busied herself at the range. Charles, puzzled, and realising that he wasn't going to prise anything more out of the housekeeper, made his way towards the woods for some fresh air, deep in thought. He knew that Katy's job as a nanny was not a permanent one, but he'd understood that she was to stay on if she wished – as Sylvia's companion. Why had she changed her mind? Why hadn't he taken the time to ring home? Then he wouldn't be in the dark now.

Sally and Elizabeth were coming up the driveway when he returned. The tiny girl darted towards him and he caught her up in his arms. 'My word! You have grown since I last saw you.'

To his surprise, his niece burst into tears. He held her close. 'Now look here, Lizzie, you are making the most hellish mess of my shirt. Let's go inside and you can tell me what's wrong.'

Elizabeth, her eyes still brimming with tears, looked up at him. 'Katy is gone! I want her back and Mamma says she can't. I want her to come back, Uncle Charles. Please ask Mamma to make her come back.'

He hugged her. 'Katy was never going to be here for ever, Lizzie. You will be going to school in four weeks' time, remember.' He looked over her head at Sally and was about to speak

115

when Sally said, 'Could you stay with Elizabeth while I go and get her tea ready, Mr Charles?' He nodded and took Elizabeth by the hand. 'Let's go up to the nursery.'

Charles broached the subject later that evening when he and Sylvia sat down in the drawing room with their coffee. 'Sylvia, what on earth has been going on? Why has young Katy resigned when she still has at least another month to go? Did you two have a row?'

Sylvia sighed heavily. 'I suppose I should thank you for not mentioning the matter at dinner. My appetite is poor enough as it is.'

Charles listened as she explained the events of the past weeks, and when she had finished he put his cup down and said severely, 'Sylvia! How can you possibly think that Katy would smack Elizabeth! She idolises the child! I've seen her tap Elizabeth on the bottom or on the wrists in admonishment, but Elizabeth accepts it. She is back in Katy's arms in no time, kissing her to say she's sorry.'

'I'm afraid it is more than that,' Sylvia said sadly. 'I would never have taken such extreme steps unless I had proof.'

'What proof?'

Sylvia crossed to the handsome inlaid bureau by the window where she kept her accounts and took an envelope from it. 'Look at this and tell me I was wrong.'

Charles withdrew a photograph and stared at it for only a second before the truth dawned. He looked at his sister in horror. 'You don't know *how* wrong you have been, Sylvia. This is worthless. I'll bet Pamela took this picture – she was the only other person there. I had no idea this was what you were referring to when you said Katy had slapped Elizabeth.'

'You can't deny that the photograph shows that Katy has just aimed a slap at the side of Elizabeth's head, which no doubt knocked her into the water. Elizabeth could have drowned, Charles.'

'It is a question of perspective, Sylvia. Katy was shooshing away a couple of persistent wasps which were terrifying Lizzie. You know how she hates them. The child stepped back too far and fell into the pool.'

116

Sylvia's face paled. She stared at Charles. 'You mean – Pamela was deliberately causing mischief?'

Charles frowned. He would like to think that Pamela had genuinely thought she'd seen the scenario as shown in the photograph, but instinct told him otherwise. It was the camera which had lied – not the naked eye.

Sylvia sat down heavily in the chair. God, what had she done to Katy! She looked at Charles. 'What can I do?'

Charles was thoughtful as he poured himself a drink. He didn't have another meeting until Thursday, which meant he had a few days free in which to pay a visit to the farm. Maybe he could limit the damage already done.

'What are you planning?' Sylvia asked.

'I thought I might go over to the farm and see if I can talk to Katy.'

Sylvia blanched. She couldn't face Katy just yet. 'Perhaps it would be better to write a letter to her beforehand . . .'

'Certainly not!' Charles said severely. 'Katy has been wronged and we owe it to her to let her know that the truth has come out. Just let's hope that she is magnanimous enough to forgive.' He looked steadily at his sister. 'This is no time for cowardice on your part, Sylvia.'

In spite of his apparent confidence, Charles did have his doubts about seeing Katy. He had to face the fact that he could get a bad reception; nevertheless he was determined to try and put things right.

Annie met him at the door as he drew up in his car, the following morning. Even from this distance he could see the look of surprise on her face. He went towards her. She greeted him stiffly. 'We have talking to do. I've just put the kettle on.'

Charles hesitated. 'I've come to see Katy, actually.'

'I was under no illusion that you had come to see me,' Annie said quietly. 'Katy is not here at the moment. The offer of the tea still stands.'

Charles followed her into the kitchen where Annie motioned for him to sit down at the large family table. Nearby, a huge Irish dresser was stacked with beautiful delftware, and above in the roofspace, a wooden airer was airing freshly ironed clothes. On the very splendid range a huge kettle belched steam.

Annie took the kettle from the blackleaded top and poured the boiling water into a dark brown earthenware teapot. 'This range is a godsend in the winter but in the summer we're killed by the heat. One of these days I'll have the thing ripped out and a new electric cooker installed,' she said.

'That would be a pity,' Charles commented. 'An electric cooker wouldn't have the same effect as the homely range. I'd give some more thought to that one.' Their conversation was stilted . . . awkward. He took the small tray from her and followed her into the other room; cool, chintzy and full of memorabilia and books, with an Irish fiddle leaning against the wall nearest the fireplace.

Seeing Charles look towards the fiddle, Annie said, 'Eddie's pride and joy. He plays like a fiend from hell for he hasn't got the natural talent but he loves the Irish music. Katy and I just close our ears when he gets goin'.'

'I love your home,' Charles said

Annie's initial frostiness melted. It wasn't this man's fault that his sister hadn't the sense she was born with.

'How old is it?' Charles took the cup from her and looked around with interest, studying the heavy beams above, which looked as though they had been there for ever, blackened as they were with soot and smoke.

'I'm not sure,' Annie pondered. 'I know that Eddie's family go back to well over a hundred years of living here.' She put the teapot down and looked him straight in the eyes. 'As I said, I'm afraid Katy isn't here and you have made the journey for nothing.'

'I can call again – or perhaps you could ask her to get in touch with me by phone? There is something important I have to tell her.'

'I hope that what you have to say will resolve the riddle of how my girl came to be accused of this dreadful act. She is living in Belfast now and may never come back home again except to visit us.'

Charles frowned. 'Belfast?'

'What happened has affected our lives severely,' Annie continued as though he hadn't spoken. 'Katy decided to go to Belfast and find a job. She is living with her friend Margaret Kelly – a very sensible girlfriend – who is studying English at the university.'

'Can I get in touch with her? I'm working at the airport – it wouldn't be a problem,'

Annie hesitated. 'I think it would be better if you gave me your number. I don't know how she would feel about me giving you hers under the circumstances. I hope you understand?'

Charles nodded. 'I do. I mustn't keep you from your baking any longer. I'm sorry to have interrupted you.' He took a small card from his pocket and handed it to her. 'What happened was all a ghastly mistake,' he said.

'I've never thought otherwise,' said Annie, and felt a sense of great relief. 'I'll give Katy your message.'

Pamela was back and already at the pool when Charles arrived home. She was alone. He parked his car. Sylvia's MG runabout was not in the garage, which probably meant that Pamela was unaware of the recent developments. With grim determination he made his way towards her, and as he reached her she opened her eyes and stared up in surprise as he towered above her.

'Charles, darling,' she said nervously. 'Cook told me you had gone out. How lovely to see you home again.'

Charles said, with deadly calm: 'Pamela, I want a word with you.'

Pamela's eyes narrowed. So he had been shown the snapshot. She had expected this and was prepared for it. Her objective had been achieved; the wretched nanny had gone. She sat up, concern showing in her eyes. 'Darling, I can see that you have spoken to Sylvia. It is all very distasteful and sad, but I love Elizabeth. I *had* to tell Sylvia what I'd seen.'

'I was there,' Charles said stiffly.

'You were on your way back to the house, Charles. You couldn't have seen what happened.'

Charles studied the lovely face, the soft mouth, the long flaxen hair, the blue eyes now looking challengingly at him, and remembered how cold her expression could be when she was thwarted. He suddenly remembered, too, that each time he visited the pool,

Katy and Elizabeth were usually banished to the other end. He brought his mind back to the moment. 'That photograph you so conveniently took gave a wrong impression. It was a question of perspective.'

Pamela gave a little gasp. 'God! You mean the snapshot made it look as though . . . Oh dear! I am sorry. I thought . . .'

Charles studied her. She was lying. She knew very well what had really happened; he could see it in her eyes. 'I don't believe you, Pamela,' he said stiffly. 'Perhaps it is time you returned to England and your friends. You did tell me just before I went that they were missing you. Besides, I think staying could be embarrassing for all of us.'

Pamela stood up, genuinely shaken. 'Charles, please . . . You must let me explain!' But he turned on his heel and made his way down the path, leaving her fuming. Discourteous bastard, she thought tearfully, and wondered if she should wait till Sylvia got back. She might be able to convince her that she had made a hideous mistake . . . No, better to cut and run. She was bored with this country anyway. She'd only come because of Charles.

Katy had been in Belfast three weeks now and she was restless. It had been grand in the beginning to wander round the city and see the sights, but the novelty had palled a bit because she had to go alone. The others were still busy with their studies and spent much of their time in the library at the university.

She had tidied up and washed down walls and scrubbed paintwork, till her arms ached and she had upset Norah, who felt that Katy was impinging on her role. Norah had complained to Margaret, who had explained that Katy had to keep busy until she came up with a job, and wasn't it better that she made herself useful while Norah caught up with her revision? Norah, appeased, had nevertheless said that she thought Katy would be better served pounding the pavements looking for a job.

Katy said that was all very well, but she was looking for the *right* job. She had made a pact with herself that she wouldn't take the first thing that came along. Nevertheless, in spite of her resolve, she was sorely tempted to do just that. When the others were all at the university, the house seemed so silent and dreary.

It was lovely when they were all there together and the place rang with the sounds of laughter and bickering and the din of banging pots as Margaret cooked the – only just – palatable meal, but when Katy was alone, somehow not even the music from her wireless was sufficient to lift her spirits. This surprised her. She had never thought of herself as someone who needed people around all the time. Perhaps it was because the city had such a different feel about it. Today, she suddenly felt that if she didn't go out and walk around the streets for a bit and get some fresh air she would go mad, so she grabbed her handbag and hat and set off.

She had been walking for some time in the direction of the university as Margaret had told her once that the Botanical Gardens next to it were a haven of peace and tranquillity on a hot day – and it was certainly hot today. She was halfway there when she came upon the bookshop. It stood at the end of a parade of rather rackety shops and houses, none of which looked as though they'd had a lick of paint since they had been built. Tired-looking vegetables visibly wilting in their boxes were on display on the pavement stall outside the greengrocer's shop. She stopped to view them. Used as she was to everything coming straight from the ground and into the pot, she was appalled to think that anyone was expected to pay good money for such as these.

She peered into the tiny grocery shop next door, where, in the dimly lit interior, two women were waiting to be served. Even here, everything looked dusty and forlorn.

Two doors away, there was a small bakery from which the smell of freshly baked barmbracks and loaves of bread drifted invitingly out of the interior, causing her to stop for a moment. Here, the window was clean, and the cakes and pies and soda bread were placed in trays and invitingly displayed behind glass covers. Katy couldn't resist the invitation. She bought some cakes and a few soda farls for supper.

It was as she emerged from the bakery that she noticed the bookshop just a few yards away. It was as grubby and as neglected and uninviting as the other shops with the exception of the neat little bakery, but she was curious. What on earth was a bookshop doing in a street like this? She could understand that the other shops would be used by the residents in the many streets around – but how many people in this area would require the services of a bookshop?

Intrigued, she walked towards it and shading her eyes, leaned close to the glass to peer in. She was disappointed. The interior was too dark and the sun too bright to see inside. She had to content herself with trying to read the titles of the sun-faded books in the window.

'Why don't you come inside?'

She turned, startled, to find a thin grey-haired man smiling at her. His glasses were perched on top of his hair and he was leaning against the doorpost holding a stack of books in his arms.

'I was just – I was just . . .'

'I know. You were just looking,' he sighed. 'That's what most of them say.'

'Who?'

'The students!' The man nodded his head towards the top of the street.

'They pass here every day in their droves but few come in. They prefer to go to the big shops in the city centre. Think they can do better there . . . Well – are you coming in or not?' Having spoken he turned and re-entered the shop.

Katy hesitated and then followed, with no clear idea why she did so. She could barely see when she came in from the bright sunlight and had to stand for a moment to adjust. 'Why do you not have stronger light bulbs?' she asked.

The man had pulled his spectacles down and was regarding her with interest. 'Too expensive!' he barked. 'When I start selling books by the hundreds instead of by the tens, then I'll think about it. Now – do you want a cup of tea? I've just made one.'

Katy grinned. She liked him. 'Do you always offer tea to customers?'

'You're no customer. You only looked in the window out of curiosity. I can spot the genuine article at ten paces.'

'Milk, no sugar, and I have some cakes here so that'll be my contribution.'

'Fair enough.' He held out his hand. 'John Reilly.'

'Katy Molloy.'

'Student?' John Reilly poured the tea and emerged from behind the curtain that hid the gas ring and the tea things in the cubby-hole.

Katy shook her head. 'I'm job-hunting, as a matter of fact.'

'Aw, b'God you're not telling me you were looking in my window on the off-chance of a job here?'

'No, I was not!' Katy laughed. 'I was wandering round the streets because I was bored with staring at a wall and listening to silence, and I ended up in this street so I bought some things at the bakery and was thinking of going back when I spotted your shop.'

John Reilly took a long slurp of his tea and said, 'And what do you think of it?'

Katy hesitated. She didn't want to hurt his feelings by being brutally honest. 'Do you do much business?' she asked instead.

'Well, that answers my question. You are too nice a person to state the truth, I can see that. The place is a holy terror of a mess. It's no wonder I don't get the students here.'

'You must do some business or you would have given up. I mean, how else could you afford to live here?' Katy handed him the bag of buns so that he could choose one.

'I have a bit put past and my needs are small. I advertise the odd book or two and I do a postal trade and I get the occasional passer-by such as yourself.'

While he was speaking, Katy studied the shop. 'You could do a lot to improve this place. All it needs is a lick of white paint to brighten it up, a few stronger light bulbs, a bit of reorganisation of the shelf pattern . . .'

'And a small fortune at my beck and call,' John said. 'And if I did all this and got no more business, then I would be truly in Queer Street. Anyway, are you an expert or what?'

'Not a bit,' Katy admitted. 'But I spend a lot of time in libraries because I am an avid reader, and it's obvious that they organise their shelves for maximum efficiency.' She felt certain that the place had potential. The university was only a few streets away, and according to John the students came past the shop on a regular basis. If the shop and its contents were

123

presented more invitingly, then it might encourage them to come in more often.

The doorbell jangled and two youths entered. Katy waited while John dealt with them and was amazed at his indifference. He shrugged his shoulders at their enquiry and when the taller of the two students spoke again, John shook his head and the students thanked him and left.

'It's ever the way. They always want what I haven't got in stock.'

'Couldn't you get it for them?'

'I could if I put myself out,' he admitted. 'But I'm not goin' to all that trouble for the sake of a few bob profit.'

'You'll never make your fortune with that attitude.'

John Reilly regarded the young girl facing him. Her eager young face looked back at him, her eyebrows raised in question. He felt his heart constrict. He suddenly thought of his late wife – it was just how Mollie used to look at him when he wouldn't shift himself. 'You are not in the business to read the books, John. You are selling them – it's how we earn our living,' she'd chided him. His eyes darkened and grew sad. Without Mollie he had gone down the road to introspection and penury. It was only because his needs were small that he managed to survive.

'You're right,' he said heavily. 'I'm willin' to listen to any suggestions for I've long given up the ghost. Maybe you were sent by some divine being for the purpose of bringing me back into life.'

Katy laughed. 'I hardly think so, but I do think that we could be of use to each other. You see, I've had difficulty in finding a job that would interest me, and maybe I have found it at last.'

'All right! Taken that you are here by divine guidance and that I am the chosen field for your endeavour, what do you propose to do with my poor body and mind? Taking also into consideration the fact that I am an old codger of fifty plus and have not the strength of purpose that you have, and that I can't afford to employ you.'

'I'm living rent free at the moment. I have a bit put past, and I live with a gaggle of students who all chip in with food, so I'll work for nothing until you are on your feet. Sure, why not? It beats cooking and cleaning the house and annoying Norah Byrne.' Katy stood up. 'This place could be a gold mine, but we would have to reorganise the shelves.'

'What's wrong with the way I have them?'

'You have all the novels at the front. We should cater for the students and put all the *textbooks* at the front of the shop under good lighting. Fiction can have its own place, but in the end it's the students we should cater for. They are the ones who are passing by and going into the centre of Belfast to buy their textbooks. I know how they must feel because I did my share of reading and studying, and the bookshop in Ballynashee was a higgledy-piggledy place with no order. I found it very frustrating.'

'Do you know anything about the business of bookselling?'

'I do not,' Katy said, 'I'm hoping to learn from you. I've always been interested in books though – and I did some work just recently with an expert who was cataloguing a collection of rare books and first editions, and I learned quite a bit from him in the short time we worked together.'

'Why should the students decide to come here, even if we did make improvements, when they have never done so before? Answer me that.'

'We advertise. It won't cost a penny. All we need is for my friends to pin up notices on the university noticeboard and pass the news by word of mouth.' Katy had not felt so motivated for a very long time. 'What do you say?'

John, fired by her enthusiasm and the fact that he would not be bankrupting himself, nodded. 'I'll shake on that!' he cried. 'Thank God you got bored and decided to go for a walk and found me before I became completely fossilised.' He pumped her hand enthusiastically.

'We will paint the woodwork – you pay for the paint – and I'll get the free help. I've a good source to tap for the chores,' Katy said, and with a last wave she went off down the street, the soda bread and barmbracks forgotten. It wasn't till she arrived back at the house that she realised she had left them on Mr Reilly's counter. She went into the bedroom and took a notebook from her drawer. She had to plan and she wanted everything down on paper while the ideas were still fresh in her mind. The phone rang. She ignored it and continued with her task, but the ringing persisted and at last with a feeling of irritation she answered it.

'Mam?' Katy was surprised to hear Annie's voice. 'Is anything wrong?'

'Not at all,' Annie said. 'Can I not ring you like any normal mother?'

Katy laughed. 'Well, what then?'

'Charles paid me a visit. He wanted your phone number so that he could contact you but I thought it better for you to ring him.'

Katy's heart was thumping. 'Did he say why he wanted to reach me?'

Annie hesitated. It was up to Charles to tell Katy the news. 'He just said to ring him on his business number. If you have some paper I'll read it out to you. He says anytime. His secretary can always take a message.'

Katy was thoughtful as she put the phone down. It seemed obvious to her that Charles had heard about her departure – and the reason for it. She felt her cheeks go hot with embarrassment. Would he be convinced that she would never hit Elizabeth, or would he take his sister's word for it? She put out her hand towards the telephone but withdrew it again. She needed time. A few more days wouldn't make all that much difference.

CHAPTER 7

In fact, a full week passed before Katy phoned Charles. It had been a week of hard work, laughter, and occasional moments of frustration. She had called a meeting to explain to the others what she had in mind for the bookshop, and they thought it was a great gas to give a hand with the decorating, and had no hesitation in offering their services.

'Sure, why not!' said Frank. 'It will give our muscles a right lashing and it will be a welcome break from all this learning.'

This statement raised a round of laughter, for Frank was the laziest slob in the group. As Donal said, Frank's idea of muscle power was lifting a glass full of Guinness up to his mouth without taking his elbow off the table.

Frank threw a cushion at him. 'I'll be working a damn sight harder than you when I start my medical practice.'

Katy called for some sense. 'This is serious. John Reilly needs our help. He has let the business fold since his wife died and I think if we can liven the place up and rearrange the shelves we will have a good chance of getting the business off the ground again – particularly if you all do a good job of passing on the news to the students next term.'

'Apart from being a great gas and all that – what's in it for us?' asked Mickey.

'You mercenary article!' Margaret said. 'Can you not help a fellow human being without tagging on a condition?' Now that Katy had found a cause, she was not going to let anyone ruin things for her friend. 'I wonder sometimes why I look on you with favour, Michael Flynn.'

Mickey grinned. 'So do I!'

'Stop clowning,' said Katy. 'Can we make a start? What are we prepared to do – and when?'

'Evenings are best, until the exams next week and then we can switch to the afternoon.' Donal looked round the group. 'Agreed?'

'Sounds all right,' Margaret said, adding, 'Is anyone going home for the whole holiday?'

'Not likely,' Frank scoffed. 'I've had enough after two weeks and m'da hates to see me idling so I end up in the bloody factory sticking labels on tin cans – working to earn some money for my keep during the year.'

The work got under way the following day, and by the end of that first week the place looked as the East End of London must have looked following a bombing raid. Katy, surveying the chaos caused by the willing workers, smiled weakly at John who was standing in his shop doorway looking on in horror. He had been shunted off for the weekend and had only just arrived back.

'It will be all right, John,' she promised lightheartedly, trying to hide her own dismay. Somehow she had envisaged everything being handled neatly – a little at a time. She hadn't bargained for the untidy minds of students who barged in and did things with great willingness and fervour but with no real thought for organisation.

'I hope you are right,' John said, with a hollow laugh. 'You are the one in charge. I'll go upstairs and change into my work-clothes and give a hand.'

Donal, having heard the exchange, caught Katy's eye and frantically shook his head and swivelled his eyes towards heaven. Katy turned back to John.

'It would be better if you didn't,' she suggested gently. 'The lads might feel intimidated if they thought you were watching them – handling the books and ripping down shelves – that kind of thing.'

John winced. The term 'ripping down' had cut through to his heart. He nodded. 'You're right. Just hearing the words is enough to give me a heart attack. I'll put my penn'orth in when everything is cleared and the new stuff is going up. I'm a dab hand with a set of tools.'

'Phew, that was close!' Donal said, when he had gone.

'We had better make the phoenix rise out of the ashes,' Katy warned. She wondered, not for the first time, if she had in a moment of madness, set John Reilly on the road to ruin and herself on the road to jail for desecration of property.

Charles was out when she rang so she left her telephone number. The following morning he rang back and when she heard his voice all her feelings for him resurfaced. The deep tones, the clipped English accent which added a touch of class to the words. The way he said her name – Kaytee – made her heart jump.

'Katy, I need to talk to you. Could we meet for lunch?'

She hesitated, uncertain that she could face having lunch with him as she still felt embarrassed about the business with Sylvia, but common sense took over. Damn it, she was innocent. Surely he knew that? Before she could reply, he spoke again.

'Katy, listen to me. I found out what happened when I was away. It was all a ghastly mistake. Sylvia was misled in her judgement by Pamela.'

Katy's heart quickened. 'I – I . . .'

'Look, I'll explain over lunch. Meet me at the Victoria Hotel tomorrow. I've got a meeting to attend but I'll leave as early as possible.'

A wave of relief flooded over Katy. She would very soon discover what the 'irrefutable evidence' consisted of. She was thoughtful as she replaced the telephone. Why hadn't Sylvia contacted her? She must know by now that she was innocent.

Next day, as she prepared for the rendezvous she felt tension rise. It didn't help that she missed a bus at the City Hall and that the next one was late. She glanced anxiously along the road, willing it to come into view. At last it did, five minutes behind schedule. She scrambled aboard and sat down near the door, her nervousness increasing with every turn of the wheels along Donegal Street.

'The nearest stop to the Victoria Hotel,' she said, handing the money to the conductor.

'We stop just a few yards away. Look out for it on the other side of the road. A man on a galloping horse couldn't miss it.'

Watching the conductor's progress down the bus, she thought, A girl in a high state of tension could, though.

Charles was standing by a revolving bookstand, turning it slowly to read the titles. She studied him. That endearing lick of dark hair that insisted on dropping down when he bent his head; the long, sensitive fingers which handled the books with such care; the immaculate suit; the air of confidence. In her imagination she saw herself running lightly towards him with delicately arched feet barely touching the thick carpet and her organza dress swirling round slim legs, in the slight breeze of her flight – a bright glorious smile lighting her face as he caught sight of her and stretched out his arms to receive her . . . The reality was that she walked slowly and solidly across the expanse of carpet in sensible white sandals, and her cap-sleeved summer print dress barely moved in the draught from the revolving door.

Charles turned at that moment and saw her. So young, so naive. He went towards her and gripping her lightly by the elbows he dropped a light kiss on her cheek. She reddened. He laughed. 'We can have a drink at the bar or we can wait and have wine with lunch.' He glanced at his watch. 'We have ten minutes before our table is ready.'

Katy's throat was drying up by the minute. She felt if she didn't get some liquid down it she would lose all vocal power. 'I'd kill for an orangeade,' she smiled.

Charles leaned towards her when they were seated on the comfortable sofa. 'I think the sooner we discuss this business the sooner we can relax,' he said.

Katy nodded and he continued: 'I only found out what had happened when I returned. I couldn't believe that Sylvia could so readily accept that you had been capable of slapping Elizabeth.'

'Sylvia wouldn't go into details with me,' Katy said. 'She just informed me that she had proof and that Elizabeth herself had confirmed it.' She hesitated and looked at him. 'You know, that hurt more than the actual accusation. To think that Elizabeth . . .' Her voice trailed off.

'Perhaps this will help you to understand.' Charles took the snapshot out of his pocket and held it towards her.

As Katy studied it her eyes dilated in horror. She had thought

Sylvia had meant she had been slapping Elizabeth for being naughty.

'Taken by Pamela,' Charles announced quietly. 'She saw it as an opportunity to damage your reputation.'

'But why? She is beautiful and glamorous. There was surely no need to do this to me out of spite.'

Charles had his own theories but he remained silent.

Katy's face hardened. 'Why didn't Sylvia show me this? I could have explained.'

'Pamela asked Sylvia not to reveal the source of her information and Sylvia promised her she wouldn't. You must remember that Sylvia was very shocked to think that you could have done such a thing.'

The waiter arrived to show them to their table and when they were seated, Charles poured the wine. Without thought Katy took a gulp of it and began to choke. When she had recovered, she stared at the tablecloth feeling foolish.

When the waiter arrived with the food, Katy used the time to gain control of her emotions. It hurt that Sylvia had been so ready to condemn.

When he had gone, Charles said, 'Sylvia is desperately unhappy about the split. She is very fond of you. She longs to set things right but she is concerned that you might not be prepared to forgive her. She really is very embarrassed.'

'Ah, so she is embarrassed,' Katy said heatedly. 'I'm sorry, Charles. Feeling embarrassed does not excuse her. Not a phone call, not even a letter have I had . . . nothing. Because of her silence I have been left with the terrible knowledge that she felt I had been cruel to Elizabeth.'

'Not cruel, never that. Just that you had been somewhat frustrated with Elizabeth. Sylvia is aware just how naughty she can be at times.'

'Sylvia has abused my trust in her fairness.'

'Are you saying that not even a late apology would mend things?'

'I don't know. I feel very hurt and – and – I've missed Elizabeth. I've been worried sick about what she must think of my apparent desertion.'

'I'm afraid Sylvia gave her the impression that you will be coming back sometime.' When the waiter arrived to take their order for dessert, Katy shook her head. Charles said, 'Coffee in the lounge, please. We'll skip dessert.' He took her arm and led her towards a comfortable sofa.

'Sylvia should have told Elizabeth the truth. It will be worse for her when I don't come back,' Katy said.

'You don't know my sister. Sylvia abhors unpleasantness. She has never really faced up to Bertie's death, you know. He is still out there somewhere – it's easier to believe that than face the truth.'

Katy frowned. 'Yet she deals with people and problems so expertly.'

'But they don't impinge on the secret troublefree life she has built for herself – the life that keeps at bay the sorrow she would feel if she confronted the fact that Bertie is gone for ever. And she has her art, which also helps,' Charles added.

'Her art? I know she dabbles . . .'

Charles shook his head. 'Dabble? She could have been a great success. When she had her first exhibition shortly after Bertie's death, the critics were unkind – although they all agreed that, given time, the talent was there. However, Sylvia read only the bad press and gave up. She came over here and went into virtual retreat until her friend Victoria persuaded her to join the charity committee.' Charles paused and smiled. 'Did you know she has got a new man in her life? I met him for the first time about a week ago. He came to dinner and I haven't seen my sister behave so coyly since we were young. He seems a nice chap. Tall, elegant, on the reserved side. Quite different from old Bertie. Sylvia adores him, judging by the way she looks at him.'

'I suspected she had someone,' Katy said. 'I overheard her talking to him on the telephone and she was twisting the cord and swinging her legs and practically cooing.'

'His name is Robert Mathews and he is a barrister,' Charles said, adding, 'I do hope you and Sylvia can be friends again.'

Katy refused to commit herself. 'Time will tell.' She rose. 'I must go. I promised John I would be back by three o'clock and it is almost that now.'

'John?'

'A friend of mine who owns a bookshop. The group of people I live with are helping me to bring it into the twentieth century. John gets worried when I am not there to supervise them. He thinks they will destroy the place,' she laughed.

Charles was disturbed by the feelings that her obvious concern for this man evoked in him. 'I'll drive you back,' he offered.

'I wouldn't dream of it. It is out of your way. I'll catch this bus.' She smiled. 'Thank you for lunch.'

'I'm very glad that we have had our talk. Maybe you and Sylvia could meet up sometime,' Charles suggested.

'Maybe,' Katy replied noncommittally.

The others had gone when she arrived back. John was upstairs in the rooms he occupied above the shop. He came down when he heard the key in the lock and Katy, looking at him, thought: The poor man is done in. She could see that the tensions of the past few weeks were showing in the lines round his eyes and in the way he worriedly eyed the remaining chaos.

'We are nearly there, John.' she said gaily. 'Once we get the mess cleared up and the name boards nailed on the various sections, we will have done. All we need do then is to step up the advertising – however, we won't worry about that now. We still have another hour or two, so why don't you and I begin clearing the place up and then tomorrow we can start nailing the name boards onto the shelves.'

John shook his head. 'Tomorrow will do. Come upstairs and have a cup of tea with me. I've had enough for today.'

She had never been in his private rooms before and was pleasantly surprised to find them comfortable and beautifully furnished.

Seeing her face, John smiled. 'How did you think I lived?'

Katy reddened. 'Sorry,' she said. 'It's just that not many men can make a place look anything more than functional. M'da, for instance, would be content with his armchair and his fiddle and the bare necessities to get by with. If it wasn't for my mam nagging him he'd be running round with his shirt-tail hanging out and his hair on his shoulders. He can see no point in putting a clean shirt on when it will be dirty again by the end of the day.'

John laughed. 'You're right. It was my Maggie who set all this up. I hate housework, and if it wasn't for the fact that I'd be letting her down if I didn't keep the place up to scratch, I would let things slide.' He sighed. 'We need you women. You have your place in the scheme of things.'

'That's a very chauvinistic remark,' Katy rebuked him.

'What does a young country lass like yourself know about chauvinism?' John lit his pipe and studied her.

'This young country lass may be naive in many things, John Reilly, but she does have a certificate that says she is proficient in English.'

John held up his hands. 'I apologise. That was a stupid remark. Let's speak of other things – such as, did you have a good lunch?'

'Excellent!' she grinned broadly.

When Katy arrived back at the house Margaret told her that Terence Coleman had rung asking for her. The tone of her voice registered her disapproval and Katy smiled. 'Margaret, will you stop worrying! If the man had designs on me he would have been quicker off the mark than this. It's been a while since the Ball.'

'I don't trust the fella. He has a reputation for breaking hearts right, left and centre . . .'

'What was the message?' Katy interrupted.

'He'll call for you on Saturday evening about seven o'clock.'

Katy frowned. 'Is that it?'

Margaret said crisply, 'It is typical of the arrogance of the man.'

Margaret was right, Katy thought. Terence had made the assumption that she would have nothing better to do. 'I'm afraid he is in for a disappointment then,' she said slowly. 'I shall be going home this weekend. I haven't been home for three weeks and last time I was there m'da was feeling depressed. I've been worried.'

Margaret had heard about Lopper's death and knew of Katy's concern for her father. 'Have you not heard anything?'

'I spoke to Mam on the telephone but I'd like to see for myself. Did Terence leave a number to call?'

Margaret grinned. 'No, he did not. I'll have to give him the bad news in person when he comes here Katy smiled conspirat-orially. 'Thank you, I would be grateful. Tell him to give me a ring when I get back and we'll start from there.'

'What happened to the sweet girl I once knew?' Margaret laughed, and felt relieved. Katy would cope very well with the devious Terence.

Charles telephoned shortly after Katy arrived home at the farm. He had heard from Sally that she would be there and wondered if it was possible for Elizabeth and her to meet as the wretched child was pestering him to take her to the Wishing Tree. 'Perhaps we could call for you at the farmhouse?' he suggested.

'I have a better idea,' Katy said thoughtfully. 'You take Eliza-beth to the tree at three o'clock tomorrow and tell her to make a wish, but don't mention that I shall be coming. We could have tea here afterwards.'

'How do we get to the tree without going through the farm-yard?'

'About two miles along the Ballynashee Road you will see, on your left, a five-barred gate leading into a field that has just been reaped. Leave your car there and make your way across two fields and over the brook. The tree is in the middle of the next field.'

'Right,' said Charles. 'See you tomorrow.'

Katy put the phone down and crossed to her mother. 'Did you understand all that?'

'I haven't gone deaf yet. What is all the mystery about? Why could you not have them come past the farm?'

'Because I have a feeling that Elizabeth is going to wish that she will see me at the tree and I want her wish to be granted. It will make the day special for her.'

'Am I to be roped in to provide the food?'

'You always do a great bake-up on Sunday. You can't act the martyr, Mam.'

'You are one devious article,' Annie replied. 'I'd better warn your father we are going to have company.'

Katy went upstairs and pulled open her wardrobe doors. She began to throw clothes onto the bed, then stopped. 'Catch yourself on, Katy Molloy,' she said aloud. 'It is the person you are that matters – not the drapery. You'll wear your slacks and your brogues and the pale lemon shirt.'

'Who are you talking to?' Annie enquired as she walked in.

'I'm talkin' to the biggest eejut this side of the Mournes,' Katy told her.

'Your da is home and he wants to know if he has to dress up to the nines tomorrow or can he wear his second best?'

'Tell him it is not the King of England coming, just Lord Charles Gilbert and the Lady Elizabeth.' Katy felt lighthearted. Her da was back on form and she was going to see Elizabeth again.

The following day, after lunch, Katy watched her mother rolling the pastry for a batch of lemon tarts. There was a tray of cakes cooling off on the window sill. Not for the first time she realised how lucky they were. In England, though the war had been over for nearly three years, food was still scarce. Here, especially in this farming area, they did so much better. 'I'm putting you to a lot of trouble,' she said ruefully.

Annie glanced at her. 'You are not! But watching you fidgeting there like a herring on a hot griddle is putting me off. Can you not go a bit early and keep out of my way? Failing that, go and finish off the dishes still left from lunch.'

Katy pulled a face but obediently crossed to the big stone sink and pushed her hands into the suds. She hated washing up but it was the least she could do. When she had finished she looked at the clock. Time to go. She took two empty jam jars and two small fishing nets from the window sill and went out, throwing a nervous smile towards her mam. They would be there by now. Her nervousness increased as she drew nearer and she had to chide herself. She was meeting a five-year-old girl, for God's sake – not an ogre.

When she breasted the small hill she could see Charles leaning against the huge trunk, his tall frame dwarfed by the enormous girth and height of the tree. Her heart leaped as he waved to her and then, as Elizabeth came hurtling towards her, she felt a surge of happiness.

'Katy! Katy! I made a wish at the tree and it has come true,' Elizabeth squealed.

Katy swung her up and small arms wound themselves round her neck in a tight hug. Charles had hunched himself away from the trunk and approached more slowly. 'Pity I'm so large,' he grinned.

She lowered Elizabeth and returned the smile. Everything had gone to plan. She held up the jars and the scoop nets. 'I thought we could go down to the stream and catch some spricks.'

'Spricks?' Charles and Elizabeth echoed.

'Tiny fish no bigger than my thumbnail and no wider than a strand of wool.'

'You mean minnows,' Charles suggested.

'You two might mean minnows – I am going fishing for spricks. Now, are the pair of you coming or not?' She grabbed Elizabeth by the hand and ran down the slope, past the tree, over the stile into the next field and down the gently sloping hill to the stream with its gurgling water.

Charles followed at a more leisurely pace and sat down on the bank to watch his two favourite women dipping their nets into the water. He listened to their chatter and their laughter and felt a quiet peace steal over him. The pressures of work seemed a long way off.

Eventually, Katy and Elizabeth trooped off over the hill to the farmhouse and tea, while Charles made his way to the road to the car, the tiny fish now floating in their lidded jar.

'Will himself be long?' Annie enquired when Katy explained that he'd gone to drive the car up to the house. 'I won't take the scones out of the oven yet or they'll go cold.'

'Is he royalty or what?' Eddie asked petulantly. 'I'm starvin' and I have been smellin' those scones and barmbracks all afternoon. I can't wait much longer.'

There was a tap on the door and Charles entered. 'Sorry I took so long. I got caught up behind a tractor.'

'That will be Patrick Toner on his way here with some fodder,' said Eddie. He turned to Annie. 'The sooner I get my tea the better as I have the milking to do.' Turning back to Charles he held out his hand. 'Do I call you Charlie?'

Katy groaned. Charles laughed. 'At your peril, Mr Molloy. Please call me Charles.'

'Call me Eddie.' They shook hands, and the state of address having been established, they sat down to what Charles later said was the best tea he'd ever had.

Annie was pleased at the way things had gone. Katy smiled conspiratorially at her. Only she knew the amount of work her mother had put in, to place such a spread before them, and she knew too how much her mam appreciated the compliment. Her da was so used to her cooking he no longer bothered to comment. It was therefore all the more precious to her mam to hear two people used to a grander style of living, speak so favourably about the repast.

When he had seated Elizabeth in the car, Charles turned to Katy. 'I think I had better warn you that Sylvia will be inviting you to dinner soon.'

Katy frowned. 'You must stop her. It's too soon. We need to meet privately to sort things out.'

'I do agree, but you know Sylvia. Doing things the reasonable way is not something she worries about. She thinks that things have been resolved and it wouldn't occur to her that you might retain some anger.'

'But I don't! I just think we need to talk together privately before sitting down at table with others. I don't want there to be any embarrassment between us.'

'I'll have a word with her,' Charles promised and climbed behind the wheel. He glanced into his driving mirror as he drove off. Katy had been joined by Tom Toner whose arm was draped across her shoulder in a familiar way. She didn't seem to mind.

Katy turned to walk back to the house when the car had turned the corner of the barn. She hooked her arm in Tom's and said, 'How are things going with your plans?'

'Well enough,' Tom replied and then added ruefully, 'There is only one snag. I have been going out with a girl from Ballynahinch way and I have sort of lost my enthusiasm for going to the college.'

Katy stopped. 'Is it so serious? Don't forget you will meet other girls when you go away. I assume that girls also go to agricultural colleges these days. After all, we proved how well we could cope during the war.'

Tom nodded. 'I met three at my interview. It's just, well . . .
Maire and I like each other a lot. Being away might alter things.'

'You will be home often enough. The college is only in the next
county. There are buses and trains.' Katy laughed and disengaged
her arm. 'There's m'da looking for you. Away you go – and have
faith in Maire,' she said.

When Katy arrived back in Belfast, there was a message from
Terence to say that he would ring her some time that evening. She
looked at Margaret. 'What happened when you told him I was
not able to see him on Saturday?'

Margaret grinned. 'His face dropped into his shoes. I don't
think that has happened to Terence ever in his life before. I did
explain, sweetly of course, that you had gone away and that he
should have given you more notice, but he wasn't a happy man.'

'Oh dear!' Katy bit her lip. Her soft brown eyes widened.
'Perhaps we were a bit mean to to him.'

'Rubbish. He was being arrogant. Don't go soft, Katy. I shall
start worrying again that you might let him take advantage of
you, just when I felt that you were toughening up.'

The phone rang as they were eating supper. Donal answered it.
'It's himself for you, Katy.'

Katy swallowed hastily and took the phone from him. 'Hello,
Terence. Sorry I couldn't see you on Saturday.'

'My fault. I should have checked.' He sounded so contrite
Katy felt worse about the way Margaret and she had behaved.
Terence continued, 'There's a good film on at the Trocadero. Can
you manage tomorrow evening?'

Katy said she could and they chatted for some time before he
rang off. Margaret and Norah had gone into the kitchen to wash
up. The men were lolling on the settee. Frank grinned at her and
made little kissing motions with his mouth.

Katy ignored him and joined the girls in the kitchen. Norah
dried her hands and walked out. Margaret raised her eyebrows.

'I'm going to see a film at the Trocadero – *The Clock*, starring
Robert Walker and Judy Garland,' Katy said.

'It's good,' said Margaret. 'Michael and I went to see it on
Saturday.' She dried her hands and they returned to the living

room. Katy was grateful that nothing more was mentioned about her being careful.

The film was as good as Margaret had said it was, and Terence and Katy walked along arm-in-arm to a restaurant nearby, discussing it earnestly, even as they were being seated. Terence watched Katy as she studied the menu, a little crease between her brows as she concentrated. Her hair, thick and curly and glistening under the lights, half-hid her face and he felt a sudden desire to lift some of it and hold it to his face to smell its freshness. He had never felt this way before, but then he had never known a girl like this before. It was her naivety that appealed to him. There was something refreshing about a girl who lacked sophistication. His blood raced at the challenge involved in winning her confidence, and it would be a challenge, for he suspected that Margaret Kelly had warned Katy of his reputation. He had been acutely aware of the reticence in Katy's manner on previous occasions.

Katy looked up suddenly, her gaze taking in the well-cut hair, the dark blazer with the crest on the pocket, the open-necked white shirt, the slim, well-manicured hands. She smiled to herself. Terence was so different from Frank and the others, who slopped about most of the time in worn trousers, wearing shirts that had lost the original colour – and their nails looked as though they had never seen a pair of scissors.

Later, when they arrived home, Katy felt nervous. Would Terence want to kiss her goodnight? God! She wasn't ready for that. However, he took her hand in his and thanked her for a lovely evening and it was all she could do not to let out an audible sigh of relief.

When she entered the bedroom she reported to Margaret that Terence had been a perfect gentleman. 'He never even tried to kiss me,' she said triumphantly.

Margaret put down the book she was reading. 'Hmmph,' she said. 'I would keep an eye on him, all the same.'

CHAPTER 8

Donal, who was spreadeagled on the settee, looked up as Katy and Margaret entered the sitting room after walking back from Mass. 'Now that the shop is ready, are we going to have a big opening ceremony?' He squinted up at Katy who pushed his feet to one side and sat down. 'Only we were discussing the idea while you were out.'

'That depends on John,' Katy said. 'He is not a man for making a fuss of things.'

'Convince him, then,' Donal persisted. 'Frank and meself were just sayin' that it's been a while since we had a hooley.'

'Since it's you and Frank who want it, are you prepared to chip in with the cost?' Katy asked.

'We'll scratch around a bit – right, Frank?'

Frank, who had been only half-listening, turned. 'Whatever,' he said, and then frowned. 'Just don't get me in too deep, man. I have other expenses.'

Katy nodded. 'I'll have a word with John. It would be nice to put the shop on the map in the right way.' She glanced towards Margaret who had not become involved in the discussion. 'What do you think, Margaret?'

Margaret said, 'Fine by me. Mind you, when this lot get started John might regret having agreed.' She looked fiercely towards Donal. 'If you two don't behave yourselves you will be in dire trouble.'

'We'll be like a pair of choir boys,' Frank grinned. 'I'll look after the lad, here.'

'That doesn't make me feel any better,' Margaret said caustically, 'just remember what I said.'

141

Katy put it to John the following morning, before they opened the shop.

'Do we need to have a party?' he said, dismayed.

'We need the good will,' Katy told him. 'Besides, it will encourage trade. Think about it. If someone walked into Mr Brown's bread shop and happened to mention that they were anxious to find a good bookshop then Mr Brown, having been accorded a kind of honour by being invited to the hooley, would say, "Why, there is an excellent bookshop just up the street run by a man called John Reilly. You couldn't do better than that. The man runs it with his assistant and they have it all done up nicely and set out like a library." '

John brought his glasses down from where they perched on top of his head and eyed Katy in amusement. 'Do you think he might even mention my assistant by name and maybe tell the customer that she is pretty and smart and John Reilly would be nowhere without her?'

'You'll do it then?' Katy grinned.

'Aye! In for a penny . . .'

'Then there is the butcher, whose name I don't know,' she continued.

'Leave the invitations to me,' John said. 'Mind you, I'm not over-keen on Dominic Rice, the publican. Do I have to ask him?'

'I don't care if he murdered your mother-in-law – he comes. He serves more students than anybody. He can put in a very good word for you.'

'He only lives two doors away. The students are not blind. They can see the bookshop.' John laughed.

'He can still speak of you as a man to be trusted.'

'You win the war. Now, how many are to come to this party? Have you remembered to invite a reporter from the *Telegraph*,' he teased.

Katy looked up from her notebook. 'Indeed I did. I'm hoping for great things there. I had a word with him before I came.'

John gasped. 'You article!'

She grinned. 'He will be here some time during the evening, for the interview, which I as your representative, will grant . . . close

142

your mouth now. I have found a path to follow and I'm on to my first achievement.'

'You are certainly more bossy and outgoing since I first met you,' John remarked. 'I'm glad you walked into my shop that day, Katy Molloy. You've coaxed me out of hibernation.'

She stared at him thoughtfully. 'You need not have invited me in, you know. I think that we were meant to meet.'

'If you hadn't come into my shop that day, I wouldn't be looking round it and feeling as proud as I do this minute. I have a lot to thank you for, young Katy Molloy – chaser of dreams.'

On the day of the party, Katy tried to hide her nervousness. All had been arranged and there was no going back. She braced herself as Margaret and the gang trooped in. 'Did you remember to bring the spare glasses?' she asked.

Margaret nodded. 'I did, you bossy madam.' She put the large cardboard box on the counter and watched thoughtfully as Katy held the door for the others to enter with the cutlery and plates and the tins containing the snack foods cadged from their parents. There was a new crispness to Katy's voice – a new air of command.

John was also observing the pile of tins and plates. 'I have a few bob myself, to pay for this party,' he said mildly.

They all turned and looked at him in amazement. 'It's a long time since *your* student days,' Donal chuckled. 'Ye never buy what you can get for free. If it's any help – and to ease your conscience – the drink is down to you.'

'That's all right then,' John said amenably.

'Has everyone who was on the list been told?' Frank took a bottle of porter from his inside pocket and held it up to the light.

'All the local shopkeepers and ourselves – oh! and the reporter,' said Katy.

'A lunchtime drink before the event, then?' Frank called to Donal to seek out the glasses.

It was a delicious stout. John nodded his head in appreciation as he savoured the liquid passing down his throat.

'We'll have to give the shop a new name, now that it has been done up all bright and new. How about calling it "The Book

Cave"'?' Mickey looked round at them all.

Donal gave a derisive laugh. 'How could you even consider such a gloomy name for a place that you have just described as bright and new. Anything with "cave" in the title conjures up a dark cavern of a place.'

'What about "Volumes" then?'

'Arseholes,' said Frank crudely and took a swig of stout. 'What the hell would that mean to anyone? I suggest "The Book Emporium".'

Katy watched the range of expressions flitting across John's face. They had taken over his life and stripped his shop and changed forever a place in which he was happy to sit and dream of Maggie. Devil the bit had he minded not being a big success. He had enough to live on and a place to lay his head. They had even chosen the colour of his walls and where the shelves and books should go – and there had been not one word of complaint. Now they were trying to strip him of his identity as well.

'Has anyone else got any ideas?' Margaret asked.

Katy spoke, her gaze resting on John, who was staring into his glass. ' "John Reilly's Bookshop" is as fine a name as you could have.' She smiled at him as he raised his head to look at her. 'One day when someone says, "I'm off down to John Reilly's" no one will need to ask where it is or what he sells. The name and the quality of service will have been well-established by then.'

Frank raised his glass. 'A drink to "John Reilly's Bookshop". Long may it prosper.'

Katy arrived home the following weekend to find a letter from Sylvia.

'It came a couple of days ago,' said Annie. 'I didn't send it on because I knew you'd be here before it arrived in Belfast. I'll brew the tea while you read it.'

Katy quickly scanned it. Sylvia wondered if she would meet her in Ballyclinchy on Saturday, at Magill's tea rooms. She realised that Katy might still feel angry about what had happened in the past, but she would be grateful if she would give her the opportunity to apologise. If Katy didn't reply to the contrary then she would assume that she would be there.

Katy blanched. *Today* was Saturday . . . she wasn't prepared . . . there hadn't been enough notice. 'Sylvia wants me to
meet her for tea in Ballyclinchy.' She looked nervously at her
mother.

'Maybe she wants to ask you to go back.' Annie placed the cup
of tea on the table and settled back in her chair. 'Would you go
back?'

'No. Too much has happened.'

'Will you go to meet her?'

'I suppose so. I'm a bit nervous about it though.'

'Why should you feel nervous?' Annie said crisply. 'You were
the victim.'

'I suppose so. But . . .'

'There are no buts. You must go and get the matter settled
between you.'

Katy sighed. 'Yes, you are right. It's not a bit of good leaving
things in the air, and I'd like to be friends again.'

'That's settled then – now tell me. How did the party go?'

'It went well!' said Katy, relieved to be discussing a new topic.
'The only one who couldn't make it was Dominic Rice, the
publican, but he was generous enough to drop by with two
bottles of good wine and six bottles of Guinness. We had a great
time.'

'I saw the write-up in the paper. I should think that if the
article is anything to go by, then John Reilly will do very well. Is
it true that it now looks like a going concern?'

'Certainly it's true. Didn't all of us work ourselves to the bone
to get the place set up and modernised.'

'I hope he pays you well.'

'Well enough,' said Katy. 'I'll be paid more when sales start to
rise.' She wondered what her mam would say if she knew her
daughter was working for nothing at the moment and using her
savings to get by.

Later, when she ran to catch the bus it was raining – a heavy
spiky autumn rain which hit the ground with such force it
splashed up again, drenching feet and ankles. By the time she
reached the tea rooms she felt chilly and mildly cross because
Sylvia had a large comfortable car and it wouldn't have crossed

her mind that Katy had to use public transport.

She walked into the tea rooms, thankful for the warmth, and put her dripping umbrella in the stand by the door. Sylvia had caught sight of her and was waving. Things didn't alter, Katy thought. Sylvia looked as elegant as ever and she still waved her hand as though it had been paralysed at the wrist. She walked towards her.

'You are wet,' Sylvia said. 'What you need is a hot cup of tea. I'll order and we can talk while we wait.'

When the waitress had gone, Sylvia put out her hand and covered Katy's. 'It's good to see you again. I can't tell you how much I've regretted our falling out. I have missed you, just as Elizabeth has. She was inconsolable for weeks after you had gone.' She drew in a sharp breath. 'If only Charles hadn't been away, all this could have been avoided. I really am sorry. Please let us be friends again. Charles told me about your new life and how much you are enjoying it. Please let me back into it, Katy.'

Katy looked into Sylvia's eyes and the entreaty in them caught at her. She sighed. 'I too would dearly love to be friends again,' she said.

'Good!' Sylvia, a broad smile lighting up her face, took up her knife and began to butter a scone. 'Now, tell me all about this new life of yours. It obviously suits you. I can't believe the change in you, my dear.' With mercurial speed her mood had altered.

Afterwards, she gave Katy a lift to the end of the lane. The heavy rain had stopped and there was now just a light drizzle which was soft and caressing. She spoke as Katy stepped out of the car. 'I'm giving a dinner party next Saturday. I would love you to come.'

Katy hesitated. 'I don't know, Sylvia. I need time to adjust. Could we make it another time – get to know each other again?'

'Please come. Then I'll be certain you have forgiven me. Charles will be there – and I'd like you to meet Robert. Remember – he was the special person I've been seeing a lot lately.' She looked pleadingly at her.

'Oh, all right, I'll come,' Katy capitulated.

'Great!' Suddenly Sylvia's voice lost the wheedling tone and became more precise. 'It will be formal – long dress, cocktails at seven-thirty, and bring a partner. Charles is bringing *his* latest.' She shot the gears and was off, leaving Katy with a feeling of having been punched in the solar plexus.

Margaret listened as Katy recounted the conversation with Sylvia and shrugged when she wailed, 'Who can I take along to the dinner party?'

'What about Frank? I don't think he has anything on. Mind you, you'd need to keep an eye on him; he tends to go over the top when he's had a bit to drink.'

Katy agreed. 'Not Frank! I still shudder from his antics on the night of John's party. This is quite a posh evening.'

'That rules out Donal, then. You know his thoughts on plutocrats. With his views he is liable to drop you in the mire.'

'Could I borrow Mickey for the evening?'

'I'm afraid not. This weekend we meet the ma.'

'His or yours?'

'His! Mine are so wrapped up in each other they wouldn't care what my brother Francie and I got up to – or with whom – so long as their little boat is not rocked. Why don't you ask that eejut Terence? I no longer fear him getting his wicked way with you, for I know you can see right through his antics. He's still keen on you, pet. He'll jump at the chance of a ritzy evening showing off in your company. See if I'm not right!'

'I don't know him that well yet,' Katy demurred.

'Give him a ring.'

'You mean now?' Nervously Katy lifted the phone and dialled Terence's number. 'Hello, Terence.'

'Katy! How are you?' The low voice sent vibrations through her. She reddened. Margaret grinned. Katy lashed out with her elbow. 'Go away!' she said fiercely.

'Pardon?'

'It's Margaret. She's being silly.'

'Forget Margaret. I hope you are ringing to ask me for a date?' Terence said jokingly.

'I am, as a matter of fact. I've been invited to a formal dinner and I need a partner. I wondered if you might be at a loose end at the weekend?'

Terence laughed. 'I'm not often at a loose end. I'm afraid I get too bored just sitting indoors.'

'Oh! Does that mean you can't—'

'No, it doesn't. It isn't so important I can't cancel . . .' He paused. 'I was going to see the parents,' he lied.

Katy sighed with relief. 'You're sure?'

'I certainly am,' Terence said smoothly. 'Much as I love the parents, sitting by the fire opposite them is not my idea of a good evening. I'm grateful to you, Katy.'

'It's formal attire.'

'Have no fear, I have the gear,' he said softly. 'I'll call for you at seven-fifteen next Saturday, if that's the right sort of time? I look forward to meeting your friends.'

'There is a snag. I will be at home, so it means you will have to meet me there.'

'That isn't a problem,' Terence said. 'I know Ballynashee – it's where we first met, remember?'

Katy gave a sigh of relief. 'Of course.' She gave him instructions on how to reach the farm, warning him about the narrow lane he would have to drive along for about a quarter of a mile.

She hugged Margaret gleefully. 'He'll make them sit up,' she said. 'I think my mam and da will get a surprise also. He is gorgeous.'

Margaret set a cup of tea in front of her. 'The girls certainly seem to think so,' she remarked.

'What must he think of me that I have to ask a man for a date?'

'This is 1947, Katy. Things are more relaxed now. And I know you will knock him out with your wit and charm. But never forget your old Auntie Margaret's words of wisdom about that young man. Once a rat – always a rat . . .'

The following Saturday, Katy sat in the kitchen with her mother waiting for Terence to arrive. When the knock finally came, she started nervously.

Annie said, 'Are you going to answer the door?' She looked over the top of her glasses at her daughter. She is dyin' with nerves, she thought, and took pity on her. 'Shall I answer it?'

With a shake of her head, Katy went forward and found

herself looking up at Terence. He seemed taller in his dark, formal wear and her heart flipped as his blue eyes looked into hers. She stood back to let him pass and Terence walked over to Annie and shook her hand. 'No wonder Katy is so beautiful. It runs in the family,' he said, with a casual smile.

Annie motioned him to a chair. The man could oil a set of wheels with that tongue. She glanced at Katy. She'd spoken of Terence as a friend. Was he more than that?

'We had better get going,' Katy said after a while. 'We don't want to be late.' They still had a few minutes to spare, however, when they rang the bell.

Mrs Skelton answered the door and Katy was dragged enthusiastically to her ample bosom. 'Katy, my girl! I never thought to see you walk through these doors again. Sally is in the kitchen and dyin' to see you. You'll have to come in for a minute.'

To the amusement of Terence, she was taken by the arm and pulled towards the sanctum. He closed the door quietly, and followed. Terence was always happy to go along with the unexpected. It was what made life interesting. He sensed a story here and he would discover sooner or later what it was. Meantime, he followed them into the large kitchen which was rich with the smell of cooking and filled with warmth. Katy was being vigorously hugged by the housemaid while a beaming Mrs Skelton looked on. He leaned against the door and waited.

When Katy had extracted herself from Sally's embrace, she pulled Terence forward. 'This is Terence Coleman.'

Mrs Skelton shook him by the hand. 'Come here and meet Sally.'

Sally grinned at Katy as she shook his hand. 'He's all right!' she said.

Terence smiled. 'Won't our hostess wonder where we have got to? She must have heard the bell.' He was impatient to meet this Sylvia and her guests.

'Mrs Sanders wouldn't hear the bell tolling the knell of doom,' said Mrs Skelton, grinning at Katy. 'She is so in love at the moment she has ears only for her man's voice.' She instructed Sally to show the couple to the drawing room.

As they entered, Sylvia swanned elegantly towards them, her

pale blue chiffon gown swirling delicately round her ankles. Katy was keenly aware of Charles standing beside a tall dark-haired man whom she guessed was Robert Mathews. She smiled shyly at him when Sylvia made the introductions.

Charles dutifully shook hands with Katy's companion, hiding his surprise. He had assumed that she would be arriving with the young farmworker. This chap was obviously used to socialising. He smiled at Katy. She looked stunning in her cream dress and he was acutely aware of the way it draped her slim young body. She looked so desirably pretty with her soft brown eyes and that smile that could melt snow.

The door opened and Katy drew in her breath. The vision of loveliness walking across the floor reminded her of Pamela. There was the same exquisite beauty . . . the same long, silky blonde hair. But whereas Pamela had invariably looked mildly discontented, this girl had a happy face. She was Helen Brooks, Charles' date for the evening. Katy liked her immediately.

Throughout dinner she was aware that Terence couldn't take his eyes off Helen but she decided, ruefully, that she held no claim to him. Nevertheless she would chide him for his neglect of her, once they were on their way home.

After dinner Terence redeemed himself in her eyes by holding her lightly by the shoulder as they awaited coffee, and it was she who moved away towards the other two women and Robert, leaving him with Charles. Terence, having discovered that Charles was involved in the airport scheme, mentioned that his father, Geoffrey Coleman, an engineer, also worked on it.

Charles was surprised. 'I understood Geoffrey's son was at university.'

Terence laughed. 'You thought I would be younger. Actually, my education was interrupted by the war. I've resumed my studies now. I'm doing an engineering degree.'

Katy glanced over and saw that the two men were deep in conversation, so when Helen motioned that they sit down on the big settee she smiled and nodded. Sylvia and Robert were wrangling amiably about where they should go for a short holiday in a week's time and didn't notice they had moved away.

Katy observed the elegant manner in which Helen slowly

lowered herself into the soft cushioned seat and how she casually shook the long blonde hair back over her shoulder. She sighed inwardly. Without thought she, herself, had practically flumped down almost spilling her drink in her enthusiasm. Helen worked closely with Charles, who had mentioned during the introductions that he considered her to be his 'right hand' and didn't know how he would manage without her, because she made life so easy for him. Katy's heart sank. How could any man resist falling in love with her! She was everything a man like Charles could want.

As the evening progressed, Katy found herself liking Helen more and more. Terence, of course, was similarly impressed. He was putting on the charm as they indulged in light banter and Katy, feeling suddenly like an extra limb, rose and joined Charles and Robert. 'Where is Sylvia?' she enquired.

Robert took her empty glass. 'She has gone to have a word with the staff and to check on Elizabeth. Let me top this up for you.'

He's a really nice man, Katy thought. A quiet gentle man – just what Sylvia needed.

'I understand your friend is the son of one of my engineers,' Charles said.

Katy started and focused her mind on what Charles had said. 'I didn't know that.'

'Have you met his parents?'

'No. I haven't known Terence very long.' Katy explained that she'd first met him at the fair and had met him again at the university Ball. She was relieved when Robert returned and the conversation became more general. She hadn't felt comfortable discussing Terence with Charles. She stifled a yawn. It had been a great evening but she suddenly felt tired and wished she was home in her bedroom tucked under her eiderdown.

'How did your evening go? Did Terence keep his hands to himself?' Margaret enquired. She was sitting on her bed whilst Katy brushed her hair at the dressing-table mirror, trying to avoid the crack which distorted her face slightly.

'We must get this mirror replaced,' she said, ignoring the

question. 'It makes me look like Quasimodo and I declare to God I'll end up going out with my lipstick halfway up the side of my nose.'

'Quasimodo was better-lookin',' Margaret grinned. 'Talk to me about the dinner party before I kill you.'

'It was a great success . . . Terence was a great success. The girl Helen, whom he immediately fell in love with, was a great success. Which was not surprising seeing as she resembled a goddess.'

'I suppose you would rather she had turned out to look like Quasimodo's twin sister, with a nasty disposition to make her unlikeable,' said Margaret wisely.

Katy sighed. 'No. Look – I could have fallen for her myself. She was God's gift to the occasion. She charmed the socks off us all.'

'Pity about Terence falling for her charms too.' Margaret cast a shrewd glance at Katy, but her friend didn't seem too concerned.

'Terence hasn't a chance with her,' Katy reflected. 'She had eyes only for Charles. I have a feeling they know each other very well . . . Oh heck! I'd better get going. The bookshop is not doing well with sales just lately and I am rushed off my feet trying to drum up business.'

As she walked along, head bent, her thoughts were busy. The bookshop had started off so well John had insisted on paying her a salary but lately, sales had begun to slow up as the students settled back for the new term having already sorted out their needs. Worried that the business would not run to two salaries, she had recently spoken to John about improving and updating his postal service.

She had suggested that the slogan could be: 'If you can't find the book, we'll find it for you.' When they had advertised the service in the press, the response had been very good, so now John dealt with the shop sales and her job was to run the required titles to earth by hook or by crook and send them – on remittance – to the person who had made the request. She enjoyed the work, which gave her a degree of mobility and interest as she scoured shops old and new for the titles. Only once, so far, had she to admit defeat. She had surprised herself by her tenacity and she had become a tough businesswoman. She prayed that this end of the business would keep them solvent until the shop picked up again.

By the end of the day she was footsore and tired. She curled up on the sofa to listen to the coverage of Princess Elizabeth's wedding to Philip Mountbatten on the wireless. Now *there* was someone who didn't have to worry about sore feet and lack of money and who had a handsome man to drape a loving arm over her shoulder and smile into her eyes. She started as the phone rang.

Donal answered it. 'It's for you, Katy.'

'Who is it?'

'I never asked his name. I should answer it if I were you,' he advised solemnly. 'This may be your big chance.'

Frank let out a whoop of laughter. 'Someone's got to hear of your goin's on and has touted your number about the town.'

'You really can be a right scut sometimes, Frank McGrady,' Margaret remarked in disgust. 'Behave yourself now and stop actin' the goat.' Katy ignored both of them and went to the phone.

It was Terence. His question intrigued her. 'Katy, do you like opera?'

'I've never been to one. I like classical music, if that's any help. Are we playing at quizzes, Terence?'

'I've got two tickets for *Tosca* and wondered if you would like to go.'

She was tempted. She'd always longed to see the inside of the Opera House and she wasn't going to pass up the opportunity. 'When?'

'Tonight! It's very short notice, but the tickets only became available today.'

'I'll come,' she said, without hesitation. 'How long have I got to get ready?'

'An hour. Not enough time to start with hair-washing and stuff. I'll be at the door around seven-thirty.'

'I'll be ready. But don't expect miracles.'

'None needed. You will look lovely.'

The overture struck up as they settled down quickly into their seats. Katy looked round in fascination. The place was a dream of red velvet and gold. The boxes had beautiful hanging drapes tied back with gold tassels, matching the curtains onstage. Chandeliers hung from the high domed ceiling, throwing off a discreet light, and now they began to dim and the curtain rose; the first act had begun.

Katy realised just how much she was enjoying herself when they were halfway through the second act, and Terence smiled and squeezed her hand. She thought that altogether it was going to be a great evening.

When the curtains closed and the lights went up, she gave a sigh of satisfaction. Terence rose. She looked at him in surprise. 'Now what?'

'Now for the refreshments. The interval lasts fifteen minutes so we don't have much time.' He pulled her to her feet and gently hustled her along. She would have preferred to stay in her seat. All the pushing and jostling quite spoiled things, particularly as all she required was a glass of lemonade. As she idly watched Terence make his way towards the bar she realised that his head was swivelling to right and left. Suddenly he veered towards the left of the bar and then turned and waved frantically at her.

It took a second to understand that he wanted her to join him, which meant having to push her way though the crush of bodies. She reached him just as the drinks were handed over.

'Katy! Look who's here,' Terence said.

She turned to find Charles and Helen smiling at her. She smiled weakly back, disappointment filling her. She suddenly realised why she'd had the late invitation and the hurried rush to the opera. She suspected that Terence had discovered at the dinner party that the other two were going to be here tonight and had hastily acquired two tickets. He had only invited her because he needed a girl – any girl – on his arm.

Charles was looking curiously at her. Terence and Helen were having an animated discussion about the last scene.

'Anything wrong? You looked quite fierce for a moment.'

She forced a normal smile. It wasn't Charles' fault. There was no reason to be churlish with him. 'I was just feeling peeved because I had to push and shove to get here.'

'Are you enjoying the opera?'

'Very much. I have never been to one before. I have no idea what it's all about but the singing was awe-inspiring.'

'All is explained in the programme. Here, have mine.' He smiled. 'I've seen it several times.'

The bell rang. They started back to their seats and prepared to watch the rest of the show. Katy felt her annoyance gradually fade as she immersed herself in the drama unfolding on stage. She turned to Terence, only to discover that he had his eyes shut. He showed no further interest in the opera at all.

They were walking back to the car when Katy stopped suddenly. 'You knew that Charles and Helen were going to be here, didn't you?'

'Why do you say that?'

'All that haste. The sudden invitation with only hours to spare. You wanted to see Helen again and you needed someone to go with you so that the meeting could appear accidental.'

'Don't be silly, Katy.' There was a faint hesitancy in Terence's voice which convinced her she was right.

'I suspected that you were looking for someone when I saw you walking to the bar with your head swivelling from side to side as though on a pivot and as soon as I saw Helen and Charles I knew I was only invited so you could meet up with Helen.'

Terence had the grace to remain silent. He had been copped fair and square. It was unfortunate that Katy had discovered his ploy.

'I'm sorry, I've behaved badly,' he apologised.

'Terence!' Katy sighed. 'Why couldn't you have been open with me in the first place? It isn't as though we are going out seriously. I would have understood. I do loathe such underhand methods. It's up to you whether we just remain friends or move on.'

When they arrived at the house, Terence saw Katy to the door then returned to the car. He slowly let the clutch in, and sat back deep in thought. True, he fancied Helen, but he didn't want to let Katy go. Katy was a very good-looking girl and he had plans for her.

155

CHAPTER 9

December 1947 had the worst weather farmers had known for many years. Drifts of snow blocked the roads, causing traffic to come to a standstill. Abandoned vehicles awaited release and sheep and cattle were trapped. Katy wasn't able to get home for Christmas because the roads were completely impassable. On Christmas Eve she phoned home to be told that her father and Patrick were out trying to rescue farm stock and lead them to shelter. Katy knew that her mother was trying to make light of it so that she wouldn't be worried.

'Patrick has been a great help. The Toner family are all staying here for Christmas so that the poor man hasn't got to trek home, for the drifts are four foot high in places. What will you do, Katy?'

'Don't worry about me, Mam. None of us could get home but we have enough food in to give us a good meal.' She laughed. 'Norah is a good cook and she says not one of us is to show up in the kitchen to throw her off. It will be quite an adventure, so you have no need to fret. As soon as I can, I will come home for a visit.'

In fact, the whole group thought it was a great laugh. 'It beats sitting by the fire listening to old records,' Donal declared, adding, 'what would the rest of you be doing?'

'I'd be helping with the stock and anything else needing doing on the farm,' Katy volunteered.

'There you are then; at least you can put your feet up here or play games with us lads,' Donal grinned.

Norah came in from the kitchen at that moment. 'Well, I would like to have made it home. I haven't seen my mam for weeks and she lives all on her own.'

She looked so worried that Mickey said in his kind way, 'She'll be all right, Norah. She lives in the middle of a row of cottages. She won't be alone.'

Frank stood up. 'I'm off to the pub for a jar even if I have to dig my way there. Is anyone else going to try for it?'

Donal jumped up. 'I'm your man.'

'I'll remind you about this if you tell me you can't plough your way through to get to Mass,' Norah called after them.

They did manage it, however. Although it was still snowing heavily, the gritting lorries were out and the streets were just about passable, and when they returned, they all tipped in and helped with setting the table and setting the few presents round the tree. Katy enjoyed Christmas Day. She hadn't expected to because of her concern for her parents and the farm animals, but the day passed well and that evening they played cards and acted out charades, until Frank, who had the largest capacity for wine, decided to stagger off to bed and the party broke up.

That night, however, Katy's worries returned. She tossed and turned beneath her blankets longing for the sleep that kept eluding her, in her mind's eye seeing the lines of weariness and worry on her father's face and going over the last conversation she'd had with her mam on Christmas morning as Annie tried to make light of their problems. At the same time telling Katy, with a little laugh, of the antics of Lazarus who had to stay indoors and hated it.

Next day, hung over with tiredness, Katy phoned John at the bookshop to explain her predicament.

'Stay where you are,' he advised. 'There is no business going here, anyway. Sure, who in their right mind would want to stagger out on Boxing Day in this weather to buy a book? I'll see you when the roads are passable.'

She felt better for having phoned. John was right – book-buying would be the last thing on anyone's mind. Thankfully, trade had improved a lot on the run-up to Christmas, helped by the fact that there had been an unexpected run on certain books that the students had not been able to acquire second-hand. She had been given a small bonus, and with it had bought her mam and da some decent records. Delighted with the gift, they had already played the records over and over.

When, two weeks later, the thaw set in, she returned to work. The experts reported that the thaw was only temporary, but she felt guilty about leaving John to manage on his own. She'd also rung her mother to say she would be coming home that weekend, but Annie insisted she should stay in Belfast. 'We will manage very well. The respite will give us time to reorganise.' She went on to say that Patrick and Tom were staying on to help out but Maura, Patrick's wife, had gone home to set things to rights there.

Katy hid her relief. Hearing of the isolation of the farm during the past three weeks had made her realise how much she had enjoyed the companionship of her friends over the Christmas period. Norah and Donal had gone home to check on things, but Norah hadn't made it back yet. Margaret explained that Norah's mam had gone down with flu and she'd stayed to nurse her.

'I'm surprised to see you,' Katy said to Donal, 'seeing as the new term doesn't start till Thursday.'

'It's perfectly simple,' he said airily. 'Much as I love the ma and da, being cooped up with them another day would have done for me, and I have a right tearaway of a brother who nearly drove me mad with his antics. As soon as I looked out and saw the first sign of weak sunshine, I was away.'

Frank remarked that he'd always known that Donal was a selfish bastard and no doubt his family were well rid of him.

'B'God! That's rich, coming from someone who couldn't be coaxed into going home for Christmas in the first place – at least the rest of us were going to try.' Donal's lips had tightened in anger.

Margaret and Katy eyed each other. Frank had gone too far in his criticism. Margaret laughed nervously. 'Donal is right, Frank. You have no room to talk – now can we stop the bickering and start getting along with each other? Donal, show us the wireless you bought with your Christmas money.'

Slightly appeased by the support he had received, Donal went to his room and emerged with the wireless. He set it on the table and awaited their comments.

'How much did you pay for it?' Frank was the first one to speak.

'Four pounds – second-hand.'

'Are you mad? You've been caught by the balls, man. I could have got you a better one for less.' The girls held their breath. Wouid Donal take offence again?

'It's a fair price – and the woodworm was for free.' Donal grinned. His good nature had reasserted itself. He was not going to let Frank rile him. 'I have no plug at the moment but m'da let me borrow his to test it out. It has a fine tone.'

Frank rose and stretched. 'I'm off for a jar while I can walk to the pub – this weather won't last. Are you coming?'

'I am indeed,' Donal said, patting his pockets for change. 'We have some serious catching up to do.'

When they had gone, Katy and Margaret settled themselves in front of the gas fire. 'They'll go mad when they get their share of the bill for this,' Margaret commented, 'but I don't intend to freeze while the pair of them sit in a warm pub with pints of Guinness ramming down their throats.'

The door opened and Mickey entered. He looked round. 'Have you killed everyone off? And what have you done with the bodies, ye pair of sadistic articles?' He ruffled Katy's hair and gave Margaret a fleeting kiss.

Margaret accepted the peck on the cheek. 'Donal and Frank have gone to the Brewers for a drink and you are to follow. Did you get a newspaper?'

Mickey took the newspaper from inside his coat and handed it to her. 'The snow has started to fall again. I had better get off. Keep the light burning till we get home.'

Margaret flicked the newspaper at him. 'Bring us back a couple of bottles of stout – or you are a dead man.'

'Mickey is so good-natured and generous,' Katy remarked. 'You've done well for yourself, Margaret.'

Her friend smiled. 'I think you have it right. Mind you, I was hoping to change my name from Kelly to something more aristocratic – Flynn is not even one step up.' She looked slightly suspiciously at Katy. It was the second time her friend had remarked on Mickey's worth. She frowned. She had also noticed the camaraderie between them.

★ ★ ★

By the beginning of March 1948, the bookshop's profits had improved so dramatically that John, his eyes gleaming behind his glasses, remarked, 'I can't believe how well we are doing. It has only been a few short months since we updated the place and here we are – in the black already.'

'Thank goodness!' Katy said fervently. 'There were times in the beginning when my heart sank as the sales fell for a while.'

John gave her a measured stare. 'I wouldn't like to think that the bookshop and its profits were the only thing in your life. Do you still see that young man you went to the opera with?'

Katy was reluctant to discuss Terence Coleman. She laughed lightly. 'I have a string of beaux waitin' in the wings – I will not want for company.'

'Are you going home this weekend?'

She frowned. She hadn't been home for ages. The fact that Charles was only two miles down the road filled her thoughts when she was there. Here, she could immerse herself in work or go sightseeing – or to the pictures with Margaret – all of which helped to keep her mind off him.

'I don't think so. You will need help in the shop. Saturday is one of our busiest days.'

'I live above the shop and I have little else to interest me. I think I can hold the fort for one day.' He gave her a shrewd glance. 'Don't use me as an excuse, Katy. If you don't want to go then don't.'

She blushed. 'There is a reason,' she admitted, 'and staying away won't solve the problem. All right – I will go home!'

She arrived just before lunch. Annie looked up in surprise. Katy hadn't phoned to say she was coming. Katy kissed her. 'I thought I'd surprise you. Is there any tea in that pot?'

'I'll brew a fresh pot.' Annie observed her daughter for a moment before saying, 'There was a phone call from Mrs Sanders. I told her you weren't here and gave her your number. Give her a ring when you've had your tea.'

'Did she say why she was ringing?' Katy was curious about the call, as she had seen Sylvia and Elizabeth on her last visit and was up to date with events in their lives.

'Sure, why would she? It's you she wants to talk to.'

Katy rang as soon as she had freshened up. Sylvia wondered if she would like to come to dinner that evening. 'I'm sorry about the short notice, but I had thought you would ring me sooner.'

'Is the seat filled?' Katy enquired jokingly.

'No! So you will come? I have something important to ask of you.'

'Can't you ask me now?'

'It will keep till this evening.'

She was intrigued. Sylvia had sounded slightly embarrassed. But then, Sylvia never failed to amaze Katy with her sudden switches of mood. She sometimes found it difficult to equate the business person with the vague woman who didn't always appear to know what was happening in her household.

When she arrived that evening, Sylvia was alone and seated by the window. She rose and came towards her, looking radiant.

'I saw you arrive. I – I – Charles will be down soon.'

She sounds nervous, Katy thought, as a slight tremor ran through her. She hadn't expected Charles to be home. Sylvia had mentioned on her last visit that Charles had been spending more time in Belfast lately. Then she became aware that Sylvia had spoken.

'Pardon?'

'I'm getting married and I want you to be my bridesmaid.' Sylvia repeated.

'Good Lord.'

'Will you?'

Katy hugged her. 'Of course I will. Congratulations! It's a step up from being your daughter's nanny.'

'It was Elizabeth's idea,' Sylvia explained. 'I was having her as my flower girl and she asked if you could be my bridesmaid – I thought it was a brilliant idea. I'm so pleased you have agreed.'

'Who will be giving you away?'

'I will.'

Katy turned, startled. 'Hello, Charles.'

'Hello, young Katy.'

She wished he wouldn't call her that, when she wanted him to see her as a desirable woman. She suspected that he didn't see

Helen in that light. She with the air of sophistication that Katy would kill for – and the gliding cat-like walk that sent men's pulses racing.

The doorbell rang. 'That will be Robert.' Sylvia left the room.

'Love's young dream.' Charles grinned. 'I never thought to see my sister in that state again – and she has taken up her painting, seriously, once more.'

'I've never seen any of her work,' Katy confessed.

'Look around. The walls are covered with her oils.'

'You mean . . . all these lovely . . . I never realised.'

Sylvia and Robert entered the room. 'Charles, will you see to the drinks?' Sylvia asked, adding, 'and do stop embarrassing me.'

Robert said to Katy. 'I hear you have agreed to be bridesmaid.' She nodded.

'It won't be a white wedding,' Sylvia warned. 'I've done all that. This time it will be a simple ceremony with family and a few friends – and a small reception to follow.'

'Suits me.' Charles handed round the drinks as he spoke. 'Let us toast the happy couple. It's a relief all round – isn't that so, Katy?'

'Indeed! I don't think my nerve would hold up for anything more elaborate.'

'You must bring your friend Terence,' said Sylvia.

'I don't think . . .'

'Of course you must!' said Charles. 'Helen is coming.'

Katy had difficulty in matching the merriment of the others at first, but as she sipped her second glass of wine she felt herself slowly relax. Sure, the battle wasn't lost till the last man had fallen. She giggled suddenly and Charles looked at her in amusement.

'I'd better run you home,' he said firmly.

Robert rose. 'I'll be passing the end of Katy's lane. It will be no trouble to take her to her door.'

Katy rang Terence as soon as she arrived back in Belfast. She dialled the number nervously and took a deep breath as she waited. He could only refuse – and it would hardly be the end of the world if he did.

'Katy!' Terence cried. 'I thought I'd spoiled it all with you.'

'There was nothing to spoil, Terence,' she said. 'In fact, I am about to ask you if you would accompany me to a wedding. I am going to be bridesmaid and the bride has invited you – I have your invitation in my hand.'

His slow laugh travelled over the line, but there was an edge to it. 'Whose wedding?'

'Sylvia and Robert are getting married on the third Saturday in April.'

'Confess!' Terence laughed. 'If Sylvia hadn't suggested it, you wouldn't have taken me along as a gift. I suspect you have a list of eligible men.'

Katy found herself smiling. He was a rogue of the first order. 'The delectable Helen will be going with Charles, which might encourage you to come,' she said mishievously.

'The delectable Helen – as you so aptly put it – has eyes for no one but your friend Charles.'

'Does that mean you won't come?'

'Certainly not! I shall pay so much attention to the lovely bridesmaid, Katy Molloy, the woman will bite her lips in frustration. But I shall be glued to your side.'

'You will not! You can play your games another way – I'll let you know more about the event when I find out times and venue.'

'Is it formal?'

'Ah no. That is the one thing I do know for certain. They want a small wedding with informal dress – but that doesn't mean you can turn up in a tweed jacket.'

'Now that is hitting below the belt. I am a man of discernment and culture,' Terence said lightly.

Katy smiled. Now that she and Terence knew where they stood with each other, she found she could enjoy his dry humour and easy manner. 'I'll get in touch when I know more.'

'I'll treat you to a meal when you do,' Terence promised. 'If you will accept.'

'If you think I would turn down a meal because you have devious qualities then you have another think coming,' Katy told him. 'I'm not one of these new women who insist on paying their share. I'll take a man for anything I can get – that is the new me.'

'You're on! I'm already intrigued.'

Margaret came in as she put the phone down. 'Anyone interesting?'

'I was giving Terence a dressing down. He is the most arrogant of men.'

'I won't argue with that.' Margaret drew her shoes off and wiggled her toes. 'I walk bloody miles from university to save money on bus fares. My poor feet are screaming. What did Terence Coleman want?'

Katy told her about the forthcoming wedding and that she'd been the one to ring Terence to ask him to escort her.

'He'll not let you down,' Margaret said. 'I'll allow him that.' She took the cups into the kitchen and Katy relaxed back into her chair and looked round. A smile rose to her lips. Her mam would have a fit if she could see the state of the living quarters – although, according to the others, it was a damn sight better now than before. Even Frank, the least hygienic of any of them, had wrinkled his nose as Donal told her about the state of the place before they had moved in.

'We had to scrub the walls down and delouse the place. It was riddled with fleas and all sorts of vermin. The furniture may not be of the best quality, but it's much nicer than the stuff that was left here. I'm tellin' you, when your man decamped, he left a right legacy behind for us to sort out.'

'Where is he now?'

'When last seen he was flogging pigs' liver and other delectable offal from a barrow in Dublin. He was duly arrested for hygiene offences.'

'How did you get to hear about it?' Katy enquired suspiciously. She wasn't sure if he was joking.

'The cod gave our names as reference.'

She looked at the threadbare carpet and the chairs that sagged in the middle and thought, I love it here. It isn't paradise but when we all separate – as one day we will – I will look back on this period as one of my happier times.

The door opened with its usual jarring creak and Norah Byrne walked in. She plonked her small case down and eyed the state of the room. 'Is there no one other than myself prepared to tidy this place up?'

165

Katy didn't reply. She had tried to grow fond of Norah but her constant griping about the habits of the rest of them and her fixation with cleanliness irritated her. It wouldn't have been so bad if Norah had been an outgoing and sociable person, but she invariably sat with her head in a book, trying to pretend to herself that she was the only one there, every now and then clicking her teeth in annoyance when one of the lads swore. She sighed. Norah, being a brilliant mathematician, couldn't see beyond the squiggles and unrecognisable things in brackets in her exercise book, and regarded the rest of them as being a bit below par.

Katy rose. Norah had gone into the kitchen and was ticking Margaret off for having the water running continuously. 'I'm off to have a long soak in the bath,' Katy called out.

Margaret put her head round the door and made a face at her. 'Enjoy yourself,' she grinned, adding in a loud whisper, 'Herself in there doesn't mean to sound grouchy. She has her heart in the right place. She grows on you.'

Katy looked quizzically at her. 'I'll try to remember that.'

When Katy arrived back at the house one afternoon, Norah called out to her that Terence Coleman was on the phone – could he please speak to her?

She hesitated and glanced at her watch. 'Could you tell him I'll give him a ring later? I'm very late for an appointment. I just stopped by to get some literature I need.'

Norah relayed the information to Terence, who said goodbye curtly and replaced the phone with a frown. No girl had ever done this to him before. What was so special about Katy Molloy? Christ! He had only rung her up because he was at a loose end and beggars can't be choosers. As Katy had suspected, he had his sights on the gorgeous Helen in the long term. Katy was too virginal for his tastes, although she was good-looking and fair enough company. What's more, she had gained him entry to the home of Charles Gilbert – a man of some influence – for whom his father worked. This alone meant he should keep in her good books.

He settled himself on the settee and lay back with his legs

draped over the arm. It would be a challenge to seduce the Molloy girl, he thought idly. He'd have to go about it subtly – but then he was an expert. He hadn't failed yet in making a conquest. What was it Marion had called him? 'The despoiler of virgins'. But she herself had not minded losing her virginity to him. Indeed, she had been grateful – she had told him so. She was married now, with two children.

He closed his eyes in thought. Molloy . . . Molloy . . . Somewhere he had met someone with that name. Never mind! It would come to him, given time.

A few days later, he phoned again. Donal took the call and, putting his hand over the mouthpiece, he called out, 'Katy! Terence Coleman for you.'

Katy gasped. 'God! I forgot to return his call.'

'That'll be a first for Terence.' Donal commented. 'The man is a walking honey pot for lady bees. The girls are never off the phone to him.'

Katy whipped the phone from him. Terence must have heard every word.

'Just be careful,' Donal went on, in a penetrating voice. 'The man is a disaster for women and he gives no quarter.'

'I'm quite capable of handling my end, thank you . . . Er, hello, Terence. I am so sorry not to have returned your call.' She put her hand over the mouthpiece. 'Go and read your dirty magazines,' she hissed as Donal continued to stand there, smirking and listening in.

Terence was speaking, his voice cool. 'Perhaps I'm wasting my time calling you.' Blast! he sounded petty and vulnerable. He needed to assert himself. 'Forget that remark. I'm just feeling a bit miffed because you haven't been in touch about the wedding.'

Katy's tone was apologetic. 'I'm very sorry. I was having rather a hectic time but I'm here now.'

Terence steadied his thoughts. 'I wondered if you would like to come out tonight and see the film on at the Trocadero? It's *Hamlet.*'

'I'd love to – I adore Laurence Olivier. Would you mind if I met you there? I have a few things to do so I will be working later than usual.'

'That's fine,' Terence said, appeased. 'I'll be there around seven o'clock. Looking forward to it.'

So am I, thought Katy as she replaced the receiver. Terence had a reputation with women, but with her he had never been anything less than a gentleman. She was very aware that he was a dangerous man, but part of his charm lay in his honesty – he admitted the fact. Katy found him exciting. After all, she had moved to Belfast for a more challenging life, and if Terence was part of it then she was happy with that. It helped also that he fancied Helen so much. He would be less likely to use his bad boy tactics on her.

Sylvia telephoned the following week to give Katy more information about the wedding and to arrange a date and time for them to meet in Belfast to buy their outfits. 'Have you asked your friend Terence if he can come?'

'He says he will be delighted. I was going to ring you shortly and let you know,' Katy said.

'I'm pleased he can come; it will even things up.'

Katy suspected that what Sylvia meant was that it would be less awkward if she had a partner as Charles and Helen would be paired. That evening she rang Terence to relay the information to him.

'Let's meet for that meal I promised you,' he said. 'We can arrange time and transport – I take it you will be going home on the evening before the wedding?'

'Yes. There won't be a lot of time otherwise. The wedding is scheduled for eleven o' clock the next day.'

'I could book us in for dinner tomorrow night,' Terence suggested.

She laughed. 'Look, the wedding is still two weeks away. The sky could fall in before then and all our arrangements would be for nothing. It would be more sensible to meet a few days before.'

'I'm sorely in need of a night out,' Terence coaxed. 'I won't mention the wedding. I just want to relax with a lovely girl and eat a sumptuous meal.'

'All right. Why am I trying to do myself out of such a meal? What time do you want me to be there?'

'I'll call for you round seven o'clock.'

Norah opened the door to him the following evening. She smiled up at the handsome young man, her myopic eyes taking in every line of him from the white shirt and the smart suit, to the shine on his shoes.

Terence gave her one of his heartstopping looks and she felt a sudden spurt of envy. What did this lovely man see in Katy Molloy? she thought, but said aloud, 'She is in her bedroom plastering her face.' She smiled archly, to show that she was making a joke but Terence ignored the words and went to stand by the window. Norah shrugged. 'I'll tell her you're here.'

Katy arrived at that moment and looked curiously from Terence to the scowling Norah.

'Katy, my darling,' Terence cried, 'how smart you look! I'll be the envy of every man in the room tonight.' He took her arm and edged her towards the door.

Katy gave him a keen stare when they reached his car. 'You were overdoing the charm bit, weren't you?'

'That was for Norah's benefit. She doesn't like you much, does she?'

Katy sighed. 'We haven't exactly hit it off since I came to live here, although she tries hard – but what makes you say that?'

'She informed me that you were in your room plastering your face with make-up.'

'The cheeky article!' Katy gasped.

'Don't let it worry you.' Terence opened the car door and waited till she was seated. He leaned in. 'I suspect that Norah is jealous of your friendship with the fair Margaret. Until you came, she and Margaret were close friends and you have posed a threat to that friendship. It didn't help, either, that you were so readily accepted by the others.'

By the time they reached the restaurant, Katy had decided she would try to win Norah's respect, for she could understand how she felt. What Norah didn't understand – or had forgotten – was that her own friendship with Margaret went back a long way.

Her gaze swivelled round the room as she and Terence trod the soft thick carpet in the wake of the stiff-backed waiter. If nothing else was in Terence's favour it could never be said that he was mean. This place had the look of money about it, and when the menu arrived, she was further convinced. It was written on heavy parchment and the napkins, cream-coloured and large, were embossed with the initials of the restaurant.

'I hope the food stands up to the décor and the napery,' she whispered.

Terence laughed. 'Katy Molloy, you are supposed to behave as though you have seen it all before.'

She leaned across to him. 'Not one bit. You would know fine well I was a hypocrite. You see before you a girl who dines in cafés that have paper napkins folded like accordions. Just because you are one of the privileged set doesn't mean I have to pretend to be one also.'

The wine waiter arrived and handed the list to Terence.

'Don't you dare ask me for my preference,' Katy mumbled.

Terence smiled and made his choice. He handed her the menu when the waiter had gone. It was written in French.

She studied it, pointed to an item and said quietly: 'What would I be eating if I chose that?'

Terence looked. 'Irish stew with a dollop of cream.'

'I'll have that,' she said.

'How about melon glâcé for a starter?' As she struggled with the idea he felt a wave of affection for her, which he quickly doused. He had no room for sentiment – but she was so honest and so perky. 'It's just chilled melon,' he said gruffly.

She put the menu down. 'Next time we dine out it will be my treat,' she said. 'I want you to teach me about such things and I will try different dishes so that I won't be caught out. I don't mind *you* being aware of my ignorance but I would be mortified if I was with someone else and couldn't hold my corner.'

Afterwards, she decided that it had been a wonderful meal. Her mam's Irish stew had a lot to live up to. She said as much to Terence.

He smiled and beckoned the waiter. 'We would like coffee now, please.'

'Here or in the lounge, sir?'

'In the lounge.'

Once seated, Katy leaned back and smiled warmly at him. 'I

can't say how much I have enjoyed this evening.'

'My pleasure! I've also enjoyed myself.'

'You had a good laugh, anyway. I doubt if you normally take a girl out to eat who doesn't know what it's all about.'

'I had to learn – and it was worse for me, for the man has to do the ordering and you should have seen the hash I made of it the first few times. I was mortified on one particular occasion because I was dining with a very sophisticated lady whom I was trying to impress, and I made a real ass of myself. Fortunately she took pity on me and gave me the low-down on the whole business.'

As they sat in companionable silence waiting for the coffee to arrive, Katy found herself recalling the time she had dined with Charles. That menu had been written in English, fortunately. 'I meant it when I said I would like you to teach me the ropes,' she said.

'And I meant it when I said I would be delighted,' Terence responded.

'Have you a girlfriend who might complicate things?'

He had two going at the moment, but that was his secret. 'No, so we can spend many happy hours together learning how to eat.'

'You are laughing at me.'

'Only a little, Katy Molloy. Only a little.'

Feeling relaxed and warm inside because of the wine, she glanced around the room. Thank goodness she had a decent dress on. It wasn't in the same class as some of those floating past on the ultra-smart women who wore them, but it was discreet and of reasonable quality. Her mam had taught her how to recognise a good outfit. 'Never go for gaudy colours and stick to a classic style that will pass muster anywhere.' Clothes rationing had put paid to most women's aspirations regarding clothes for so long now, but things were beginning to change.

She looked at Terence, who was watching her with a tiny smile hovering on his lips. 'I'm so pleased you are coming to the wedding. I hope you manage to make your mark with Helen.'

'Oh,' he shrugged, 'I think I may have lost interest there. I am a fickle man.' What he didn't add was that he'd had more fun with Katy Molloy, this evening, than he'd had for many a long day. As

171

the evening progressed he had come to realise just what a lovely young woman she was – and her eagerness to learn had enchanted him. He felt a sudden desire to make love to her – a desire quickly squashed. He stood up, suddenly. 'Time to get you home.'

CHAPTER 10

Sylvia, looking stunning in her cream satin wedding suit and the little matching hat with its wisp of feathery decoration on the side, smiled demurely as she turned to face her new husband for his kiss. Katy stole a look at Elizabeth who was staring at her mother in awe. She felt the tiny hand creep into hers and she squeezed it gently as they followed the bride and groom into the vestry to sign the register.

'Mamma is beautiful, isn't she, Katy?'

'Very beautiful!' Katy whispered and held her hand to her lips as they watched the signing. The formalities over, the wedding party began the walk up the aisle and as they did so, Katy became aware that Charles had joined Helen; her face was even more beautiful than usual beneath the large black picture hat of stiffened lace. She looked glamorous and sophisticated in a red suit of soft pure wool which clung to her, emphasising the slim figure. Charles whispered something to her. Probably telling her how gorgeous she looked, Katy thought.

Sylvia had wanted an understated wedding with just a few of her friends and family present, but later, at the reception at the Cashmore Hotel, Katy sipped her drink and studied the guests. The clothes they wore were by no stretch of the imagination discreet. The smell of money was everywhere. She was thankful that she had been asked to act as bridesmaid for she could never have competed. As it was, her own dress of blue moiré fabric was exquisite – thank God the bill for it was not hers to pay. She recalled how Charles had looked at her as she walked down the stairs. His eyes had said it all, but then he spoke the words that set her heart alight.

173

'Katy Molloy, you are beautiful! What more can I say?'

'You can stop embarrassing me,' she said, as pink colour stained her cheeks.

'I'm stating facts. You look absolutely sensational.'

She had held onto his words, hugging the compliment to her, until she had glimpsed Helen in the church and realised that she was no competition for the Helens of this world with their confidence and hourglass figures. She shrugged. Today they were looking at a Katy Molloy they had never seen before, and she was pleased enough for her mirror had not lied, judging by Charles' compliment. She didn't begrudge Helen her beauty. She was a lovely-natured girl and she liked her.

At the reception, Terence drew her across to where Helen stood alone. She explained that Charles had gone to replenish their drinks. Terence said smoothly, 'Katy and I are popping into Belfast later this evening. Why don't you and Charles join us?' Katy was pleased that he had now thrown his arm casually over her shoulder – it made her feel part of their scene – but she was less pleased at the statement he had just made for she hadn't been consulted.

When Charles joined them, Terence repeated his invitation.

'What do you say, Helen?' Charles raised his eyebrows at her.

'Fine by me.'

'That's settled then.'

Katy spoke. 'There is a problem. I am visiting my parents at the moment and—'

'That isn't a problem. We can take both cars, and if Helen doesn't mind Terence seeing her home at the end of the evening, I can drive you back. Don't forget that I live here.'

'I think it's a brilliant idea,' said Helen. 'Oh do come, Katy.'

'I've already phoned through to book a table for four at Gresham's,' Terence put in. 'I only managed to get a sitting because I'm a regular customer. It's an unpretentious little restaurant and tables are much sought-after.'

Katy gave in. 'I'll phone Mam and let her know.'

The evening was a most enjoyable one. Terence, in an effort to make up for his earlier high-handedness, paid a great deal of attention to Katy and she, under the influence of a couple of

174

glasses of fine wine, began to mellow towards him. As he'd promised, the restaurant was one of those understated haunts which had become popular for that very reason. Everything about it was discreet, from the service right down to the lighting and the soft music.

Later, on the way home, she lay back against the soft upholstery of Charles' car and felt her eyelids drooping. She was wine-happy, and content. The soft drone of the engine was lulling her into sleep; she fought to keep herself from succumbing but the battle was lost and halfway home she gave up the fight.

Charles reduced the speed so that she wouldn't wake and his eyes softened as he stole a glance at her. Having watched how she and Terence reacted to each other this evening he had felt a little envious of their closeness and rapport. She sighed in sleep and turned towards him, pillowing her head in her palm to make herself more comfortable. He couldn't bear it. He pushed down on the accelerator. The sooner he got her home the better. It was utter madness to compare a girl like this with someone like Helen. She was pretty where Helen was exquisitely beautiful. She was short of stature where Helen was tall and willowy. She was perky and funny where Helen was smart and sophisticated. Helen was of his world. Katy was not.

He slammed on the brakes so suddenly that Katy woke with a start. She pushed her hair from her eyes, struggling to remember where she was. Charles was looking at her oddly. She drew her cream shawl round her shoulders and said sleepily, 'Have we arrived yet?'

Charles felt suddenly annoyed with himself. What the hell was the matter with him? 'Yes, we're here. I'm sorry I woke you so abruptly.'

'That's all right. Thank you for bringing me home – it's been a grand evening altogether, hasn't it?'

'A wonderful day – and evening,' Charles agreed.

She sat up. 'I've been wanting to ask you how things went with moving Barney Fogarty's cottage.'

Charles cut the engine, slightly bemused by the sudden turn the conversation had taken. 'We did end up with a few problems,' he said. 'When we took the cottage apart we found that many of the stones had begun to crumble – then we realised that if we introduced new stones, they would show up against the weathered ones. We were short on ideas until the old man himself came up with the answer. There was an old barn at the back which was 'tumbling round his ears' he said, and as he had no interest in bringing it with him he suggested we knock it down and use those stones that were worth using. It worked brilliantly. Even after we had built a toilet and a bathroom onto the new cottage we still had enough left to build him a small outhouse.' He smiled ruefully. 'I think Barney did very well out of us.'

Katy yawned again and chuckled. 'Trust an Irishman to get the best of a bargain! I'd better get inside. I daresay my mam is peering through the window at this very minute wondering what we are doing here.'

Charles said, 'I'm sure she knows her daughter better than to worry. Well, Katy Molloy, as I said, I have enjoyed the evening.'

'So have I,' Katy agreed. 'We do seem to meet up, eventually.' She laughed nervously. 'Perhaps at another wedding?' She hoped to God it wouldn't be his. She stood there in the moonlight and watched the car until it disappeared round the corner of the barn before entering the house.

Later, as undressed she ran through the evening in her mind and found herself savouring every look that Charles had thrown her way. Terence was fun, but Charles was the one she wanted to be with. She curled into a ball beneath the bedclothes. There was little point in wishing. Then sleep crept up on her and stole her thoughts.

Charles drove off fast and let in the clutch clumsily, his mind dwelling on the past few minutes as Katy stood there outlined in the moonlight, her riotous curls endearingly escaping from the grips that had kept it under control for most of the evening. There was something about her that brought out the best in him. She was so young, so wonderfully naive. He glanced at his watch. It was two o'clock in the morning but he still felt restless and wide awake. When he arrived back at Beresford House he threw his keys on the hall table and went into the drawing room to pour himself a double whiskey. Stretching out on the settee he allowed his mind full rein. His thoughts were unsettled and surprising ones.

Although he had spoken the truth when he had said that he had enjoyed the evening, he had nonetheless found himself disconcerted by the secret messages passing between Terence and Katy – such as the time when the waiter had come forward with the menu and Katy had glanced at it in amusement and remarked to Terence, 'Good heavens, a menu written in English for a change.' Terence had smiled back conspiratorially but made no comment.

She had looked so young and yet quite at ease. He rose to pour himself another whiskey. What was the matter with him? Why was he bothered about her relationship with Terence, when a lovely girl with a heavenly body was interested in him? Helen had made no secret of the fact that she liked him more than as a friend, and he suspected that he only had to say the magic words and she was his. On Monday he would send a large bouquet of flowers to Helen because . . . because she . . . His mind became muddled and he felt suddenly drowsy. Tomorrow he would sort out his life and his relationships. Tomorrow . . . The whiskey glass slipped from his hand.

Katy woke with a start the following morning. Her mother was shaking her awake and telling her she was going to be late for Mass if she didn't get a move on. She looked round dazedly and then remembered that she had come home for Sylvia's wedding. She rose and slipped into her dressing gown. She still felt tired and she had a slight headache. In the bathroom she slopped some cold water over her face. Her mouth felt dry – she had drunk too much wine. God! Her parents would go mad if they knew that she drank alcohol. They were very strict on that score.

She paid a visit to Vincey's grave after Mass. She hadn't been there so often of late, and it was with a feeling of regret that she knelt down on the turf to say a prayer and remembered the joy they had all felt when he came home from the war safe and sound . . .

Her thoughts were interrupted by the sound of her mother's voice calling to her.

177

She hurried towards her and apologised. 'Sorry! I lost track of time.' She took her mother's arm and they dashed to catch up with Eddie, who had gone on ahead.

'What were you thinking about while you knelt there?' Annie asked gently. She had seen the look on Katy's face and was intrigued by her tender expression.

'I was remembering how we felt on Vincey's return,' Katy told her. 'I was also remembering the times when he told me to stop dreaming and make things happen . . . and that once I couldn't have knelt there without bursting into tears.'

She's over the worst, Annie thought. Eddie was right when he said that the day would come when the grieving stopped and the memories took over. She sighed. If only she could say that about herself.

After lunch, Eddie settled down with the Sunday paper as he'd done a hundred times over, while the two women got on with the washing up, but when some time had elapsed he entered the kitchen to complain. 'Where is my mug of tea?'

Annie said, 'It's on its way. Away back and read your paper.'

He returned to his chair where he lit his pipe and puffed on it with enjoyment before falling into a slight doze. The hot ash from his pipe nearly burnt the hand of him as it slipped from his grasp and he hastily tapped the ashes out and placed the pipe in the rack before settling back into his chair. His eyelids drooped again. He was off.

It was some time later that the soft hum of conversation pierced his consciousness. As he began to stir, he heard Katy mention Donal, Mickey and Frank. He sat up, suddenly alert.

'Who are these men?'

Annie and Katy started in surprise. 'In the name of God, Eddie Molloy, are you trying to give me a heart attack?' Annie snapped.

Eddie ignored the reproof and looked straight at Katy. 'You speak as though you see these men on a daily basis.'

Katy swallowed. She had foolishly been telling her mam about Christmas and how they'd nearly ruined the meal because Frank had turned the oven off when the turkey had still half an hour to go before it was cooked – and how Donal and Mickey had rescued the situation just in time.

Annie said quickly, 'They are friends of Katy's.'

Eddie was not to be sidetracked. 'You spoke of them as though they were living in the same house . . . are they?'

Katy stammered, 'Well – yes . . . and no. They live upstairs . . .'

'You live in a house not a block of rooms,' Eddie said accusingly.

Katy felt herself flushing. 'They – they – live upstairs, but we – er – share the kitchen and food . . .'

Eddie heaved himself out of his chair and stood over her. 'I was persuaded against my will to let you go to Belfast, but I was never entirely happy with the idea. Now you are coming back home. I won't have my daughter living like this.'

'Stop right there, Eddie Molloy.' Annie grabbed his arm.

Eddie shook it off. 'Home!' he repeated. 'Where you will *not* be able to get into mischief.'

Katy, eyes blazing with hurt and anger, faced him. 'I will not come home to live with a father who has so little faith in me. You brought me up to live by a certain code. How could you think I would abuse that code?'

'You cheeky article,' Eddie fumed.

Tears of anger filled Katy's eyes. 'I would never do anything to disgrace you. More than that, I would never let Vincey down.' She walked from the room.

'Come back here!' Eddie made a move to follow but Annie blocked his way.

'Never!' she ground out fiercely. 'I have never gone against your judgement in all the years we have been married, but in this instance I am taking Katy's side. She is right. We brought her up with a set of principles to follow and she would never do anything to shame us. How could you think for one moment that she would?' Annie's heart bled for Eddie at that moment. He loved Katy dearly and she could understand his concern, but he was wrong to condemn her.

'The lads live upstairs but they all eat together – it's cheaper that way and if they didn't share the rent then they would all be stuck in little rooms at the university.'

Eddie stared at her. 'You knew all about this arrangement?'

'Yes,' she admitted. 'It seemed easier not tell you because I knew fine well what your reaction would be.'

'You didn't think I had a right to know?'

Annie sighed. 'I'm, sorry, Eddie. You did have that right, but you can see by your reaction why I took it from you.'

'I'm away out to do the milking. I'll be back once the girl has gone.'

'Eddie!' Annie called, but her husband went out without a backward glance.

The house was empty when Katy arrived back. There was a note propped up on the mantelpiece. *We are all over at McCarthy's place*, she read. *Join us if you are back early enough.* It was signed by Margaret who had added a P.S. *Norah isn't back either. If you don't feel like coming you can be company for each other*.

Katy scrumpled the note. The last thing she needed was Norah with her observations about the state everyone had left the place in. She lifted her case and made her way into her bedroom. For her it would be a lukewarm bath – she knew the others well enough to know they would have used up all the hot water – and an early night.

She was just drifting into sleep when a sound from the other room roused her. She yawned and reached for her book. Once disturbed she knew she would have to wait for tiredness to hit again. The sound occurred once more and this time she realised that it was a sob. Tentatively, she opened the door into the sitting room. Norah was huddled into the corner of the large settee, clutching a hanky to her mouth. Katy crossed to her. 'What's the matter?'

Norah shrugged. 'Nothing, absolutely nothing. I'm just having a fit of the blues.'

'God, Norah, I never thought I'd see the day. You always seem so strong and capable.'

'Is it only the weak can cry on an off day?' Norah asked bitterly. 'I realise you all think I'm built with a heart of stone and a pair of ears stuffed with cotton wool so that you can all make remarks that I am not supposed to hear.'

'What do you mean?'

'Oh, I've heard the remarks about my bossiness and my fixation about tidiness – and the way I set out rotas for the everyday running of the place. And I also know that when there is anything going on I'm not always invited.'

Katy curled up beside her. 'But Nora, you don't always like the things we do. You don't like dancing. If you remember, you were invited out for a drink not long ago and you gave us a lecture on the evils of it – and you do tend to make a scene if the house schedules get out of kilter.'

Norah sniffed. 'I'm not able to rattle on about things in a sociable manner. I only know about co-signs and numbers and I'm not pretty like Margaret and you.'

'Norah, I won't have you say that. I know for a fact that Margaret would give anything for that hair of yours – it's so shiny and manageable.' Katy was seeing a different Norah and she was intrigued. The spectacles had been discarded and she was surprised to discover soft hazel eyes that set off the auburn hair.

To give the other girl time to compose herself, Katy made her way into the tiny kitchen and busied herself making the cocoa. When she got back, Norah had stopped sniffing and was staring into space. She turned to Katy.

'Look, I'm sorry about this. Take your cocoa into your room. I'll be fine now.'

Katy shook her head. 'I'm going to drink my cocoa here and you are going to tell me what brought this on. For the first time since I came to live with you all, I'm seeing a different – and indeed more human – side to Norah Byrne. I've always had the impression that you were impregnable when it came to emotions. Now I see a person who is just as vulnerable as the rest of us – and who is a more attractive personality when she sheds the fussy manner and tells the truth about herself.'

'I've not always been nice to you, have I?' Norah asked, shamefaced.

'No, you haven't,' Katy said honestly. 'I've never understood why.'

Norah sighed. 'Jealousy! You waltzed in here and immediately clicked with everyone. You were particularly close with Margaret and I felt I had been replaced in her affection. You see, Maggie and I were the only girls in the group and it was us against the lads – but when you came she changed and I felt left out.'

'But Norah! Margaret and I . . . we grew up together . . . fought each other, even. You were still her friend all the same.'

The other girl shook her head. 'Not in the same way as you were. I noticed how close you were as soon as I saw you together and it helped to fuel my jealousy. Things happen for you. You have such confidence.'

A burble of laughter rose in Katy. Norah stared in surprise.

'Oh Norah, if only you knew what music those words are to me . . . because I came here feeling as green as a grasshopper. I knew nothing. The only way I kept going was to continually tell myself that I was no worse than the next and no better than most.' Katy paused for a moment and a wry smile lifted her lips. 'I'll tell you something that no one knows and which I am only now admitting to myself. I am in love with a man who is not in love with me and who is in a different league altogether – and I've just had a terrible row with my father whom I love dearly. So you see; all the things that happen for me are not always great news.'

'Do you know for certain that he doesn't love you?' Norah asked.

Katy smiled. 'Never mind that now. What are we going to do about you?'

'I feel better already.'

Katy said thoughtfully, 'Margaret helped me; I will help you – firstly to alter this fixation you have for orderliness.'

'That's the maths fanatic in me,' said Norah ruefully. 'Everything has to match or add up.'

'You'll change,' Katy promised. 'Now the first thing we have to do is to stop you tidying up after everyone and moaning about having to do it.'

'But we'll be living in a pigsty! You know what the lads are like – they'd be happy to drink out of dirty cups.'

'So let them. We'll bring Margaret in on this. We'll hide a couple of saucepans and some crockery in my room and if the lads don't do the washing up when it's their turn, then they won't have anything clean to eat off. They'll soon get the message.'

Norah laughed shakily. 'I'll never be able to keep my hands off the dirt, or my tongue from going on about the untidiness,' she said.

'Yes, you will. See that bracelet you wear?'

Norah looked down at the silver bracelet on her wrist.

'Every time you have the urge to tear a strip off anyone or you itch to tidy up the kitchen, you will rub the bracelet with your fingers till the feeling wears off.'

Norah threw back her head and gave a hearty laugh, and Katy thought that if her hair were taken down from that severe plait and allowed to drift over her shoulders . . . and if she dumped the sloppy jumpers and the heavy-duty shoes . . . Norah would look so much less formidable.

She grinned and pulled the other girl to her feet. 'I can hear the key in the latch. We'll talk another time. I'm off to bed before the gang come in. I suggest you do the same.'

Three days passed before Frank McGrady suddenly became aware of the state of the kitchen. This evening the sink was piled high with dirty dishes and the worktop with pots and the debris from the last meal. He poked his head round the door. 'Whose turn was it to do the washing up last evening?'

Donal got up and glanced at the rota. 'Mine,' he said sheepishly.

'Well, you can get your fat arse in here and do it. We haven't a plate clean enough to eat off.'

'I've forgotten to wash up before. What has happened?' He looked over to where Norah was sitting.

'Don't look at me,' she said sweetly.

Frank leaned against the door looking curiously at her. 'Is there something behind this?' he asked. 'Only Donal is right. Somehow the lot got done even if we did forget.'

'You didn't forget, not one of you. You just got used to me clearing up after you because you know I can't stand mess so you didn't bother in the first place.'

'So what has changed?'

'I have,' said Norah, with a feeling of satisfaction.

'When the meal is cooked what are *you* going to use?' asked Frank triumphantly.

'I have a spare set of equipment,' Norah said smugly, adding, 'I don't mind doing the cooking – that way I won't die of food poisoning – but I'm not going to swan round after you lot any longer.'

'Come to think of it,' said Dolan cautiously, 'you haven't done any nagging lately. Are you sickening for something?'

'I wondered what was missing in my life,' said Mickey, with awe. 'You haven't been telling me off about the state of my clothes either.'

'Donal!' Frank yelled. 'Are you going to sit there or are you going to get in here and give a hand? I wouldn't recognise an offending microbe if it was doing a war dance on your sausages, therefore we can't take any chances.'

Norah smiled to herself. The plan was working well. She'd have something to report to Katy when she came in from the bookshop. It was a pity Margaret was away; she would be amused. She settled back onto the cushions and became immersed in her study again.

When Katy breezed in half an hour later, Norah looked up with a smile and nodded towards the kitchen, from which the sound of banging pots and raised voices was issuing. 'They've discovered that there isn't a clean pot in the place. I've told them we don't eat till I have something to cook with and in.'

Katy grinned. 'Told you so. I'm off for a nice soak in the bath before they catch on that I'm here.'

'If they haven't used all the water. I'd give it half an hour. Seeing as they can't ruin the kettle I'll bring you in a cup of tea.'

Katy went into the bedroom and threw her things on a chair. Terence was due in an hour so she didn't have a lot of time. She took her dress from the wardrobe and laid it on the bed in readiness and when Norah brought the tea she sipped it hastily and went upstairs to the bathroom to test the water. It was hot enough and she set it running while she gathered up her underwear.

Later, as Katy sank gratefully into the soft water she closed her eyes and relaxed, allowing her thoughts to take over. Her relationship with Norah had altered dramatically over the past few days, as the girl unloaded her insecurities and sought her advice. She felt she couldn't let Norah down, mainly because it wasn't so long ago that she had been troubled by her own insecurity and had been grateful for Margaret's help, but it puzzled her why, when she was so fond of Margaret, Norah hadn't spoke of her unhappiness to *her*.

In the kitchen, Norah was preparing the meal while Donal and Frank argued amiably in the next room about the most effective way to skin a rabbit. Norah cringed. She hated violence and particularly against animals. She closed the door of the kitchen and concentrated on her work. The doorbell rang but she ignored it. Let that pair of rabbit worriers outside deal with it.

Seeing that Frank wasn't making a move, Donal rose reluctantly to answer it and stared at the man on the doorstep. 'Can I help you?'

'I understand that Katy Molloy lives here.'

Donal nodded. 'Come in. I'll tell her. She is in the bath at the moment.' He noticed the man's lips tighten and a deep frown crease his brow. 'I'll get her for you,' he repeated nervously. He raised his eyebrows at Frank as they entered the sitting room. 'A friend of Katy's,' he explained and Frank rose and shook the stranger's hand and offered him his seat.

Donal went out of the room and knocked on the bathroom door. 'Katy, there is a visitor for you,' he bellowed.

'I'll be as quick as I can.' Katy hurriedly climbed out of the bath. Terence was about half an hour too early – he was normally late.

Eddie had taken a seat and was regarding the young men with interest. He was the first to speak. 'I understand you all live together,' he said quietly.

Frank laughed and drew his large form up, resting his hands on his knees. 'Chance would be a fine thing. We three poor kitters live upstairs. We are only invited down for meals and for a bit of the old crack when the girls get fed up listening to each other.'

'Is that so?'

Donal said sourly, 'We are welcome enough when we have to do the chores.'

185

'Away on with you,' Frank scoffed. 'It is only fair. If the girls didn't cook for us then you would be the worse off. You like the old grubbo, my lad.'

Donal grinned. 'Look who's talkin'. You would eat the hind leg off a donkey.'

Norah came out of the kitchen as Dolan finished speaking. She stopped in surprise at the sight of Eddie. She had thought that it was Terence at the door.

'This is Katy's father,' Frank told her.

Norah gasped. 'How do you do? Would you excuse me? I'm cooking the meal – er – I'd better tell Katy to hurry.'

'I've told her she has a visitor,' Donal said.

Norah glared at him. 'I'll hurry her along all the same.'

She tapped on the bedroom door. Katy opened it. 'I'm coming,' she said crossly. 'I'm sure Terence said half-past seven. He can jolly well wait.'

Norah groaned. 'It isn't Terence, it's your *father* He is being entertained by Donal and Frank.'

'Oh my God!' Katy hastily pulled on her dress and drew a brush through her hair. She fumbled for her shoes. Her nerves were shot to pieces. What on earth was her da doing here?

She stopped in surprise as she entered the living room. Her father was laughing uproariously at something Donal had said. He looked up at her and rose, saying awkwardly, 'I needed to talk to you. The lads have been keeping me amused.'

'We can go into the bedroom.' Katy looked weakly at Norah.

'You'll join us for a bite to eat, won't you?' Norah smiled at Eddie.

Eddie held up his hand. 'Not for me. The lads and I are going for a jar as soon as they have eaten.'

Bemused by it all, Katy led the way out. She couldn't have been hearing right.

Eddie took her hand and held it tight. 'I know this is a shock for you, darlin', but I had to do it this way. Your mam gave me a terrible battering for all I said that day, and ever since I have been going over it all and I now know I was wrong. You were right. I brought you up to a certain standard and I should have trusted you. It was wrong of me . . .' He drew breath and continued. 'I like the lads. I can see that they are decent fellas. Can you forgive your old da?'

Katy's eyes misted. She knew only too well what it had cost her father to make such a statement, and indeed to be the one to come to her to make up the quarrel. She threw her arms round him. 'Oh, Da!'

'Enough of that!' Eddie said gruffly. 'Trust a woman to overdo things. You can come home now without worrying. Your mam has missed you.'

Katy gave him another hug. 'I can't tell you how glad I am that we have made up. I also said some things that I regretted. We really are quite respectable, Da.'

'I know, I know. I may not be the world's greatest brain-box, but I know a decent man when I see one and I can trust those two boyos next door with my daughter.'

Katy said curiously, 'Why didn't you give me a ring? We could have made an arrangement to meet.'

Eddie looked his daughter straight in the eye. There was no point in lying. 'I wanted to see what the set-up was. I know it was a devious move, but I needed to know you were safe.'

'I should be furious with you,' Katy sighed. 'However, it has been for the best if it has put your mind at rest.'

Eddie looked at his watch. 'I'm dyin' of thirst. Do you think that fifteen minutes is long enough for the pair of them to have finished their meal?'

Katy laughed. 'They'll have shovelled it down and be ready and waiting by now. What about yourself?'

'I had mine at six o'clock like I always do. Patrick is going to round things up for the night for me and I'm goin' to enjoy a rare evening out. Now! If you're done castigating me I'll be off with the lads. You can have your meal in peace.'

Katy refrained from telling her father that she was dining out with a young man. No sense in ruining a lovely visit. She didn't think, somehow, that her father would look on the racy sophistication of Terence with the same equanimity as he had on the pair of scallions in the other room. She ushered him out. She had ten minutes left in which to see him on his way before Terence arrived.

Frank and Donal stood up when they entered the sitting room. 'Don't you two lead my father astray,' she cautioned. 'He is not used to city ways.'

'Thank the Lord for that,' said Donal. 'We can fleece him and he won't know what has hit him.'

Eddie chuckled, enjoying their company which reminded him of sparring with his beloved Vincey. 'I'm too long in the tooth for that to happen. It's more than likely you two will come home the poorer.'

Terence arrived within minutes of their departure, and Katy, relieved that things had worked out in more ways than one, greeted him with more warmth than usual.

Terence grinned. 'Does this mean I can look forward to a successful evening?'

'If you mean a good film followed by good food,' Katy said mischievously, 'then yes – I think so.'

CHAPTER 11

It was Frank's idea to have a holiday. They were lolling about in the Botanic Gardens next to the university at the time, eating a picnic lunch and discussing Katy's suggestion that now she was a fixture in the house, she should start paying rent.

Margaret spoke for all of them. 'We still have a month to go before the refrigerator is paid for. Don't forget, you would only take a pittance from all of us.'

'The bookshop is doing well and I am earning a good salary. I think I should pay my way – and then there is the telephone. I should contribute to that.'

'That is already fixed,' Donal reassured her. 'How do you think a gaggle of students could afford to have one? Most other households could never dream of having a telephone. Frank's father had it installed for us, for his mother's sake. She wanted to be able to keep in touch with her boy. And anyway, you do pay for your calls. Also, you tip in for other expenses.'

'If she wants to start a month early then she can,' Frank granted. 'I'm all for easing the burden.' He winked at Katy. 'You're on, love.' He stretched his tall form along the grass and leaning on one elbow, continued, 'What does everyone think about the idea of going over to England for a holiday?'

They all stopped eating and stared at him – 'as though he had commited a mortal sin,' Margaret said later.

It was Donal who spoke first. 'Are you mad or what? We can't all go over to England. The girls' reputation would never stand the strain.'

'Sure, who will know? It would be more fun to have some female company. Men on their own tend to drink too much, and having the girls with us would keep us from getting into trouble. Those English girls are quite bonnie . . .'

'Jaysus, Frank, sure you have no need to worry. They wouldn't bid you the time of day, you big cahoun. Look at the size of you. You look like a bare-chested wrestler,' Donal chuckled.

'That's not true,' protested Margaret. 'He's just a big teddy bear.'

'Thanks, Margaret,' Frank said with dignity, and tensed his muscles. 'These are the arms of a dedicated rugby player, Donal m'lad – one look at me and no one will try anything on. And as for you, I haven't seen you with your girl on your arm for a while, whereas I have two trying to beat a path to my heart. Big is beautiful, my brave boy! For all your command of language you don't know how to sweettalk a girl, that's your problem.'

Katy said thoughtfully, 'It would be a bit of a gas. As Frank says, sure, where would the harm be in us all going?'

Donal sighed. 'I can't go. I promised m'da I would give a hand in the factory for a couple of weeks. We're behind with the orders.'

'Ach away! He'd let you off for a week, surely.'

'I also need the money,' he admitted.

'Your loss then.' Frank looked around. 'What about it then?'

'I'm willin',' said Katy, 'if Margaret and Norah come.'

Norah blushed with pleasure. 'I can come as well? I mean, that will be an extra female. You might want . . .'

'We aren't going as couples, Norah,' said Margaret. 'Have you not been listening?'

'I – I didn't quite mean that. It's just that I don't always join in with what you get up to and I just assumed you would not have considered me.'

'You're more human now,' said Mickey. 'A few weeks ago you were goin' on like you were our mother but lately . . .'

'Shut up, Mickey,' interrupted Frank. 'It's settled then. We are all going – except the poet here.' He clapped Donal on the shoulder. 'Unless you change your mind.'

But Donal ruefully declined the invitation. 'I can't afford it.'

'That's a point,' said Frank 'How are we all off for money?' He had assumed charge since the trip had been his suggestion.

It was agreed that it had to be done on the cheap. It would be rucksacks with minimal apparel because they would be doing more walking than travelling by bus or train once they got there, so suitcases would be cumbersome. They must only take one pair of decent shoes for social occasions and a sturdy pair for walking. The same went for clothes.

'You girls can't bring a load of dresses and undergarments,' Frank warned.

Margaret put her hands to her head. 'God!' she cried. 'You mean I can't bring an evening dress?'

'Very funny,' Frank said, and continued, 'we can go cheaply on the ferry if you are all prepared to sleep on deck. I've done this before – and by the way, I have a few contacts over in Sussex to take care of our social life in the evenings.'

'Where exactly are we going?' Margaret enquired.

'We shall make our way to Brighton. The train for London will be at the docks at Heysham, and then we'll travel by tube to Victoria to pick up the train for the trip down to the Sussex coast. You'll love it down there. It has everything. Seaside . . . the Downs . . . the Brighton Pavilion . . . and it's only an hour by train back to London should we want to pay a visit.'

'What about accommodation?' Margaret ventured.

'That's no problem. There are lots of cheap boarding houses in Brighton. I tell you, we will have a ball there. It's such a lively town. In the evenings we can meet up with my friends for a bit of fun . . .'

'How come you know people down there anyway?' asked Mickey curiously.

'Two friends who were at school with me went over there to Sussex, to study at art school – but I opted for Queens. We keep in touch after a fashion and I've already been over once and spent many a sozzled hour at a social club they use in and out of term-time. It's a good laugh and the drink is subsidised so it's cheaper than the usual pubs.'

Katy was secretly thrilled that they were going to Brighton. Sylvia had mentioned just recently that Charles was attending a big architects' exhibition there, and their holiday would coincide with it. She made her plans. She informed her parents that she

191

wouldn't be home for a couple of weeks at the end of June, and she phoned Terence to explain where she was going and with whom. When she arrived for work she spoke to John Reilly, who listened carefully, noting her discomfiture as she explained that she would like a week off to go on holiday.

'Is there something you aren't telling me?' he asked.

Katy reddened. 'I'm going with some friends – that's all.'

John calmly removed the pipe from his mouth. 'Anywhere exciting?'

'England.'

'With Margaret?'

'Yes.'

'And the others?'

'Yes,' Katy said. 'And why not?'

'No reason why you shouldn't.' John leaned back.

'I didn't actually mention that the lads were coming when I told my parents.'

'You think they would object?'

'I don't think so,' Katy said thoughtfully. 'My father came to terms with the fact that we are all living in the same house. It's just . . . well, going on holiday isn't quite the same, is it?'

When he had gone, Katy sat deep in thought and that evening she phoned her mother and explained the situation.

There was a pause before Annie answered. 'You're going with the lads?'

'Actually, Mam, the lads are taking us – it was Frank's idea. He has been over there a few times to visit some friends at art school. He asked us if we'd like to go with him this time and we thought it would be a good idea. Donal can't come, though. He has to do some work for his father as he's short of cash. Of course, if you think I shouldn't go, then I won't. I will understand your reasoning. I would respect it.' Katy became aware that she was gabbling and stopped.

'You weren't going to tell us, were you?'

Katy sighed. 'I was afraid you might put the block on it and I do want to go so badly, Mam.'

'Katy, if your father can live with the idea that you are sharing a house with the lads then I doubt that he would see a holiday

192

together as being any different. He thought they were a fine bunch. Both of us would have been more concerned at your deviousness if we discovered that you had kept us in the dark.'

'I'm sorry, Mam.'

Annie relented. 'Perhaps another time you will have as much faith in our judgement as we have in your ability to behave decently.'

Katy's heart lightened. 'Oh Mam, thank you! I am so looking forward to this holiday.'

Katy informed the others that she had been given the green light, and two weeks later with great excitement, they boarded the ferry and found a corner of the deck to sleep on. Not even the cold dampened their mood. Apart from Frank, it was their first visit to England, and when he arrived with hot tea and some buns from the tiny cafeteria, they drank and ate heartily and then using their knapsacks as pillows they settled down to try and get some sleep.

The journey was not without mishap. Norah was seasick and Frank mislaid his knapsack, but in spite of it their sense of adventure was undiminished – even when they arrived at Heysham to find the place enveloped in thick fog with the quayside treacherously slippy.

Once on the train, Katy folded herself into the seat and closed her eyes. The others did likewise, and when the train whistle blew for the 'off' she was so tired that the shriek of the whistle and the pungent smell of soot from the boiler and the hiss of steam as they gathered speed was only momentarily intrusive.

By the time they arrived at Euston, the sleep they'd managed to get on the train had helped, and excitement mounted again as they stepped onto the platform and got caught up in the bustle of the busy mainline station. Frank took charge and like sheep they followed obediently as he led them to the nearest subway.

Katy was nervous as they travelled down the escalator into the bowels of the earth. She had known about the subway system in London but the reality of it was a bit frightening to someone who couldn't look down a deep hole without feeling dizzy. She stole a glance at the others and Norah's gaze caught hers. She smiled faintly. She wasn't alone in thinking there were other ways she would prefer to travel.

To her intense relief they reached Victoria station quite quickly. 'That was a bit like riding a bullet,' she remarked. Norah and Margaret said nothing but Mickey smirked at them.

'I could see your faces,' he said. 'The three of you were wondering if your hour had come, weren't you?'

Margaret grabbed him by the arm. 'Shut up, Mickey,' she said grimly.

They were lucky in that they found accommodation to meet their needs at the third attempt. The guest-house, situated off the main road that sloped all the way down from the station to the sea was run by a Mrs Compton. After she had grilled them as to why they were holidaying in a group and why they had chosen Brighton, she showed them to their rooms with the admonition that she would put up with no hanky-panky. 'However,' she added, 'you look a decent lot and as you are from Ireland and we all know that everyone over there is very religious and under the influence of the church and the Virgin Mary, I'll put the girls in one room and you big chaps in another.'

'God? What books has *she* been reading?' Frank laughed, when Mrs Compton had gone. He had poked his head into their room to see what it was like.

Margaret told him to get out. 'If the dragon lady sees you here we'll be out on our ear before we have had time to unpack.'

'There isn't a lot of room in here,' Mickey remarked as he joined Frank.

Margaret crossed to the door. 'That's because there are three of us sharing – count yourselves lucky there is only two of you. Now will the pair of you get out of here! We'd like to unpack.'

Later, lying on their towels on the pebbly beach basking under a hot sun, plans were made to cover the next few days. Frank, knowing the area, had drawn up a timetable to take in walking on the Downs, paying a visit to the Regent's Palace, taking a bus to Lewes and other villages of interest, and in the evenings they would meet up with his friends for a drink or two.

'We'll want a stroll round the town,' said Margaret.

Frank's mouth dropped in horror. 'I'll go round the Lanes with you – they are worth it for the antiquity of them – but I'm not trailing round shops. Mickey and I will wait for you in Willy's Bar.'

'Wherever that might be,' said Margaret with a touch of sarcasm. She often thought Frank was too fond of the drink.

He laughed. 'It's on the corner before the entrance to the Lanes at the seafront end. You can't miss it.'

Katy and Margaret strolled down the wide and busy main road overlooking the promenade. The whole place was festooned with fairy lights from the pavement on one side of the road across to the other. Margaret remarked that if nothing else, she was going to make this walk again by night to see them in all their glory. Katy was more interested in the many hotels that lined the road. She wondered which one was hosting the event that Charles was attending. With a tiny jolt of shock, she remembered Pamela Goodman saying that she owned a weekend property in nearby Hove. Katy gave a shudder. Now that was *one* person she had no wish to see ever again . . .

As they passed the Grand Hotel, Margaret paused to look. 'Now there is the place to spend a week,' she said, in awe.

Katy giggled. 'There wouldn't be a Mrs Compton there. Just think! We would be so anonymous we could be with Jack the Ripper and nobody would take a blind bit of notice.' They sat on the wall outside for some time, watching the top-hatted doorman arrange for luggage to be brought in from the cars and taxis that dropped off the elegant guests, and then they made their way to the Lanes.

Katy and Margaret were enchanted by the higgledy-piggledy narrow alleyways that constituted the Lanes, with their many antique shops and tiny cafés. They stopped outside one, tempted to go in but Margaret said they'd better not as the lads would be waiting for them. She looked at her watch. 'In fact, we only have fifteen minutes left to reach the pub.'

Katy said, with a sigh of regret, 'We must come back another time. There is still so much to see.'

Next day, Katy was gazing up at a cloudless blue sky when she announced that she thought the holiday was proving to be a success. Margaret agreed with her, but Norah said she felt she should be doing some work to prepare herself for next term.

'Relax, Norah, for God's sake. It's only one week out of the year. You'll manage to catch up. With your brains what have you to worry about?' Margaret scoffed.

The day was a scorcher and they were lying on the dry tufty grass halfway between Lewes and Ditchling Beacon on the top of the Sussex Downs, in the partial shade of a large thorn bush. They were waiting for Frank and Mickey who had lagged behind to watch a farmer and his dog catching rabbits in a nearby field. 'You are coming with us when we go to meet Frank's friends at the social club, aren't you?' Margaret asked Norah.

Norah groaned. 'I hate going into bars, Margaret. Must I?'

'Yes, even if I have to drag you. We never get such chances in Ireland. The only time we get to go to a bar is if we have a big do on, so I'm going to make the most of the opportunity – and so are you. Besides, I'm sure they'll do lemonade as well.'

'I'd be mortified to ask for a lemonade when you are all drinking the hard stuff.' Norah was aghast at the idea.

Margaret sighed in frustration. 'When we put in our orders sure, no one will know who is having what. Now give over and enjoy yourself.'

That evening, as they sat with Frank's friends at a pub near. 'The Level' in Brighton, they were joined by others, and Katy and Margaret were so busy glowing with delight at the attention they were receiving that they didn't notice what Norah was getting up to. Norah, in her usual way, had quietly acknowledged all the greetings and then retreated from the general conversation. She had taken a corner seat and was partially hidden behind a large post.

It was Mickey who first realised that she was deep in conversation with a bespectacled youth who was gazing at her earnestly while she was rattling away there. He nudged Margaret. 'Look at herself over there,' he whispered. 'She hasn't stopped the mouth goin' for the past fifteen minutes by my watch.'

Margaret in turn nudged Katy. 'Look at Norah,' she mouthed. 'She hasn't drawn breath, according to Mickey.'

Katy giggled. 'They're a perfect match. The boy looks as serious and dedicated as she is.'

When they were all saying goodbye, having arranged a further meeting, it was noticed that Norah and her new friend were still absorbed in their discussion. Mickey called out to her. 'Norah! We are all off now. Are you staying or what?'

Norah started and looked embarrassed. She hurriedly said goodbye to her new friend and joined the group. 'You didn't have to make a remark of that nature, Mickey Flynn. Have you no sensitivity? I was only being polite.'

'What's your boyfriend's name?' Mickey continued to tease, and laughed when Norah spat out: 'His name is William, he is from Cornwall, he is studying maths like myself, but at London University. He has two sisters and he is working part-time in a newsagents shop in London to earn some money before the new term starts and to pay for this break – *satisfied*?'

'Jaysus, I don't want his history and his pedigree. I was only codding you.'

Margaret hissed at him, 'You have as much finesse as a bull in a field full of cows. I wonder what I see in you. Leave her alone and get along there.' She grabbed him by the elbow and gave him a push.

Norah, now in an even quieter mood than usual, walked by Katy's side on the way back to the boarding house. Her feet were red raw from all the walking earlier in the day.

Next morning when they had made their plans for the day, she took Katy aside. 'Katy, William has asked me if I would like to go and visit a few places with him. I wonder . . . could you sort of make my excuses?'

Katy smiled. 'Of course I will, but why not just say so yourself?'

'Mickey will only start with the teasing. I can't stand that.'

Katy nodded. 'Away you go. I'll tell them and by the time we meet at the end of the day, he will have got used to the idea.'

It was virtually the last they saw of Norah. Each day she was off as soon as they had breakfasted, while they made their own plans. Margaret dared the two men to make any attempt to tease her. Katy was listening half-heartedly to the exchange that morning, her own thoughts turning to Charles, wondering where was he at this moment and what was he doing? And later that day, as she lay on the beach under the hot sun, she wondered dreamily if at some time during his busy schedule, he ever gave a thought to one Katy Molloy.

Next day she had her answer. She and Margaret had elected to spend the day on the beach again as it was gloriously sunny and the sea temptingly cool. The lads had gone walking on the Downs and Norah was with her boyfriend.

By teatime, when they'd had enough, Margaret suggested that they make their way to the Lanes once more and take tea at a little tea room they'd spotted. They made their way up to the main road, and just as they were about to cross it, Margaret cried: 'Blast! I've left my cardigan behind. Wait here for me.'

Katy sat down to wait on the low, broad wall that ran along the road above the promenade, swinging her foot to and fro as she glanced idly towards the imposing entrance of the Grand Hotel, opposite. Suddenly her heart leaped as she realised that the man coming down the steps towards a waiting taxi was Charles. She stood up and began to wave excitedly. Charles did not notice, as he was busy handing his case to the driver. She made an attempt to cross the road but the traffic was heavy. Soon it would be too late. She hopped about in frustration.

At last there was a break. Keeping her eyes on the taxi, she stepped off the pavement and then froze at the sight of another tall, elegant figure coming down the steps with an overnight bag in one hand and a light jacket over the other. Her heart chilled as she watched Charles bound up the steps to take the bag from Helen's hand and within seconds they were in the taxi and on their way.

She started back to safety as horns blasted at her, and as she reached the wall again, Margaret joined her, remarking, 'You look as though you've seen a ghost.'

She turned. 'No! no. I definitely did not see a ghost,' and tried to make her voice sound less leaden than her heart.

On the eve of their departure, Katy and Margaret declined the invitation to go out to the pub. 'You two will be swilling all evening. You will be no company for us,' Margaret told Frank and Mickey sternly. 'Katy and I have arranged to see a film and go for a super meal afterwards.'

'That should be exciting,' Frank remarked, and winked at Mickey. He had noticed that Katy had gone very flat since yesterday.

'Let's see what happens tomorrow, me laddoes. *We* won't be the ones travelling with a fierce hangover,' Margaret retorted.

Later, as the girls strolled back to Mrs Compton's, they linked arms. The film had been mediocre but the meal superb, and it had helped in a small way to lighten Katy's mood. It was a warm balmy evening, and as they walked, dodging the crowds on the pavement who were admiring the coloured lights strung along the seafront, Katy sighed. There was a cosmopolitan air about Brighton; an air of suspense and excitement. Buildings were lit up and the noisier pubs blared forth music. Small cafés left their doors welcomingly open and some had placed chairs and tables just outside. The lights on the Palace Pier made it look as though a cruise ship had docked. A lot of the war damage inflicted on the town had been repaired, and what defence mechanisms had been set up on the beaches, removed. It was a perfect night for a stroll.

By the time they reached the boarding house, they were pleasantly tired. Margaret begged to have her bath first. Katy said she didn't mind, although it meant she had to wait till the water heated again. Later, when Margaret returned she continued to lie on her bed and read, until she judged it was hot enough. The hour was now late and Margaret had sleepily laid her own book down and snuggled against her pillow, so Katy gathered up her nightdress and sponge bag and made her way to the bathroom.

She felt her body respond to the warmth of the soft water, and for a long time she lay there, allowing her thoughts to stray to pleasant things. Determined to blot out the picture of Charles and Helen, she concentrated her mind on the holiday and the fun they'd all had . . . the walks up on the fabulous Downs overlooking the beautiful countryside, the nights out, the beach and the shops and the café in the Lanes. She lifted her watch and glanced at it. It was after midnight. Time to get out.

She felt deliciously languorous as she stepped out, and she wiped the mirror with the edge of her towel in order to study herself. Her face was rosy from the steam and her hair clung damply round her face. She pulled it back and, wrapping her towel round her, she tucked it in and began to brush her teeth. She was rinsing her mouth when the door burst open. She turned, startled, to find Mickey standing in the doorway, staring vacantly at her with a foolish smile on his face.

'Hello Katy, you lovely g-girl,' he stuttered.

Katy held her towel close to her and spoke severely. 'Mickey, you're as drunk as a stoat. You had better get out of here.'

'I m-may be drunk but I can sh-sh shtill appreshiate a lovely woman like yourself. You were kind to me when Margaret rowed with me. If it hadn't been for – for – I musht give you a h-hug Katy, to sh-ay thank you.'

Alarmed, Katy stepped smartly to one side as he lurched towards her. She tried frantically to tuck the edge of the towel into the top, and desperately anxious that the others didn't hear him, she said in a fierce whisper: 'Will you whisht, Mickey. Margaret is only next door and she has ears like a rabbit. She won't be amused.'

Mickey, all sense gone, grabbed at her. 'T'hell with them all. You look delish – delish – great, Katy Molloy.'

Katy reached out her hand to stop him from falling into the now empty bath. Mickey grabbed her to steady himself and the towel became unwrapped and slid to the floor.

'You beautiful crayture!' Mickey yelled, in delight, as they struggled.

'Will you whisht, Mickey.' Katy pleaded again. 'Margaret will hear us.'

'Margaret already has.'

Katy whirled in alarm. Her friend was standing in the doorway, her face suffused with anger. Mickey, having relinquished all hope, sagged in a heap against the wall and regarded the two women owlishly.

'You don't think . . .' Katy began.

'I do!' Margaret broke in, with bitterness in her voice. 'I've noticed how friendly you and Mickey are.'

'Margaret!' Katy cried. 'I'm fond of Mickey but I would never—'

'You should have locked the door.' Margaret nodded towards the hapless heap that was Mickey. 'That eejut is a red-blooded man. He reacted to you and – and will you cover yourself up!' she suddenly hissed.

Horrified to find she was still naked, Katy hastily wrapped her nightdress round her and ran past Margaret. The room they shared was only a few yards along the corridor but it could just as well have been miles. She suddenly felt faint and had to lean against the bannisters. The awfulness of the scene swept over her and she felt tears smarting behind her lids.

She climbed into bed and huddled beneath the sheet, aware of the raised voices coming from the bathroom. She glanced at Norah who was snoring lightly beneath her bedclothes, and felt dismayed at the swiftness with which everything had fallen apart. She tried to block out the raised voices in the bathroom, and the sound of scuffling as Margaret hauled Mickey to bed. At last there was silence. She tensed as she heard Margaret return, and then lay awake for what seemed like hours, feeling thoroughly miserable.

Next day as they packed for the return journey, Katy stood by the window and looked out over the rooftops towards the sea. Behind her Margaret was stuffing clothes into her knapsack with jerky angry thrusts. They had been so close, now they were miles apart, divided by antagonism. She wanted to close the gap between them . . . to touch her and try to convince her of her innocence, but she didn't move. She felt suddenly angry herself that Margaret could so easily condemn her. Instead, she shrugged her rucksack onto her shoulders and waited.

Mickey and Frank walked into the room. 'Are we all packed and ready then?' asked Frank in a loud, jovial way.

Mickey groaned. 'Play the noise down, Frank.'

Katy moved from the window.

'It's been a great holiday, hasn't it?' Frank asked anxiously.

'I've never had a better one.' Katy smiled. None of this was Frank's fault, she thought. 'Where were you last night?' she asked.

'I stayed with a friend.' He turned to Mickey. 'You look bloody terrible,' he said candidly. 'I don't suppose you remember much about last evening.'

Katy tensed.

'Not a lot!' said Mickey with a rueful look towards Margaret.

'It will all come back eventually,' Frank grinned. 'Trust me. I am nearly a doctor.'

Margaret said nothing.

Norah beamed at everyone. 'It was the best holiday I have ever had.'

Charles placed the phone down thoughtfully. Katy's mother had just told him that Katy was on holiday in England with some friends. He lifted his briefcase from the table and made his way out. According to Annie Molloy, Katy was due back in a couple of days; she promised to ask Katy to give him a ring.

Helen was waiting for him by the car. He was giving her a lift home from the office in Belfast. She did possess her own car, but said she found it less nerve-wracking to use public transport during the rush hour. He frowned. Just lately the lifts had become more frequent. Surely the solution lay in moving nearer to the job?

She smiled as he approached and the smile was so enticing he was tempted to ring Sylvia and say he would be dining in Belfast this evening; however, it was but a transitory thought. He had too much work to do, so it was a glass of brandy and the use of Sylvia's study for him.

Living at Beresford House had become more interesting of late. Sylvia had taken up painting seriously again, and when she wasn't painting she was playing the perfect wife and mother. Elizabeth was ferried to school and back again with fervour, but Lizzie had confessed to him that she preferred to go with her new friend Bernadette, whose mother took them in a very interesting old car which popped and banged its way along the road with the exciting possibility that it might not reach its goal. To keep the children amused, Bernadette's mother insisted on them singing at the top of their voices and jumping up and down so as to, 'Let this crayture know we mean business and that it has to keep going.'

Elizabeth adored it all. She told Charles that when Mummy took her to school it wasn't nearly so much fun. The large car with the purring engine was so boring to ride in and her mother kept asking her if she was all right. She also mentioned that she still missed Katy very much. Sally was nice but she didn't know any good stories.

Tonight Sylvia looked serene. Charles glanced from her to Robert. Sometimes he was mildly embarrassed by the soppy looks they threw at each other; at the same time he suspected that he was envious of their newfound happiness. For his part, marriage had eluded him. There had been a couple of near-misses, but his nerve had gone at the crucial moment.

Sylvia spoke. 'Charles darling, Robert and I have something to tell you.' Her normally pale skin was pink. She reached out for Robert's hand and held it as she made her announcement. 'I'm going to have a baby.'

Charles smiled. 'Congratulations!'

'Of course we haven't told Elizabeth yet. We wanted to wait for the right moment.' She stood up. 'Which reminds me. I'd better go and have a peek at her.'

When she'd gone Robert said, 'The news came as a big surprise to me. I rather hoped we would have some time on our own before having children.'

Charles couldn't suppress his grin. 'You should have thought of that before you took action.'

'Blame nature and the way it takes its course,' retorted Robert, but he returned the smile.

When Sylvia came back Charles stood up. 'Do you mind if I use your study for a while? I have a lot of work to get through.' Sylvia nodded absently, her eyes already on Robert.

When he entered the study he set his papers out neatly and started to work on them. On the whole, things were going well. Now that the problem with Barney Fogarty had been settled, work had begun on the new runway and the few niggling problems that did occur were quickly resolved. Now the job was finished and his firm had managed it on time. There were still some refinements to add, but the runway itself was successfully completed and the engineers had tested it for strength and vibration level. Charles worked solidly for an hour and then with a tired sigh, stretched his arms above his head and flexed his shoulders. He leaned back in his chair, and at that moment Sylvia popped her head round the door to say that she and Robert were off to bed, and Robert wondered if Charles was going for a stroll because if not, he would lock up for the night.

'I'm off to bed myself,' Charles said. 'I think a soak in the bath would be my preference.' He gathered up his papers and put out the lamp and followed Sylvia from the room.

Katy phoned Charles at his office two days after she arrived back. She was intrigued by his request to contact her and felt nervous as she dialled his number. Helen answered.

'I'll find him for you, Katy,' she said. 'It might take some time, so hold on.'

Katy sincerely hoped not for long. Phone bills were kept to the minimum at her shared household. Then Charles' voice interrupted her thoughts.

'Katy! Hello! Have you had a good holiday?'

'Thank you, yes,' she said. 'Mam told me you wanted to talk to me?'

'Yes. We are having a lunch party to celebrate the opening of the extended runway. I wondered if you and your friend Terence would like to come?'

Katy hesitated. 'When?'

'Two weeks from today.'

'That's quite a good day, actually,' Katy said. 'We aren't so busy on Wednesdays, so thank you – I'll ask Terence.'

'Your mother told me you went to Brighton. That's quite a coincidence – I've just been to a conference there. We must have been in the town at the same time.'

'Really,' Katy said evenly. 'Where did you stay?'

'The Grand Hotel.'

'A tiny mite more luxurious than our boarding house. But we had a wonderful time.'

'It was mostly hard work with me,' Charles said ruefully.

Katy frowned. Not all work and no play, though.

Charles continued: 'Sylvia was wondering if you would be coming home this weekend? She says she hasn't seen you for a while.'

'I am going home. Tell her I'll give her a ring.' Katy felt pleased with her performance. Her voice had been friendly and cool. She lifted the phone off the hook again and rang Beresford House. She might as well sort the weekend out now.

Mrs Skelton answered. She was pleased to hear from Katy. 'I'll not waste your money chatting now, girl,' she said. 'I know you are to be invited up, so if you are goin' to accept the invitation then we'll have a talk when you get here. Come a bit early and we can have a word before I tell herself you have arrived.'

To Katy's amusement, Mrs Skelton had it all planned out. She was to come round to the side of the house and slip into the kitchen so they could have a bit of a crack, and then she would announce her as though she had just appeared. 'Otherwise we don't get to see you or hear what is happening in your life.'

'Quite a lot!' Katy laughed. 'I have just been on my first holiday in England and had a grand time.' Until the last night, she added silently.

'You can spill the beans when you get here. I'll away and tell herself you are waiting on the phone.'

Katy heard the phone hit the table and waited for Sylvia to lift it.

When she told John that she had been invited for lunch by the pool on Saturday, he was very good about it.

'Away on home, girl. I can manage here.'

'But I've just come back from a week's holiday,' Katy objected. 'I feel guilty about taking Saturday off.'

John grinned. 'Aha! Knowing that I have made you feel guilty will make me feel better about having to do all the work. I wonder how I ever managed before Katy Molloy set foot in my shop.'

Katy laughed. 'I'll say no more, and next week you are going to take yourself off somewhere nice to relax.'

'Sure, where would I want to go?'

'I don't care if you only walk upstairs to your sitting room – so long as you are not working down here.'

'You're on! Now away and get those book orders that you were talking about the other day or you're dismissed.'

Katy worked especially hard for the next few days so that John would have little more to do on Saturday than answer the bell and wrap up a purchase. Indeed, by the time she reached Beresford House on the appointed day she was feeling tired, but the sun was high in the sky and there was a haze over the countryside and she felt a lightness of spirit she hadn't experienced since they had all arrived back from England. Margaret, although managing to hide it from the others, was still polite and cold towards her.

Katy was amused to find when she arrived that things hadn't worked out as Mrs Skelton had planned. Sylvia, on her way to the poolside, had seen her open the large gate and had waited for her. 'Come straight down to the pool when you have changed into your costume,' she said.

Katy whipped in to let Mrs Skelton and Sally know that she had arrived and they would have to have their chat at the other end of the day as Sylvia had caught her as she came in.

'That's all right,' said Mrs Skelton. 'Anyway, Sally has taken Elizabeth over to her friend's house and they won't be back for a while so it works out better this way.'

Sylvia was alone at the pool. 'Charles and Robert have gone for a game of golf at the club and will be back soon,' she explained, omitting to mention that it had been her idea so that she could have a quiet word with Katy.

'Do you mind if I take a dip before we have our chat?' Katy pleaded.

'Of course not.' Sylvia had noted the pink face and the beads of perspiration.

Later, as they relaxed into their deck-chairs, Katy studied Sylvia. There was a certain glow about her. A smile was playing around her mouth. 'You look like the cat that stole the cream,' she remarked, and Sylvia's smile widened as she told Katy about the baby.

When the men arrived back for lunch, Robert went to help Mrs Skelton lift the trolley up to the poolside. Charles sat down beside Katy. 'It seems ages since I saw you,' he said. 'Tell me all about your holiday.'

Katy smiled lazily and lay back. 'Later, when we've had lunch.' She had made the decision that she wasn't going to ruin the friendship that existed between them because she had witnessed Charles and Helen coming out of the hotel together. She had no right to make judgements that might jeopardise their friendship. After all, it wasn't Charles' fault that she had been foolish enough to fall in love with him.

After lunch, while Robert and Sylvia dozed, Katy and Charles went for a stroll. Katy had slipped a dress over her swimsuit. Charles was wearing a towelling robe. They walked towards the little copse from which Pamela had taken the offending photograph. They were silent as they walked through, but as they emerged into the sunlight again, Charles spoke.

'I'm going to ten-thirty Mass tomorrow. Will I see you there?'

Katy stopped in amazement. 'I didn't know you were a churchgoer,' she said.

'Actually, I'm a lapsed Catholic. Being a fighter pilot during the war didn't leave much time for regular attendance at church. We had to make do with a blessing by whatever padre happened to be on duty at the time, and when we weren't in the air we were either drinking ourselves into a stupor or sleeping for days to catch up. One tends to become lax about religion after a time.'

'Surely your faith would have grown stronger under the circumstances. Didn't you pray when you were in danger?'

Charles grimaced. 'We didn't have time. One doesn't stop to pray when a Messerschmitt is coming straight at you or a colleague is bawling in your ear that one is creeping up behind, about to shoot the hell out of you. You just hope the Almighty is on your side and understands your dilemma.'

'I've often wondered why you decided to go into aviation design in view of the fact that you had such a hair-raising war,' Katy remarked.

'I found ordinary architecture too boring. I love planes. Being around them gives me a thrill.'

'Why do you not fly them commercially then?'

'Because flying transport planes would become just as boring as commercial architecture eventually. Besides, the working life of a pilot is limited. This way I get the best of both worlds.'

When they arrived back at the pool they found that Sylvia and Robert had returned to the house. They followed in companionable silence. This is the man I love, Katy thought tenderly. I know that it is not returned, for he loves someone else, but I am a stronger person now and I will cope. In real life one has to compromise. She made another important decision on the way back to Belfast that evening. She was going to set things straight with Margaret.

When Katy walked into their bedroom, Margaret began to do what Terence called a 'smart about turn' but Katy gripped her by the arm. 'We have some talking to do,' she said firmly. 'You don't leave this room, Margaret Kelly, until we sort things out.'

'We have nothing to say. My eyes didn't lie.'

'Yes, they did. Also, how is it that Mickey is forgiven and I get cold-shouldered?'

'Mickey is an affable eejut . . .'

'Mickey was drunk. He barged in on me – and before you say it – I know I should have locked the door, but it was late and I was tired. I would never do a thing to hurt you.' Katy cried. 'You are the one stable relationship I have. I value our friendship more than anything and I'm not goin' to see it destroyed because of a stupid misunderstanding. You are not leaving until I have given you the true picture of what happened that night.'

When Katy had finished explaining the situation, Margaret's face had lost its closed look but she remained silent. I've wasted my time – I'm gettin' nowhere, Katy thought, and was about to make another plea when Margaret, with an explosion of mirth said: 'God! Didn't he look like a right fool lying there with his eyes out of focus.'

Katy's eyes crinkled up and she laughed heartily. 'He was so drunk he would have found a toad desirable,' she giggled.

'He can't take the drink at all,' Margaret said, with sudden seriousness. 'I think on reflection that the others must have spiked his drinks, for I've never known Mickey to get in to that state since I've known him.' She looked at Katy and sighed. 'I lost my wits. Welcome back, Katy. I've hated being at odds with you, but I was so jealous when I saw you both . . .'

'Oh Margaret!'

Her friend looked sheepish. 'I know. I'm as daft as the boyo himself – but seeing you standing there naked as a plucked chicken, but looking lovely I—'

Katy groaned. 'God, let's forget it! My only consolation is that Mickey was so cut with the drink I have hopes he'll not remember a thing about it.'

Margaret rose. 'I'll make us both a cup of tea,' she murmured. There was no point in telling Katy that Mickey now remembered the whole episode. She had threatened him with annihilation if he so much as breathed a word.

CHAPTER 12

Katy and Margaret went shopping in Belfast for a dress for Katy to wear at the airport luncheon party. It was Margaret's idea. 'You've got to make an impression,' she said. 'There will be a lot of style there and you don't want them to think you are a country cousin, now do you?'

'Don't mind at all,' Katy said truthfully. 'I'd hate to play second fiddle to a dress. Besides, instead of me causing a sensation because I am wearing some creation I have bankrupted myself for, they might take one look at the dress, take a second look at me, and say, "God, what a waste!" '

'Ach, away on!' Margaret scoffed. 'I have every confidence in you.'

'Nevertheless, I shall dress well but discreetly.'

'As ever!' Margaret sighed. She was disappointed. She had been looking forward to transforming the virginal Katy into a femme fatale. Those boardroom toffos wouldn't give her a second glance; they were used to more sophistication in their women. Still, Terence had an air about him, and just being with him would give Katy some clout.

For the next hour they wandered round, trying on outfits and discarding them. Margaret remained patient. Katy's dithering, although driving her mad, was a small price to pay for the resumption of their friendship. They entered their third store, Robinson Cleaver's, one of the largest in Belfast and at last Katy saw two dresses with possibility. Margaret waited while she tried both on at least twice and was relieved when she settled for a pretty floral dress with short sleeves, the new mid-length flared skirt and a broad belt which showed off her tiny waist.

Katy, too, was pleased with the choice and she had just the right shoes to go with it. 'My first "New Look" dress. Have you any designs on my hairstyle?' she asked, noticing that Margaret was looking at it speculatively.

'There isn't much you can do with a bird's nest except leave it be,' Margaret said tartly. 'Come on! Let's go for some tea.'

When the waitress had dealt with their order, Margaret said, 'You mentioned some time ago that Terence Coleman has invited you to meet his parents. Is that still on?'

Katy nodded. 'This weekend, in fact. Why?'

Margaret shrugged. 'You haven't mentioned it lately – or him, for that matter.'

'Which is not surprising since you and I have not been on the best of terms since we came back from England. I've been out to dinner with him on two occasions just recently.' She frowned. 'I don't know why you all distrust him. He is a perfect gentleman when he is with me.'

'Maybe you have reformed him,' Margaret said. But secretly, she doubted it.

Terence called for Katy late on Friday afternoon and they set off with Margaret's admonition that he was to drive safely and not like the racing driver he thought he was.

The route out of the city was heavy with traffic as it was the rush-hour, and steering the low-slung sports car round trams and buses proved hazardous but Terence was a good driver. Nevertheless Katy was glad when they were on the open road and she could relax. His parents lived in a rented house about thirty-five miles from the city on the road to Donaghadee and he was familiar with the route. The sun was still hot but Terence had rolled the top down so there was a welcome breeze cruising round them which kept them cool. Katy was nervous at the prospect of meeting Terence's parents but she chided herself. Terence and she were very good friends, not lovers, and it was a normal friendly visit. The object of her thoughts was concentrating on his driving so she concentrated on settling her mind so that by the time they reached his parents' house she would feel less agitated.

The house sat in complete isolation by the side of the road, surrounded by a wall, into which was set a green-painted gate and a short path leading up to the front door. Katy waited while Terence put his key in the lock and pushed the door open and then followed him into the hall. There was a curious emptiness about the place. Not a sound . . . no feeling of warmth . . . and no one came forward to greet them. She glanced at Terence, who was fumbling at the telephone table. He turned to her, holding an envelope in his hand. Katy waited as he tore it open and withdrew the handwritten page, and scanned it while she stood there with her nervousness increasing by the second. Could Margaret and the others be right about Terence? Had he duped her?

He handed her the letter. 'Apparently my parents have had to leave suddenly. They couldn't contact me to let me know, but they say we are to make ourselves at home. They have left some wine and salad for supper, with fresh fruit for afters.'

'We can't . . .'

'I'm hungry even if you aren't,' Terence said coaxingly. 'We might as well eat and drink and enjoy the evening before we go back.' He ushered her into the sitting room.

Katy chewed her lip in thought. 'It does seem silly to turn back with empty stomachs – and feeling weary,' she admitted.

'Excellent!' Terence said. He pushed her gently onto the couch and went to fetch the food. When he returned, he set the tray on the table. 'The only thing missing is music,' he remarked, and rose to turn on the wireless sitting on a table in an alcove.

Katy ate the food with enjoyment. His mother had prepared an excellent ham and cold potato salad which was followed by fresh fruit salad and cream. She drank the wine slowly. She was still a relatively new convert to wine and it didn't take much to make her feel mildly tipsy. Terence, on the other hand, drank deeply and Katy found herself becoming a little uneasy.

'Don't forget we have to drive back,' she said. 'I couldn't drive a car to save my life so you need to stay relatively sober.' She laughed lightly in an effort to play down her concern.

Terence smiled. 'Don't worry. A cup of strong coffee is all it takes to set things right.' He rose. 'I'll make one and then perhaps you would like to take a walk round the place? There is quite a nice garden at the back.'

'Why don't we take the walk first, before it gets too dark. The sun is already well down.'

Terence shrugged. 'Fine by me.'

It was indeed a nice garden, although the lawn looked overdue for a cut and some of the flower beds were in need of attention. 'Do your parents look after the garden?' Katy asked.

Terence shrugged. 'I have no idea. It certainly looks as though it has been neglected.' He said hurriedly, 'My father has been very busy on the airport project – I expect things got behind. Let's walk to the end. See – there is a stile leading into a meadow with the proverbial babbling brook on the other side.'

By the time they arrived back at the house, darkness had begun to close in. Katy stole a quick glance at her watch and said tentatively, 'Shouldn't we be getting back?'

'We have time for another glass of wine, followed by coffee,' Terence coaxed. He did a little jump in the air and executed a pirouette and grinned at Katy disarmingly.

'Very well. But we really must think about getting back soon.'

'Into the living room with you,' Terence said firmly. 'I'll put the kettle on and bring in the wine.' He shooed her out of the door and stood for a moment in thought. If he played things right, the fair Katy would be sleeping here tonight. He opened the new bottle of wine and set it on the small tray with two glasses and then hesitated. He had never felt this nervous about seducing a woman before, but then it had been a long time since he'd been with a virgin – and he was totally convinced that Katy Molloy was one. He stooped and opened the cupboard and withdrew the precious bottle of Napoleon brandy that his father kept there for special occasions. This was one such occasion, he decided. He threw back his head and drank the tot of brandy in one gulp. His father would have had a fit. According to him, brandy was a drink to savour. What the hell! Terence poured another tot and this time drank more slowly. He felt the amber liquid do the trick. He was calm and relaxed now.

Katy looked up as he entered the room, smiling at her. She smiled back. There was something different about him, she thought. She felt ashamed of her suspicions, but her heart thumped wildly and she glanced at the bottle of wine on the tray. It was still full. Terence sat down beside her and handed her a glass. She began to sip and continued to observe him. He had a strange look in his eyes.

After a few minutes he rose. 'I think we'll have that coffee now.' He noticed that Katy had not drunk much of her wine. 'Drink up,' he admonished.

In the kitchen, Terence poured the coffee, hesitated, and then took the brandy out of the cupboard. Christ, he was nervous. What the hell was the matter with him? He was an expert in the art of seduction. What was so different about Katy Molloy? He hastily threw the brandy down his throat. That was better. He shook his head. He mustn't get too relaxed or the whole plan would be banjaxed. He entered the room and put the coffee down on the table before sitting down beside Katy and putting an arm round her shoulder. He gave it a squeeze.

Katy, surprised, wasn't sure what to do. Terence had kissed her lightly and had put his arms round her many times, but there was a proprietorial feel about the action this time. She inched away. He gripped her shoulder more tightly. There was no gentleness in the action and a feeling of alarm gripped her as she smelled the alcohol fumes on his breath. 'Terence! What are you doing?'

'I'm trying to make love to you,' he said bluntly, all pretence gone.

Katy stiffened in his grasp. 'Terence, we are very good friends – please don't spoil things. I'm not ready for this.'

'Poppycock!' His voice had hardened. 'You have got it wrong.' Blast it, his words were slightly slurred – that last brandy was one too far; he mustn't ruin it now. He steadied his breathing. 'It's time we got to know eesh other better,' he said, and lowering his voice seductively, he added, 'We could make love.'

Katy gasped. 'I have no intention . . .' She pushed him away with sudden strength. 'My God! You had this all planned. Your parents were never going to be here. That note – it was planted there by you!'

Terence moved back to take her in his arms again. 'This could be your greatest . . . oh, stop struggling, Katy . . . be glad you are going to be initiated into the joys of love by an expert.'

So – it was all out in the open now. All those meals, the visits to the pictures, the Opera . . . they all had to be paid for now. She shuddered. 'Terence, you wouldn't . . .'

He gave a loud guffaw. 'Three brandies and half a bottle of wine says otherwise.'

'Three brandies?' Katy was horrified.

Terence leered. 'I needed Dutch courage. It's been a long time since I seduced a virgin – and you are one, are you not, Katy Molloy?'

He tried to force his mouth on hers and the smell of his brandy-laden breath washed over her. Katy pushed her head back against the cushion and looked beseechingly at him. 'Terence, don't do anything to destroy what there is between us,' she pleaded.

'Katy Molloy. I want you. Shimple ash that.'

'But you are going about this the wrong way!' Katy tried to force his weight off her arm. 'Please listen to me. You will be so angry with yourself.'

Terence tipped more wine into his glass. 'This is the big seduction scene, Katy Molloy. Why is that name so familiar? It has been worrying me for some time. I think I knew a Molloy once . . .' He sat up suddenly and his eyes narrowed. 'Just sit quietly and listen while I tell you why I am so sure of it.'

'You're drunk, Terence . . . Please . . . I know it's the wine doing this. I have never known you be other than a gentleman.'

He took his hands away. His lips curled. 'You have a brother called Vincey, haven't you.' It was more a statement than a question.

'Yes.' Katy's heart began to beat faster. Now what? Would this nightmare never end! 'How do you know my—'

'Listen and I'll tell you.' The shock of his remembering caused his mind to clear.

Katy shrank back against the cushion, her eyes dilated in fear. His tone had altered. Suddenly he seemed more alert. She feared him more now than before.

'I could cause you and your family acute embarrassment and ruin their lives for ever,' Terence said slowly. 'You see, your precious brother was not the hero you all thought he was. I was in the same action as a medical orderly, and I saw what happened. I saw your cowardly brother leave his best friend to die a horrible death.'

'No-o-o . . .' Katy moaned.

'To save his own skin,' Terence continued. 'A shell burst nearby as they were making their advance and when his friend fell, with his leg shattered by the blast, he screamed for Vincey to save him, but your precious brother took one look back and then hightailed it to sh-afety . . .' Terence felt himself sliding back again. Hastily, he swigged some coffee before continuing. 'The young lad died before we could get him to the field hospital. Now, I wonder how your parents would feel if they knew about *that* little episode?'

Katy, ashen-faced, tried to speak. 'I – I don't believe it,' she whispered, her voice raw with despair.

'It's the truth.' Terence looked at her with disgust. 'I know I have a reputation with women, but I would – would –' he hiccuped 'would never do a thing l-l-like that to a pal. I intend to tell your mother how her precious boy let his friend die. Don't worry – I w-wouldn't touch you now. The man who died was also my friend.' Terence rose from the sofa and staggered upstairs towards the bedrooms.

Katy stared numbly into space. Terence was drunk. He couldn't really have meant what he said. Oh gracious God, how was she ever going to get home?

Rising from the sofa she tiptoed up the stairs towards the bedrooms and listened. The rhythmic sound of snoring was coming from one room. She opened, the door quietly. There was Terence lying across the bed, dead to the world. Oh God! Why had she never learned to drive! It would be so easy to sneak his keys. She might have had a problem finding her way back, but anything was better than spending the night here. She looked at her watch. It was ten minutes to midnight.

There was only one more hope. The telephone. She might be able to get a taxi. She groaned – at this hour? But it was worth a try.

She found the local Donaghadee telephone book and frantically looked up the services. In her haste she dropped it twice and swore under her breath. At last she found a number and dialled. It rang and rang till she thought she'd scream. At last a voice spoke.

'Please! I'm in a bit of a pickle,' she babbled. 'I need to get back to Belfast in a hurry. Could you help me?'

'It's midnight, miss.'

Katy's voice became more urgent. She tried not to, but a sob broke through. 'Oh God, please. I've got to get home. I'm in trouble, *please*.'

'Where are you?'

Katy blanched. She had no idea. 'I'm in a large house about a mile past a factory.'

'That's the old Kelvin Hall ballroom on the main road to Donaghadee. It isn't a factory. Can you tell me the name of the house, young lady?'

'No!' Katy wailed. 'I could walk towards the fact – er – Kelvin Hall . . .'

'No,' the voice said, 'I remember now. If you didn't pass any other houses until the one you are phoning from, once you went past the Kelvin Hall, then I know where you are. I'll pick you up in ten minutes' time.'

Once outside, Katy strode up and down, keeping in the shadows where possible, and glancing anxiously, first towards the house and then down the road. When the taxi arrived the driver, a small, balding man, came over to her and, seeing her agitation, took her arm.

'Are you all right, miss,' he asked.

Katy nodded. 'I am now. I was shocked and I panicked.'

Bob Kelly doubted, it was as simple as that, but it was not his business and the girl seemed to be calmer now. He led her to the car.

The journey back was fraught with worry. She had to get to her mother before Terence did. At least she could break the news gently, maybe soften the incident in the telling. Katy had felt heartbroken herself at the revelation – even though she could swear Terence had made it up to spite her. God knows how her poor mother would react.

When she arrived back at the shared house, Katy tiptoed

noiselessly past a soundly sleeping Margaret and sank gratefully into her own bed. In the morning she would make her way home to Ballynashee. What a nightmarish evening – and what a lucky escape she had had.

Annie was in the kitchen preparing the hen feed as Katy walked in. She looked up in surprise but hugged her daughter warmly and offered her the usual mug of strong tea. 'Why didn't you tell me you were coming?' she asked.

'I have something important to discuss with you,' Katy said. 'Could you leave the hens a bit longer?' She drew her mother into the sitting room.

Annie listened in silence as her daughter related the cruel story she had been told. She watched the pain flitting across the young girl's face as she spoke of the dreadful evening she'd had with Terence and when she had finished, Annie put her arms round her. It had taken a lot of courage for Katy to relate her tale, and Annie knew the sorrow her child must be feeling at having to hurt her by its content.

'I knew all this.' She gently stroked the dark hair.

'How? Did Vincey . . .'

'Do you remember the nightmares that Vincey had when he came back from the war? The weeping . . . the walking around in the dark?'

Katy nodded. She had comforted Vincey herself once.

'I went in to look after him during a particularly bad one,' Annie explained. 'That night he told me the story of when they stormed the beach. He felt so riddled with guilt and remorse because he couldn't save his friend that his mind wouldn't let go. His nightmares were always about that dreadful day. The poor lad's right leg had been blown off and he was bleeding to death rapidly. Vincey stopped to help, but realising there was nothing he could do, he carried on running.' Annie paused. 'If Vincey had gone back, there would have been two dead lads on that beach instead of one. Thank God I was able to make him understand that he had nothing to feel guilty about.' Her eyes grew sad. 'It was the last comfort I ever gave him. He was dead six months later.' She dashed away a tear and rose.

'Are you not supposed to be at work today?' she asked and made her voice sound brisk.

Everything is back to normal. Katy thought, and felt proud – proud that she hadn't let Terence Coleman get the better of her. She'd ring John and explain that she'd had to rush home on family business and would be in later.

When she got back, Katy held a meeting in the house. The luncheon was in a few days' time, and now that she had sent Terence packing she was without a partner. The prospect of attending on her own held little appeal. She must find a substitute.

She explained to the others that for personal reasons Terence and she would not be seeing each other again, but that she was now in a spot because she had no one to partner her to the do at the airport.

'I said it wouldn't last – didn't I say that? I knew you were too sensible to be taken in by that slimy toad.'

Margaret butted in. 'Shut up, Mickey. It isn't any of your business. What we need now is a volunteer to attend the luncheon with Katy. If you can't help, then away and make us all some tea.'

Donal said he was sorry, but he had to work. His father was away on business and they were short-handed at the shop because two of the staff had had to go with him.

'That leaves you, Frank.'

Donal laughed. 'Ye can't take m'laddo. He hasn't a suit to his name. The only rigout he possesses is holey at the elbows.' Margaret glared at him.

Frank, who had listened to them all, placed his textbook on the table and leaned forward. 'I'm your man, Katy. I'll borrow my da's best Sunday-go-to-meeting togs. He is the same size. The wrists might be a bit high but sure, who will notice.' He looked pityingly towards Donal. 'You'd be better with me in a set of rags, anyway, than with a fella who can't spell his name backwards.'

Donal grinned good-naturedly. 'Well said, man. Inaccurate – but well said.'

220

Katy had insisted on working as usual at the bookshop. When Frank arrived in a borrowed car to pick her up, she told John Reilly that she would come back afterwards to finish the day. 'So but me no buts,' she said sternly.

John shrugged and turned his gaze to heaven. 'It's like talking to a brick wall,' he told Frank. He had never seen the student look so grand – taking into account the fact that he was dressed for a walk in the countryside rather than for a luncheon.

'Try livin' with three of them,' Frank sniggered.

Katy pulled Frank away. 'Never mind the sarcasm. We had better get going.'

She was grateful to the big fella for baling her out but she was nervous. She hoped he wouldn't tip the wine glass up too frequently.

When they entered the large room where the luncheon was being held there was no sign of Charles but Helen, having observed their arrival, came over to greet them. She led them to the drinks table and the buffet. 'Do help yourselves,' she said. 'I'll pour you both a drink.'

'Red wine for me,' Frank requested. He turned to Katy and raised his eyebrows.

'Oh – er – white, I think,' she said.

'Sweet, medium or dry?' asked Helen.

'Er – medium, please.'

While Frank was filling his plate, someone spoke to him and Katy watched in fascination as the two men walked along, balancing the plates and laughing, easy in each other's company. Helen returned with the wine. 'He isn't shy, is he?' she gestured at Frank. Then: 'I thought Terence was coming with you?'

'I had to change the arrangements,' Katy said quickly. Fortunately at that moment Helen was called away when a man in a pinstriped suit signalled to her. Katy filled her plate and joined Frank by the window where they chatted amiably and idly scanned the room to see what was going on around them. Eventually, Frank put his empty plate on the small table by his side and said, 'Well, I think it's time to start circulating.'

Katy gazed at him in horror. 'Do we have to? Can't we just stay here and observe?'

221

'Not at all. It's the done thing to circulate at parties,' Frank said airily. 'There isn't anything to it.'

'You go on. I'll stay and finish my drink and get further acclimatised.' Katy was feeling nervous.

'Join me later. By that time I'll have got into the swing,' he promised.

Katy watched Frank join a group which opened out to receive him. Within seconds everyone was nodding in turn as introductions were made. She smiled in amusement tinged with surprise at the ease with which the big man had integrated. If only Donal and Mickey could see him now. Frank looked sartorially at odds with the others, certainly, with his wrists dangling beneath his cuffs, but they were laughing uproariously – probably at one of his jokes – and they obviously didn't give a toss for his odd attire. Katy had been so deep in thought she hadn't realised that Charles had joined her.

'Glad you could make it. Sorry I wasn't here to greet you,' he said coolly, just as Frank arrived.

'I'm afraid your assistant has injured herself,' Frank informed Charles. 'Helen was picking up some broken glass and she cut her hand. It's quite a deep cut.'

Charles frowned. 'I'd better go to her.'

'I think she will need stiches. Look, if you like I could run her along to Casualty so that you can carry on here.'

Katy broke in: 'Frank is a medical student. Helen would be in safe hands.' She said to Frank, 'Don't worry about me. I'll make my own way back to the bookshop.'

'I'll see that Katy gets there,' Charles said. 'You're sure Helen is all right?'

'Just feeling a bit faint,' Frank assured him.

'I can take a taxi,' Katy insisted. She had begun to realise with some surprise that Charles' manner was rather cool.

'Certainly not! In any case, people are beginning to drift away.' Charles had summed up the situation.

A small group of businessmen joined them to shake hands and express their gratitude. 'Good luncheon, man,' said the tallest and the most portly. 'Best smoked salmon I've tasted since before the war.'

222

Twenty minutes later, Charles escorted the last of his guests to the door. When he joined Katy again he said, 'You'll have to direct me. You've never told me where you live.'

'Actually, I'm going back to the shop. I promised John I would help finish the day out.'

'Surely your employer could have given you the rest of the afternoon off.' Charles frowned.

Katy rose to John Reilly's defence. 'He did offer, but I insisted. I couldn't let him do everything himself. There is a lot more than you may think to locking up for the day.'

Charles, surprised at her defence of John, said politely, 'I'm sure there is.' He excused himself to have a word with the catering manager.

Katy was thoughtful during the journey. She stole a look at Charles, puzzled by his manner. She couldn't pin down a reason for it, but the usual warmth between them was missing. She spoke only to give directions before lapsing into silence again.

Charles too was silent as he concentrated on his driving. Every fibre in his being was conscious of the girl by his side, whose soft voice stirred him so as she gave directions. Her voice with its musical cadence had always charmed him.

At last Katy said, 'We're here. I did wonder if I would get us lost as I've never come from the direction of the airport before.'

Charles followed her into the bookshop. His gaze swiftly travelled round the interior, noting the light décor and the attractive shelves with their rows of books all neatly catalogued according to genre. He was still examining the layout when a man in his fifties emerged from a curtained alcove in response to Katy's call that she was back.

'John, I would like you to meet a friend of mine, Charles Gilbert.'

John Reilly came forward and held out his hand in greeting. 'I've heard much about you,' he smiled.

'This is my boss, John Reilly,' Katy said.

Introductions over, John offered them a cup of tea.

Charles shook his head and thanked him. 'I really must get back, but I would like to take you up on the offer another time.' He instinctively liked this man.

Katy saw Charles to the car and watched as he settled himself comfortably behind the wheel. She desperately wished he would say something that would pierce the formality that lay between them. Instead, he produced a brown paper bag from the back seat and handed it to her. 'Terence Coleman asked me to give this to you,' he said tonelessly. 'It would appear you left it behind when you spent the weekend with him.'

Katy paled, but before she could reply Charles put the car into gear and drove off. She slowly re-entered the shop and John handed her the latest consignment of books which he had catalogued and entered in the ledgers. Silently, she climbed the ladder to place them on the shelves. It was one of the jobs John couldn't do because of his arthritic hips and the knee that had been shot to hell in the first war, which caused him to limp.

'I like your friend,' he remarked.

She looked down from her height and reached out for the book he was holding up towards her. 'How can you tell at such short notice?'

'I can look into a man's eyes and see his soul,' said John smartly. 'I liked his manner and his bearing. The man is cultured and he has integrity.'

'And you can tell all that just by looking into his eyes for a few minutes?'

'Yes I can, you article – and I can also shake this ladder and give you a bad moment if you don't stop making fun of me.'

Katy came down. 'That's the lot.' She looked curiously at John. 'Can you really do that – make a snap judgement about someone? I mean, there are men who are adept at hiding their true selves.' Like Terence Coleman, she thought bitterly.

'True, but in fifty plus years I've not been wrong yet. I think that says it all.'

'He has been kind to me,' Katy agreed.

'You are very fond of him.' It was a statement.

She stared into space. 'As a friend.' A friend who had handed her a nightdress in a paper bag and condemned her without trial; who appeared to have double standards which said it was all right for him to spend a night in an hotel with a woman, but not for her to do likewise with a man.

Picking up the large empty boxes, she took them out to the small yard at the back of the shop, leaving John to deal with the till. For a moment she stood with her back against the wall to compose herself, for her heart had dipped in despair.

On his way home to Ballynashee, Charles was feeling equally disturbed because he knew that what he was feeling was jealousy – red-eyed jealousy. When Terence Coleman had handed him the parcel, his first reaction was one of disbelief that Katy could have spent a weekend alone with the man. It went completely against everything he knew about her. The lively but shy young girl brought up on a farm who was a regular churchgoer didn't fit the picture that had emerged. The second reaction was that he wanted to punch the salacious bastard to the ground, but common sense took over. Why condemn the man for being red-blooded? Katy must have known what she was doing. Charles banged the steering wheel. Could Katy have changed so much in the short time she had lived in Belfast?

He changed the gears down roughly as he reached the gates of Beresford House, his thoughts still in turmoil. He knew that Terence Coleman's parents were in Germany. He knew, because he was the one who had sent Geoffrey Coleman on ahead to work on a project on which he would be joining him later; and Mrs Coleman had accompanied her husband as she always did. Terence must have been aware that they would not be there. He scrunched to a stop on the driveway and made his way to the kitchen to check that Mrs Skelton had left him some sandwiches and a flask of soup as Sylvia and Robert were dining out with some friends.

The housekeeper had gone, but Sally, clearing up some dishes from the nursery, informed him that Mr and Mrs Mathews were upstairs getting ready to go out and Elizabeth had been put to bed half an hour ago.

Charles straightened and managed a tiny smile. 'But not asleep yet, if I know my niece.' No reason to make others suffer for his moods and disappointments.

'Don't you wake her if she is, Mr Charles,' Sally said, with some severity. 'You'll only make it harder for her to get back to sleep and I'm the one who has to lull her back into the mood again after you get her excited,' but she smiled as she said it. She would run to the ends of the earth and back again for Charles Gilbert. For all his wealth and his high position, he always treated the staff as equals – unlike that nose-in-the-air madam Pamela. Still, she'd had her comeuppance well and truly and the divil serve her right.

Charles took the stairs two at a time and peeped into Elizabeth's room. As he'd suspected, she was lying on the bed with her knees up and a book propped against them. She could read most of the words herself now, she had informed Charles not long ago, and nothing pleased her more than to be able to retire to her room to do just that.

He tapped lightly on the door. 'Prince Charming wishes to converse in private with the Lady Elizabeth Sanders.'

'Uncle Charles! I thought you weren't coming back this evening,' Elizabeth squealed, joy lighting up her face. 'That's what I was told.'

'A dastardly plot to keep us apart,' Charles grinned. 'I shall find the culprit and then it is off with his head.'

'It was Sally!' Elizabeth cried, with delight. 'It would be great fun to see Sally running around, putting clean sheets on the beds, with no head on her shoulders.' The idea set off a fit of giggling.

'You will make a fine dark Queen, my lady,' said Charles soulfully. 'You have no pity, no soul, no heart.'

'I'm only joking!' said Elizabeth, aghast. 'Really, I am.'

'Of course you are, and so am I.' Charles ruffled her hair and lay down beside her. 'What is your greatest wish, oh desirable one?'

'What are you now, Uncle Charles?' Elizabeth giggled.

'I am the second cousin of the second cousin of the genie in the bottle. My powers are limited but I can still conjure up a good result if necessary.'

'I wish Katy would come here. I haven't seen her for ages – and I would like to visit the Wishing Tree.'

'I can only grant one wish at a time so I will grant you a visit to the Wishing Tree, but there is a chance – just a chance, mind – that if the wind is in the right direction, the other one could be granted as well.'

'Really, Charles. The things you fill my daughter's head with.'

They turned. Sylvia was leaning against the lintel of the door looking exquisite in a black dress. Not even pregnancy could make her look less than what she was – a very lovely woman, her brother thought fondly.

'I stand accused,' he grinned, adding, 'You're off then?'

Sylvia nodded. 'I just popped in to see if Elizabeth was asleep and if not, to say goodbye.' She leaned over and gave her daughter a careful hug. 'Sweet dreams,' she murmured.

Charles rolled off the bed. 'She's in good hands,' he said. 'And as you heard, if she is good she will be visiting the Wishing Tree some time.'

'What about work?' Sylvia asked as they went downstairs.

'My work is more or less finished now. I'm giving myself the rest of the week off but I shall be here if needed.'

'Have you seen Katy since she was home last?'

'I was with her today.'

'Did she mention if she might be coming up this weekend?'

'No, but then there was no reason why she should mention it. I got a feeling that she might though, by something her employer said – which is why I told Elizabeth her second wish might happen.'

Robert arrived just then. 'Ready, darling?' He turned to Charles. 'Evening, old man. How did the luncheon go?'

'Extremely well, actually. I'm sorry you two couldn't make it.'

'Yes, rather unfortunate. But two huge meals in one day is not on and we had made this prior arrangement a long time ago.'

'I understand. Go on – enjoy yourselves. I will guard the Lady Elizabeth.'

When they had gone, he slipped upstairs to check on his niece and found her fast asleep. When he returned to the kitchen, Sally had finished tidying up and was donning her coat.

'I'm off now, Mr Charles. Is there anything you want before I go?'

Charles took the sandwiches from the sideboard. 'No, but you must tell me where the mustard is, or you're dismissed, without a reference.'

Sally laughed, fetched the mustard, showed him where the

soup was keeping warm on the range, and departed.

Charles took his tray into the sitting room, grabbing the evening paper off the hallstand on the way. He was thankful to be alone with his thoughts, a glass of wine, and a light but palatable meal, and no one to disturb the quiet that was pervading the house. He leaned back against the soft cushions. There was much to think about; a few decisions to make businesswise and personally. He took a sip of wine and nibbled on a sandwich and let his thoughts have full rein. Later, when he started to work on his papers, he found his concentration interrupted by the mental picture of a rosy-cheeked face fringed by a wealth of curly black hair, and he groaned. There was no point in going down this road. Katy was fourteen years younger than him and her upbringing was so utterly different; her values . . . he rose abruptly. There was no future in it. No future at all. He was a foolish man with impossible dreams.

The following morning, Katy struggled into the farmhouse kitchen and dumped the large bag down on the floor. Annie looked up in surprise. 'You didn't tell us you were coming. Your da would have met the bus.' She eyed the heavy bag. 'What in the name of God have you got in there? You haven't come home for good, have you?'

Katy made a face. 'It's my washing. I thought to make use of your boiler. My underwear is becoming greyer by the week because of the quickie wash it gets in the sink. Anyway, are you not glad to see me home again?'

Annie held her face up for a kiss. 'Of course I am, but I need warning so that I can air your bed.' She ran her hands under the tap and lifted the kettle off the hob. 'I'll make a cup of tea. I could do with a rest from baking – I've been at it all morning. We'll sit down and you can tell me all your news.' She took a packet of Rinso from the cupboard and handed it to Katy. 'Go easy on this – I won't be able to get to the shops for a few days.'

Katy packed the clothes into the boiler and set it going before joining her mother. She sipped at the strong tea in silence. She had some news to impart and she was worried as to how it would be received. At last, she took a deep breath and put her empty cup on the side table. 'Mam,' she said gently, 'I'm thinking of leaving the bookshop.'

Annie gave her daughter a startled look. 'But I thought you were so happy there.'

'I am,' Katy nodded. 'But it is time to move on. John has the place running on oiled wheels now. He only needs some enthusiastic person to work for him and he can manage fine.'

'Have you told John about your decision?'

'Not yet. You see, there is something I need to sort out with you and m'da before I do so.'

Annie hoped Katy knew what she was doing. It had been so comforting to see her settled and enjoying life. The small niggling worries that Eddie and she had had in the beginning had been allayed just lately, and now, just as they were enjoying a bit of peace of mind . . . She sighed inwardly.

Katy continued, 'Mam, I would like to go to university to study English.'

'Can you still do that? You will be twenty years old when you start.'

'I have the necessary certificates and my age is no problem.'

'The others – won't they be finishing soon?' Annie frowned. 'You can't live in that house on your own. Your da gave in once and felt better when he had met the lads, but I can't see him wanting to go through the worry again.'

'Frank goes this year to do his clinicals, and Donal also finishes, but Margaret and Mickey have another year yet. Frank and Donal will be replaced and we hope that the new pair will fit in with us.'

'It all seems a bit up in the air,' Annie said slowly. 'And I think your father will be less keen on you living at the house when Margaret and the others are gone.'

Katy found herself bristling. 'Mam, if I can cope with a situation like the one I've just got out of with Terence, then I can cope with anything.'

Annie said crisply, 'Don't forget that you were naive enough to get lured to that house in the first place.'

'That's unfair. I thought his parents were going to be there. But

I coped – that's the important thing. That should prove that I am able to look after myself now.'

Annie rose. She had heard the sound of a tractor. 'At least your da doesn't know about that incident,' she said thankfully.

Eddie had dropped by to let his wife know that Patrick and he would be late stopping for lunch. She wasn't to bring it down to the field for another hour. 'How's the girlie then?' He turned to Katy.

'I'm well, Da.' Katy looked up into his eyes. 'You look wrecked. Have you not replaced Tom yet?'

Annie handed him a cup of strong tea, now cooled. 'Get that into you. You have time to sup and have a quick word.'

Eddie took the mug gratefully, before answering his daughter. 'No. I hope that college he has gone to can teach him more than we could or I'll have broken my back with the extra work for nothing. We tried out a few lads but they were useless. We'd have spent more time re-doing what they had done and chasing them up for what they hadn't done to make it worth the candle. It was easier to buckle down and get on with it ourselves.'

'It's too much for you and Patrick,' Katy fretted.

'Your mam does the milking and all the other things we don't get around to,' Eddie said. 'I'm just grateful for a good harvest and top sales. I can't complain.' He put the mug down. 'Well, I'm away off. Patrick will tear a strip off me if I chunter on here any longer.' He tapped Katy on the shoulder as he passed. 'I'll see you later.'

Katy turned to her mother. 'I sometimes feel guilty about leaving the farm when I see m'da looking so tired and over-worked,' she murmured.

Annie shrugged. 'Your da is all right. He is busy it's true, but it is only for a short span. When the hay is in he'll be able to relax a bit.'

'I'll give them a hand after lunch.'

Annie smiled. 'That would help. You're a grand girl.'

By the end of the day, Katy felt that every muscle in her body had twisted itself into a burning knot. She hadn't realised just how out of condition she was, but she kept the knowledge to herself, going wearily upstairs after supper to soak in a hot bath.

Now more than ever she had cause to be thankful that three years ago her da had had a bathroom installed when electricity had come to the farm, although, for months after, he had continued to moan about the harshness of the light. He yearned for the soft glow of the paraffin lamps of the past, but he'd got used to it though, when he discovered how much easier it was to milk the cows without having to set up the lamps in the barn of a winter evening.

Next day, after she had helped with the washing up, Katy made her way to the Wishing Tree. She hadn't been there for a long while, and the thought of curling up on her branch to do a bit of thinking and dreaming, was heavenly. Life had become so hectic with the see-saw progress of the shop she hadn't had a chance recently to sit and think things through.

Because the day was hot she was wearing a thin cotton dress and carrying her sandals in her hand, revelling in the feel of the warm grass brushing her feet. She was so absorbed in her sensual enjoyment she started when she heard her name.

'Katy! Katy! You came!' A breathless little figure hurtled towards her when she was some way from the tree.

She stopped as Elizabeth reached her and threw her arms round her. 'Uncle Charles told me you would come. He was right! Clever Uncle Charles.'

Katy hugged the tiny figure with one arm and shaded her eyes with the other. Her heart flipped as Charles walked towards her, looking debonair in a white shirt and grey flannels. He was bareheaded and the soft breeze that had helped cool her feet as she walked was lifting his hair.

'I hope you don't mind,' Charles said. 'The Lady Elizabeth desired to visit the Wishing Tree and I thought it would be all right as you hadn't mentioned that you were coming up this weekend.'

'I don't mind a bit.'

Charles said lightly, 'I try to keep her happy. I half-guessed that you might be home this weekend. I just mentioned that if she was good, the tree might grant her second wish – which was to see you.' He had a longing to take Katy in his arms, but he shook off the feeling.

231

So much for her afternoon of dreaming, Katy thought, but at least Charles was trying to be friendly. 'Shall we climb the tree?' she asked, and took Elizabeth's hand.

Later, they wandered down to the little brook that flowed through the bottom field, and as Elizabeth paddled happily, Katy and Charles talked.

'I shall be leaving soon,' he said.

Katy kept her voice casual. 'I thought you would be here for at least another six months.'

'I have another job to set up in Germany. This one is rolling along nicely, and it's up to the workforce and the foremen to keep things moving now. If I'm needed then they can phone me and I can be back in a few hours. Helen has managed to find me an apartment near the airport in Berlin.'

'I'm sorry you're going.' She tried to keep her voice steady and impersonal, but was aware that there was a slight quiver in it.

'I hope you are,' said Charles, and with an attempt at levity, added: 'If I happen to get involved with the German equivalent of Barney Fogarty, I hope you won't mind if I give you a call.'

'You'll probably find a German girl who will understand the situation,' Katy said, with a little smile. Inwardly her heart was plummeting. Would Helen be going with him? The question was answered by Charles' next words.

'I won't be leaving for a couple of weeks yet. Helen will be going ahead to set things up.'

Katy leaned back on her elbows and idly watched Elizabeth as she paddled in the stream. The thought of Helen chasing round Europe with Charles was hateful, and the fact that she liked Helen made matters worse, for she couldn't feel bitter towards her. God! Was she mad or what? What had she, a gormless Irish girl, brought up on a farm in the middle of nowhere, got to offer a man like Charles Gilbert, with his sophistication and his experience? She rose and joined Elizabeth.

'I'm looking for fishes and frogs,' Elizabeth explained solemnly, as she approached.

'I think you would need to go further upstream. The water is a bit shallow here,' Katy explained. 'Let's build a dam, instead.' They set to and became so engrossed in their project they

232

completely forgot the man who sat with his back resting on the low bank, watching them.

After a time Charles rose abruptly. 'We had better be going soon. I promised Sylvia I would have Elizabeth home in time for tea.'

Katy stole a quick glance at her watch. 'I was hoping you would have tea at the farm. Mam would love to see Elizabeth.'

'Please, Uncle Charles. Ple-e-a-se.'

Charles hesitated. 'I'd have to ring Sylvia.'

'All right. If she says not, then at least we tried.' She turned to Elizabeth. 'You may have to wait for your farm tea.' She traced her finger along the pouting lips.

'Hey – don't let the deely bobber see that scowl. He'll have the shoes off your feet in a tick and the nails removed.'

Elizabeth laughed. '*Please* tell Mummy that I'll be very good at bedtime if I can stay to tea.'

When they arrived at the farm house, Charles asked if he could ring Sylvia. Katy smiled and nodded, and put her arms around Elizabeth.

When he'd put the phone down Charles turned to the two expectant faces. 'The answer is yes, but the Lady Elizabeth has to keep her promise or she will not be allowed such licence again – so be warned.'

'What does licence mean?' Elizabeth asked.

'It means that you won't get your way another time if you don't keep your promise.' Charles swung her up and they all went into the kitchen where Annie had prepared a large tea.

'I hear tell you are going away soon,' Eddie remarked, halfway through tea.

Charles looked at Katy. ''Fraid so. I have a new commitment in Germany.'

Eddie stopped, his hand halfway to his mouth. 'Should you be helpin' that lot?'

'The war is over, Mr Molloy,' Charles said with a trace of impatience. 'Towns have to be rebuilt – airports and runways re-established. We need the access as much as they need the help. We won the war. We now have bridges to build between our two nations. There has been a lot of sorrow for both sides but we can't dwell on the past. We must just make certain that it doesn't happen again.'

'Did you lose anyone in the war?'

Katy and her mother glanced at each other.

'As a matter of fact, yes. I lost both my parents – and my brother-in-law.' Charles had gone white.

'I'm sorry about that, lad,' Eddie said gently, 'but I still think we should let the jerries get on with the job of building their own towns and cities. We have enough to be doing rebuilding our own desecrated areas before we start helping those who started the whole shebang in the first place.'

'I understand how you feel,' Charles said quietly, 'but I tend to take a different view. I hope that fact doesn't ruin a newfound friendship.'

Eddie rose. 'Not one bit, son. I attach no blame to you for your views. You flew planes during the war, I understand?'

Charles nodded.

Eddie grimaced. 'Just give me time. It's hard to forgive a race that yielded such power and committed such carnage. I will in time, though. The people of Germany were following a bad leader, after all.'

'Sorry about that,' Katy apologised later. 'M'da is convinced that Vincey's brain haemorrhage was triggered off by all that he suffered during the war years. He still feels bitter because the Germans started the whole thing in the first place, and we lost so many young men because of Hitler's crazy ideals.'

'I gathered that. Don't worry – I have a great respect for your father.' Charles helped Elizabeth into the car, said, 'Goodbye,' and drove off without a backward glance.

Katy walked disconsolately into the house. 'I'm just going up to my bedroom for a while, Mam,' she called out, and as she climbed the stairs she felt such an ache where her heart was she lay down on the top of the bed and folded her arms across her chest to try and ease it.

CHAPTER 13

When Katy arrived back at the house, Margaret met her at the door, and bundled her into the sitting room. 'Thank God you're here. Maybe you can shed some light on this.'

'On what? What's happened?'

'Norah's gone!' Margaret flumped down onto the settee beside Donal.

Donal bawled her out. 'This bloody settee has been filled with concrete by a previous owner. Another pound of flesh on you, Margaret Kelly, and I'd have ended up on the floor with a fractured hipbone.'

'Oh, shut up Donal,' Margaret said. 'This is no time for you to be sounding off.' She turned to Katy.

'Where has she gone?' Katy asked.

'She left a note to say that she has gone to England.'

Katy gasped. 'She must be mad! She has another year to do at Queens. Show me the note – surely Norah wouldn't be so foolish.'

Margaret fished in her pocket and brought the note out; Katy read it. Norah wrote that she was sorry to dump this on them in such a fashion, but she couldn't face being away from William for a whole year. They had worked out that she could leave university here, find a job for a year in London and then try for a place at a university in England to finish her studies. She apologised again for the way she had set about things and hoped that they would forgive her. She remained 'their faithful friend Norah'.

'Donal and I found the envelope sitting on the fireboard there, when we came in,' Margaret explained

'What did Frank and Mickey have to say – and where are they?'

'They haven't come back yet.'

Katy frowned. 'There isn't anything we can do about the situation, apart from wishing her luck. What we have to think about now, is how this is going to affect us as a team.'

'We'll be one down on the rent-sharing again,' Donal moaned.

They were still drinking tea and nibbling half-heartedly on cheese sandwiches when Frank and Mickey arrived.

'Has the cat died?' Frank asked, looking at the faces confronting him. No one answered.

Mickey crossed to Margaret. 'What has happened?'

Margaret explained about Norah's departure.

'I say good luck to her,' Frank shrugged.

'What are you grinning about?' Margaret asked Mickey.

'I'm just imaging our Norah having a fling with your man over there. I mean, can you imagine Norah kissing a man and making him tremble all over.'

'Norah may be no Marilyn Monroe but she isn't as naive as you might think,' Margaret protested. 'She kept this place going and we are all going to miss her – meself most of all.' She gave Mickey a killing look and went off to the kitchen to shed a few private tears and make some fresh tea.

For the next twenty minutes they argued about rotas and cooking and who would take on which job, and as they did so they began to realise just how much organising Norah had done. Katy said that in answer to Donal's concern about the rent, there wouldn't be a problem. Had he forgotten that she had been paying rent for some time?

'Great! That settles that. Now can we all agree on the proposals and then I can get off to my bed,' Margaret yawned.

Katy glanced at the clock and was shocked to find that it was now well past midnight. 'I'll sleep in my own bed tonight and move my stuff into Norah's room tomorrow,' she said, and added, 'I'll miss Norah, too. She was good company in the end, wasn't she?'

Margaret smiled. 'She was indeed.' Once in their bedroom, she looked thoughtfully at Katy. 'Speaking of company, what really happened to the big romance with Terence Coleman? Which reminds me, Donal was saying just the other day that he hasn't been seen round the university just lately.

Katy knew she couldn't pretend. She closed the door and sat down on Margaret's bed and began to tell her what had happened on that fateful evening.

Margaret listened open-mouthed, and when Katy had finished she shot off her bed and began to pace the floor. 'The bastard!' she said. 'I never liked the idea of you two together. You were just a chicken to be plucked, as far as he was concerned. Mind, I warned him what would happen if he tried anything . . .'

'You discussed me with Terence? You spoke about our relationship?'

'Calm down. I told him while he was waiting for you one evening that I'd have something to say to him if he didn't treat you properly. He has a bad reputation with women, Katy. I was concerned for you.'

'I think I managed very well under the circumstances. I am not a complete culshie.' Katy glared at Margaret, who glared back. Suddenly they burst out laughing.

'As it turned out – you were just that,' Margaret giggled.

Katy sighed. 'That's true – but it taught me a lot.'

'Well, I suppose it is one way of learning about life. You won't be caught out another time,' Margaret said.

Katy laughed bitterly. 'I'd rather read about it in a book. It was quite unpleasant at the time – and very frightening.' She took her sponge bag and made for the bathroom.

Margaret watched her go. She was heartily glad that Katy had come away unscathed.

Charles flew to Berlin at the beginning of September, a week earlier than anticipated, and for the first two weeks after his departure, Katy missed him dreadfully. She had known that his going would affect her, but the depth of her feelings surprised her. She tried to submerge herself in work but wasn't entirely successful.

To John Reilly it was patently obvious that Katy's mind was elsewhere. He observed her as she climbed the steps to fill the shelves with the latest deliveries, noting the listless way she went about doing the job, but he shrugged off the temptation to ask if there was anything amiss. She would tell him if she wanted to.

Aware that she was being watched, Katy called to him to hand her up another set of books. 'Are you stuck to that seat or what?' she enquired.

He rose and handed her several heavy books. 'You look a bit peaky. Why don't you have some time off? Go home for a rest.'

He has noticed something, she thought. 'I'm fine!' she said, adding with a light laugh, 'Haven't I only just come back from there? And besides, I will end up helping out on the farm and that is a lot harder than stacking a few books.' Katy hesitated and then climbed down the steps.

John, still holding some books, remarked with a puzzled look, 'There are still some more to put up on that shelf.'

Katy took them from him and placed them on the counter and took in a deep breath. 'I'll make a cup of tea and then there is something I must tell you.'

John's heart sank. Judging by the tone of her voice and the look on her face, Katy was going to tell him something that he was not going to like. He sighed. 'I'll make the tea while you sit on the chair and work out the best way to give me the bad news.'

Katy reddened. 'It isn't that . . .'

'I can read bad news on a person's face at twenty paces,' John said, and smiled ruefully.

Katy had been agonising over her decision ever since she had come back from a visit to the farm, and when they had all been reassessing their living arrangements she had been even more certain that she had to restructure her life. Change was becoming inevitable. Frank had already made arrangements for his clinicals, which meant that he would be living in at the hospital some time in the near future, and Donal's finals were coming up next year, he was already spending more time at his father's pharmacy.

Luckily, Margaret and Mickey still had another year to do – but after that? Katy knew that she had to move onwards, herself. She didn't want to sell books for the rest of her life, and also, when the others had gone she couldn't see herself living in the house alone. The set-up was an unusual one, and not many parents would sanction their offspring living in such unconventional circumstances. *They* had managed it – but only because Margaret and Mickey's parents knew each other and they had trusted them. 'They regard us as more like brother and sister,' Mickey had grinned. Frank's parents 'couldn't give a toss' so he said, and Donal and Norah had never mentioned to theirs that they were living in a mixed-sex situation . . . Katy started as John arrived at her side with a steaming mug of tea.

'It's our half-day. The door is locked,' he said. 'Now what is it you want to discuss with me?'

Katy put the mug down and looked straight at him. She explained haltingly that she had started thinking about the future; she had decided to go to university, and would therefore have to give up her job at some time . . .

John broke in. 'It was going to happen one day – I knew that.'

Relieved at John's acceptance, Katy said, 'You have everything under control now. I've come to the end of my usefulness, and just think how you will enjoy having someone else to teach and boss around!'

'How soon were you thinking of leaving?' John asked.

'Not for a long time. There are various things to sort out, you see. I have already applied for a place at the university here to study English . . .'

'You couldn't start this autumn, then? That's a shame.'

Katy pulled a face. 'I may not get in for next year – so you will have plenty of time to find a replacement.' She grinned. 'Who knows! One day someone might walk through the door just as I did.'

'It would never be the same, my girl. Never in this world. There will only ever be one Katy Molloy, chaser of dreams.' John grinned. 'What I really need is for some older lady to walk in and beg for a job as housekeeper . . .' He stood up. 'In the meantime, we have some work to finish.'

Sylvia telephoned to invite Katy to dinner. Nothing formal, she explained. They hadn't seen her for a long time, and Robert had suggested it was time that they did.

Katy accepted without hesitation. She would miss Charles'

presence, she thought sadly, but she looked forward to seeing Sylvia and Elizabeth again. They were part of her family now.

She took the early bus home to the farm, shivering slightly as she sat down on a Rexine-covered seat and turned her gaze to the passing scenery. It was now late November and the trees, although practically leafless, still looked good, bathed as they were in the wintry sunshine. She wondered how her own tree was looking now? She hadn't been to it since she had last gone there with Charles and Elizabeth. She hadn't heard a word from Charles and felt hurt about that. Towards the end of their afternoon spent by the stream, things had seemed a little easier between them. She had looked at the post each morning hoping for a postcard, at least – but there was nothing.

'Are you getting off here or not, miss? You did ask for Ginty's Corner.'

She turned with a start. The bus driver was new on the route. 'I didn't realise we were here. Thanks.' She grabbed her small weekend case and made her way off the bus.

The following morning, she asked Annie if she would mind if she took herself off for a walk.

'Ach away on, Katy. There is no need to ask. I manage when you are not here.' Annie knew fine well that the walk would be across two fields to the tree. Katy had something on her mind, for she had noticed how quiet the girl had been since her arrival.

Once she reached the tree, Katy settled herself onto her favourite branch, smiling wryly as she did so. Time had altered the childish body of her youth and her rounder figure made it more difficult to perch in the fork. Now she had to hold onto the branch above for balance, but as she sat there she felt a kind of peace sweep over her. The gentle soughing of the breeze through the branches was soothing to her mind. She closed her eyes the better to enjoy it and wrapped her jacket round her to keep out the chill.

So much had happened in the past couple of years. Some good things, some bad, and she had learned to deal with them. She felt more in charge of her life. She was no longer the child whom Vincey protected, and who had spent most of her time wishing and dreaming and doing nothing to make the dreams come to fruition. 'If wishes were dreams, Katy Molloy, you'd never wake up.'

Well, she *had* woken up – and she had progressed from the shy aimless person she once was. Everything that had happened in the past two years had helped the transformation. She had experienced joy and intense happiness ... had plunged to the depths of despair when her beloved Vincey had died ... had been helped by John Reilly to see that death doesn't mean the end of a relationship. She had survived a bad experience with Terence Coleman and learned that she could still trust men like Charles. Best of all, she had discovered that she was a survivor.

Over at Beresford House, Charles Gilbert was sitting in the drawing room with Sylvia who, now well advanced in pregnancy, was lying on the sofa, rifling idly through a magazine. He never ceased to be amazed at the change in her since her marriage to Robert. She looked young again, and the smile that had always been her most endearing attribute, was back.

Conversation between them had petered off and Charles was feeling restless. He was going to meet Katy at dinner tonight for the first time in many weeks, and he was nervous. This in itself was unusual for Charles, who was a man with the ability to meet problems of any kind with a degree of equanimity. His job was a demanding one and at times exceedingly tricky, and there was no room for panic or nerves. It was unsettling to feel as he did now.

Suddenly he felt an urgent desire to see Katy. He needed to settle what was between them before he faced her across the table. Needed to know how she felt about him. Needed above all to try to make her understand how he had been feeling when he so readily condemned her ... the hurt ... the disappointment when he had thought she had spent that weekend with Terence Coleman. He'd been so jealous, so foolishly hasty to assume that she had slept with that blackguard ... His faith in Terence's father had blinded him to the son's flaws. Whatever the explanation for the nightie in the brown paper bag, it would have been an innocent one. He knew it now with all his heart. If Katy would give him a chance, he would tell her how much she meant to him. My God – he hoped it was not too late.

Charles knew when he went to Germany that he had to tell Helen their relationship must end, because he was in love with someone else. It had been a difficult thing to do because Helen's feelings for him ran more deeply than his for her, and the guilt he felt was the greater for that knowledge. He had been so wrong to let the situation get out of hand, and as he suspected, the confrontation had been an emotional one with tears and recriminations. He rose. 'I'm going for a walk,' he said abruptly. Sylvia just nodded, absently.

Annie looked up in surprise as Charles stepped onto the porch, where she was sweeping up the leaves. She leaned the brush against the wall and invited him in. She always enjoyed his company and she hadn't seen him in an age.

'Is Katy around? I need to see her about something. It's rather important,' Charles said politely.

'She has gone for a walk. She went off about fifteen minutes ago.'

When disappointment flitted across his face, Annie relented, although she knew that Katy had wanted solitude. 'She may be down by her tree,' she suggested.

'Thanks,' Charles said gratefully.

Annie watched him go. She rubbed her arms as the cold bit and when Charles had climbed the stile into the first field she went indoors. She hoped that whatever he wanted to say to her daughter would bring on a smile. Just lately, they had been scarce, and the ones that did make it looked as though they were pasted on.

Katy was so wrapped up in her thoughts that she nearly fell off the branch as a noise startled her, and she opened her eyes to the sight of Charles, gazing up at her with a look of tenderness, tinged with anxiety. Her heart leaped in her breast. She had not thought to see him.

'Hello Katy,' he said softly.

'God! You gave me a fright. How did you know I was here? Did you know I've been invited to dinner?' Oh dear, she was gabbling. If Charles only knew the turmoil and the elation that his unexpected appearance had wrought in her . . .

'I called at the house and your mother told me you might be here. And yes, I did know that you would be dining with us, but I wanted to see you beforehand. Can we take a walk down to the stream?' He helped her from the branch and continued to hold her arm as they made their way across the field towards the burn.

The unexpected joy of having Charles arrive beside her was tinged with curiosity as Katy wondered why he had sought her out.

'Sylvia didn't mention that you were coming home when she invited me to dinner,' she began.

'She was told not to tell you. I wanted to surprise you.'

'Well, you certainly did that.' Aware that her hand was still being held, she tried to draw it away but Charles pulled it back. Firmly, she withdrew it again.

They sat down on the large boulder that he had hauled from the stream during the summer and Katy gave a slight shiver. It was cold by the water, away from the warm shelter of the tree. She gathered her scarf round her neck and was about to put on her gloves again, when Charles pulled her closer to shield her from the cold. Katy stiffened. Her body was trembling at the nearness. She moved away again.

'Don't worry, I am not Terence Coleman,' Charles said,

Katy gasped. 'Who told you about that?'

'I called at the house two days ago and your friend Margaret more or less informed me I wasn't welcome. She said you were just beginning to make something of your life, and she was not going to let you see anyone who could believe that "a shite" – and I quote – like Terence Coleman could possibly have persuaded you to stay the night with him. Such a person – meaning me – was not fit to tie your shoelaces.'

Katy was bewildered. 'I can't believe she—'

'She was very concerned about you and wanted to make certain no one else would break your heart.'

Katy turned her head away. 'Margaret got that wrong. Terence Coleman would never have broken my heart – I felt nothing for him but friendship and he destroyed even that – just as you marred my friendship with you by being so quick to believe any lies he told you.'

'What else could I believe when he had given me your nightdress?' said Charles. 'I know it was stupid of me, but my jealousy blinded me. I was angry – but I should have given you a chance to explain.'

Katy said in a low voice, 'Yes, you should.' But as she said it, realised with a pang that she was just as guilty as Charles in drawing conclusions. She glanced at him.

'I never mentioned that I saw you coming down the steps of the Grand Hotel in Brighton and getting into a taxi with Helen. I jumped to all the wrong conclusions myself.'

'Why on earth didn't you wave or shout – or something?' Charles asked.

'I tried to cross the road but the traffic was too heavy. By the time I could have managed it you had gone.'

'That was a most productive week,' Charles said. 'And I can recommend the hotel.' He added softly, 'I stayed there alone. Poor Helen had to stay at one in the centre of Brighton with all the other secretaries and make the trip to the conference twice a day. She wasn't best pleased.' He rose. It was time to go back. He and Katy would get to know each other slowly again, now that mutual trust had been re-established. They had made a start today and his instinct told him not to rush things, but one day soon he would tell her that he wanted more than friendship. He wanted her love.

When Charles had finished telling her about the stay in Brighton, Katy felt such a rush of relief go through her that she had to look away again. She thought, I love this man, but he is only part of my life – not all of it. If it ended tomorrow, I know that I would survive the hurt. My life belongs to me . . . not to Charles, not to Vincey, not to anyone – but to me.

EPILOGUE

Katy stood at the casement window and looked thoughtfully out over the pretty garden. Today was Donal's wedding day. He and Maraid had waited three long years for this because Donal wanted everything to be perfect and had refused his father's offer of the rooms above the pharmacy. He wanted his own house.

It had been a time of change for all of them. Margaret and Mickey were married now and would be there with Chrissie, their little girl. Mickey was teaching at a school just outside Belfast but Margaret was content to be a mother and a housewife.

Katy smiled wryly. Funny, that. Margaret had always been the forceful, go-ahead one. Now she had become a brilliant mother and was as contented with her home-life as a cat with cream.

Frank was senior houseman at the Belfast Hospital and was, as ever, running after any girl that could nod her head in an up and down manner. Any girl, he was quoted as saying, who could only shake it from side to side, had no chance. He was still big and good-natured and as popular as he had always been. He was convinced that he would never marry. The nearest he would ever get to a wedding ring, he had vowed recently, was when he handed it to Donal today to put on Maraid's finger.

Norah too was married and living in England. She sent the occasional card but no one had had any other contact with her since the day she had run off.

John Reilly, the rogue, had married Mary McCoy his new assistant, and was living a leisurely life in a cottage at the foot of the Mourne Mountains just outside Newcastle, while Mary spoilt the life out of him.

Katy looked at her watch and frowned. And what of Charles

Gilbert? Where was he at this moment? Time was passing; the journey ahead was a long one. She looked at her watch again and was about to shut the casement doors when she felt a hand on her shoulder. She twisted round. 'It is about time, Charles Gilbert. We have an hour's drive to the church!' Katy looked up at her husband with shining eyes. 'You look very grand,' she said softly, adding proudly: 'I have the handsomest man of them all.'

Charles kissed her thoroughly. 'And the most amiable.' He grinned. 'There aren't many men who would let a wife mingle with handsome, immoral students on the pretext of getting an English degree – and employ maids and a nanny to look after his precious son.'

'A king among men.' Katy grinned back. 'Now, we must get going.' She knelt down and picked up her sleeping son in his carrying basket. 'And you had better behave yourself at this wedding. Anthony Vincent Gilbert.' She laughed, and led the way out of the room.

Following the wedding they would spend a week at the farm where Charles would be in his element helping her da in the fields while her mam lovingly fussed over her grandson. At some point they would visit Sylvia and Robert, and Sylvia and she would compare notes about Vincent's and William's progress and laugh at Elizabeth's bossiness with her little brother. And best of all, Katy would have Vincent all to herself with not a nanny in sight, as Sylvia had opted to look after William without help and had said that she was loving the experience. As the large car purred along Katy hugged her tiny son close to her. 'Your Uncle Vincey would have been so proud of you,' she whispered.